THE BOSTON SYNDICATE

FINN

Book Cover by Y'all. That Graphic

Edited by Victoria Ellis, Cruel Ink Editing and Design

Proofread by Rosa Sharon, Fairy Proofmother Proofreading, LLC

CHECK YOUR TRIGGERS

Your mental health and emotional well-being matters to me. You can find a list of possible triggers on the book's page on my website katerandallauthor.com or by scanning the QR code below.

Xoxo

To my husband. Don't mind my google search history. Love you, babe.

Contents

1. Finn   1

2. Alessia   19

3. Finn   35

4. Alessia   51

5. Finn   69

6. Alessia   87

7. Finn   105

8. Alessia   119

9. Finn   137

10. Alessia   155

11. Finn   173

12. Alessia   189

13. Finn   207

14. Alessia   219

15. Finn   237

16. Alessia   249

17.	Alessia	263
18.	Finn	273
19.	Alessia	287
20.	Finn	303
21.	Finn	317
22.	Alessia	329
Epilogue		343
Also By Kate		349
Acknowledgements		351
About Kate		353

CHAPTER ONE

FINN

THE LAST THING ANY man who's the leader of a criminal organization wants to do is admit when he fucked up, but I did. And it nearly cost a man—a man I've come to respect—his life and his woman's life. That's not something I take lightly. Being the head of the Monaghan family, the oldest Irish mob outfit in Boston, doesn't make me exempt from making mistakes—and I made a big one. The MC I work with had been having a problem with the Italians, and I didn't move fast enough. I've been putting plans in place to take care of the Cataldis well before they started shit with the bikers, but the time I thought I had has run out.

The relationship between the Black Roses MC and my family has been fruitful and very profitable for each of us. That's why I'm headed to their clubhouse on a bright Monday morning instead of getting head from the blonde I took to a hotel after the underground fights my brother Eoghan runs. Sometimes, I like to go a few rounds in the ring, and last night, I demolished some gym rat who thought his steroid-induced muscles would make up for his lack of skill. It did not. It was the stress relief I needed leading up to the meeting at the clubhouse. The fight and the blonde.

Speaking of Eoghan, he looks a hell of a lot worse for wear than I do as we travel down the highway between Boston and Shine, Massachusetts, to meet with the president of the MC.

"You okay over there? You're looking a little green around the gills, brother." I attempt to swallow my laughter, but there's no use hiding my smirk at his obvious discomfort. I may be driving a little faster than necessary, taking turns a little sharper, but I wouldn't be the loving older brother I am if I didn't give him all the grief I could.

"Fuck off," Eoghan groans, trying to shift in his seat to find a more comfortable position with his blond head resting against the window. "Why isn't Cillian with you again? I don't see why you had to drag me out of bed at this ungodly hour."

"It's ten in the morning, you lazy asshole. And Cillian isn't here because he's been searching for Carlo Cataldi while simultaneously covering the casino. The man needs some sleep."

"I need some fucking sleep," he mumbles, closing his bloodshot blue eyes. My brother and I share the same eye color, but that's where our familial similarities end. Eoghan takes after our mother with his blond hair that he keeps longer, whereas I have short dark hair that touts our Black Irish roots.

Carlo is at the center of the Italian problem I've

let fester long enough. He was the one who took Ozzy, the Black Roses MC president, and his woman, Freya, hostage a few months back. Cillian would be here in a heartbeat if I'd asked, but my lieutenant has been burning the candle at both ends. Running the casino and finding Cataldi are vital to the future of our organization, and Cillian is as dedicated as they come.

My brother cocks his head then shakes it, sighing heavily. He is not a fan of how I've handled the Italian situation. If it were up to him, we would have gone in guns blazing months ago and taken care of them.

There has never been any love lost between the Cataldis and the Monaghans, but I can't justify an all-out war with them. My brother would have preferred a show of extreme force, but we aren't prepared for it—yet. Even though I'm only older than Eoghan by a mere fourteen months, I'm still the boss. I make the calls on this kind of shit, not him.

Thank fuck for that.

Since he isn't commenting further, I let the conversation drop. We'll just go round and round if I engage. After my fight and the subsequent fuck from last night, I'm not wound tight enough to give Eoghan the argument he's looking for. Besides, I have more pressing issues weighing on my mind than worrying about my inaction with the Cataldis the last few months. Things not even my brother knows about.

When we pull up to the clubhouse situated at the edge of Shine, I wave at the prospect manning the gate and he lets us through. This is only the second time I've been to the clubhouse in the handful of years Ozzy and I have been doing business. Usually, they make their way into Boston for the night, and my brother and I show them a good time. But since this visit is more of a personal matter, I decided coming to Ozzy was the right call. It's my way of showing the MC president the respect he deserves.

Knox, the club's VP, meets us at the door after we've parked in the gravel lot and clasps my hand in a firm shake. "Good to see you, Finn." He releases my hand and shakes my brother's. "Eoghan."

"Knox," my brother replies. Eoghan is one of those guys that everyone likes to be around. He's easygoing, at least until you piss him off. Knox, on the other hand, has always struck me as a man of few words who doesn't need more than a look and a few grunts to effectively get his point across. It doesn't surprise me when he doesn't return my brother's friendly smile.

Walking into the clubhouse, Eoghan spots Jude, one of the club's enforcers, playing a game of pool with one of the other enforcers, Linc.

"Oi!" Eoghan calls with a wide smile.

Jude spins around and returns his smile with one of his own. "Fucking wanker. You didn't tell me you were coming with Finn. I had to find out from this arsehole," he replies, pointing to Linc.

"Last-minute decision. I call winner," Eoghan says, walking over to the table and fishing a quarter from his pocket before slapping it on the table. Who the hell carries change these days? My brother, that's who.

Jude and Eoghan have built a friendship over the years we've been doing business together. He's even come out to Boston a few times to partake in the fight nights my brother sets up. When Jude came over from jolly old England, he'd just gotten out of the Royal Marines and hooked up with the Black Roses through an old family connection. His training in the service makes him one hell of an opponent in the ring. To my knowledge, he hasn't been out our way since he shacked up with a little spitfire of a woman and settled down. Pity. His fights brought in a shit ton of money—especially if he was fighting one of my guys. The English versus the Irish is quite the old rivalry.

"I'll let Ozzy know you're here," Knox says before disappearing down the hallway.

I take a moment to look around the clubhouse. Several of the brothers are milling about or sitting at the bar and nursing hangovers. I nod to the few I've met before and spot a picture on the wall with a prospect patch next to it. The photo showcases a young man in his early twenties with a bright smile. Cooper Reed. He was killed trying to protect Jude's old lady, Lucy. A feeling of heaviness settles in my chest. The kidnapping didn't have any confirmed connection to the Cataldis, but when Lucy was taken, she mentioned the pilot of the plane she was on spoke Italian. It doesn't take a genius to figure out the Cataldis were most likely involved. That kid was so damn young, but age doesn't mean much in our world. Once you're in, the enemy doesn't give two shits about cutting your life short. It's what we all signed up for, the score we all know too well. Doesn't lessen the responsibility I feel toward his death, though. I should have handled this Cataldi shit when we knew what was going on after Linc's old lady was taken and almost sold by one of Cataldi's men. Fucking scum.

"Come on back," Knox tells me before I can beat myself up more than I already have.

I follow the quiet man back through a hallway, and he opens the office door for me but doesn't enter.

"Good to see you, Ozzy," I say to the president of the Black Roses MC. We shake hands over his desk and the piles of paperwork strewn about. Looks an awful lot like mine.

"You too. Drink?" He points to the bottle of whiskey sitting on the edge of his desk. My lip quirks up, noting it's the same whiskey we sent over here months ago.

"Please." I'm never one to turn down a fine Irish whiskey, regardless of the fact that it's barely eleven in the morning. "And let me know when you're running low."

He pours us each a couple fingers, and we get settled back in our seats on opposite sides of his dark mahogany desk. His office reminds me of my father's, minus the skulls and old beer signs. Pictures line the walls. Photos of his grandfather—the man who started the club—and the generations of Black

Roses who followed. Their club is similar to how our family runs things in that the firstborn son will inherit the leadership role when their father retires. Like the Monaghans, the Black Roses value family and loyalty above all else and proudly display and honor the previous generations.

"I wanted to talk to you about two things. First, my contacts in Nevada have heard some rumblings from the Bone Breakers. The men who came out several months ago to discuss doing business out west? The Bone Breakers think you know what happened to them."

When I was looking at working with a club that had more contacts on the West Coast, I asked Ozzy to have the Bone Breakers out for a few days and get a feel for the type of MC they ran. I trusted his judgment and wanted to make sure the two clubs could work together with the gun business I had the Black Roses handling. Three of the Bone Breakers went missing, so I assume shit went down and the MC handled it.

"Now, I'm not going to ask what happened. That's between your clubs." When I asked Ozzy about the meeting, he said they weren't interested in doing business with the Bone Breakers and they weren't the type of club my organization wanted to work with either. It's what he *didn't* say that had me looking into other avenues to get a stronger foothold in the Western market. "But since they were out here on my behest, I thought I would let you know it sounds like there's trouble brewing on that front."

"Thank you for letting me know." He clearly doesn't plan on elaborating. If Ozzy's club had anything to do with the disappearance of the Bone Breakers, I'm certain there was a good reason for it, and it probably saved me a future headache.

"The second is Carlo Cataldi."

Ozzy's nostrils flare, and it looks as though if his jaw tenses any further, he's likely to break a molar. Can't blame the man. That fuck Carlo threatened to sell off his woman, Freya, and nearly killed Ozzy after destroying his cabin. Freya was working as a US attorney in Boston and built an airtight case against Carlo's father, Francesco Cataldi. Francesco was head of the Cataldi family until a few months ago. After the Italians busted into this very clubhouse just over fifteen years ago and shot Freya when she was barely eighteen, she had a score to settle—and settle she did. If there's anyone in the state of Massachusetts who hates the Cataldis as much as my family, it's probably Ozzy and the rest of the Black Roses.

"There's been no sign of him," I continue. "My source on the inside tells me his capos have no idea where he slithered away to, but he doesn't think Carlo's down for the count. It's only a matter of time before he resurfaces. Right now, his organization is still floundering with him in the wind. It doesn't hurt our cause that he was the one making deals with the skin traders. Thankfully, his capos don't have his connections, but that could and probably will change."

My hope is we can prevent any of them from taking over the trafficking empire Carlo was trying to build under our noses. It's no secret that my family doesn't stand for anyone hurting women, especially the sick fucks that buy them. That asshole kept his crew tight. Even my inside man didn't know details about who Carlo was dealing with, and he's been there for a few years now.

"Not that I don't appreciate the visit, but you could have told me this over the phone. Why the face-to-face?"

I study the whiskey in my glass and take a sip before answering as honestly as I can. "Because I'm a man of honor, Ozzy. I told you we would handle the Italians, and we failed. You and I have always had a good working relationship, and I let you down. The Cataldi situation took us by surprise. I don't like surprises, especially when they get my friends kidnapped and nearly killed." I especially don't like this weight of responsibility I've been carrying around. "I wanted to make the trip out here to tell you personally, man to man, that we're more determined than ever to handle the Italian situation. It won't touch you or your club again." And I'm about to make a move that will ensure I can keep my word.

Ozzy stretches his arm over the desk and holds out his hand for me. "Thank you, Finn. I appreciate the heads-up. If you need us, you know where to find us."

Grasping his hand, I nod. "Appreciate that, Ozzy. We'll

be taking it from here."

When I release his hand, I lean back in my chair and take another sip of whiskey. "How's Freya?" I heard through the grapevine, a.k.a. my brother, that she wasn't doing very well after the attack. The wide smile on Ozzy's face tells me that's no longer the case.

"She's good. Been working with the women at the shelter, helping them sort their legal shit." He chuckles and shakes his head. "The assholes who hurt those women won't know what hit them once Freya is through with them in court."

I was relieved when Eoghan told me Ozzy's old lady had decided to leave the US attorney's office after putting Francesco Cataldi, Carlo's father, behind bars. She'd made a name for herself as a battle-ax during her time there. Doing business with a club with such close ties to a federal prosecutor had my old man and brother on edge.

"Good to hear. I hope she gives them the hell they deserve."

One of the reasons I've always liked working with the Black Roses is they feel the same way my family and I do about the pieces of shit who hurt women. There aren't a lot of men like us who hold their business partners to such a high standard, but I wouldn't have it any other way. And I know the man across from me feels the same.

"Now, let's talk some business. There's a new shipment coming into port down South in two weeks."

"Not that I don't mind the work, Finn, but with Cataldi

in the wind, have you considered moving on the ports in Boston? It seems like a hell of a lot less risk for everyone involved."

Our shipments have never gone through the Port of Boston for that exact reason. Cataldi controls those ports, and I refuse to give that man a dime in taxes. "I'm working on something." Nothing has been solidified yet, but an offer, shall we say, has landed in my lap that would push Cataldi out for good.

We hash out the details for the run in a couple weeks and finish our drinks before I stand to head for the door.

"I'll walk you out," Ozzy says, coming around his desk.

When we step into the main room of the clubhouse, I spot my brother looking at the pool table with a frown marring his face and a smile of triumph on Jude's.

"One of these days, I'm going to beat you at pool," my brother grumbles.

"But not today," Jude replies with a satisfied smirk.

"Don't gloat, brother," Linc says, smiling at Jude behind his cup of coffee. "Or I'll call Lucy down here and tell her you wish she were here so you had some stiffer competition."

Jude stiffens and lifts his chin before shooting his friend a narrow look. "I'm not afraid to play Lucifer."

Linc laughs. "You might not be afraid to play her, but I'll certainly enjoy watching her knock you down a peg or two."

I remember Eoghan saying something about Jude's old lady being some pool-playing phenom.

"She doesn't win every game, mate."

"Sure she doesn't," Linc drawls out. "There was that one time six months ago..." He looks off into the distance as though he's trying to recall a memory, then snaps his fingers, turning back to Jude. "Oh wait, no. You lost and stomped off with your panties in a twist then, too."

Eoghan and Linc share a laugh at Jude's expense, but the Englishman rolls his eyes, brushing off their ribbing.

"You should bring her to the next fight," Eoghan offers.

Linc and Jude both shake their heads. "My woman and fight nights probably wouldn't mix. It would only take one remark from a meathead who has something to prove before she'd be laying them flat on their back," Jude says with an affectionate smile.

Eoghan laughs and smacks Jude on the back, shaking his hand then Linc's. "Well, the offer stands. I'll just make sure to have more security on hand if you come."

My brother and I say our goodbyes and head to the car.

"How was your meeting?" Eoghan asks after we've driven out of the parking lot.

"Fine. Let Ozzy know that we're taking care of the Italian situation."

Eoghan lets out a breath and nods. "It's about damn time, brother."

"It's not as easy as you seem to think it is, Eoghan."

My brother whips his head toward me. "You don't

think I know that? My problem with the inaction you've taken isn't because I don't know what it would take. My problem is that you haven't done *anything*. If we thought Francesco was bad, he's nothing when it comes to Carlo. Now that the old man is in prison"—he shakes his head and blows out a low whistle—"I'm afraid we haven't seen how bad things can get."

What he's saying isn't wrong, which is why I've been entertaining the offer from Mario Amatto, head of one of the Italian Mafia families who hold territory in Massachusetts.

The Italians split the state in three. The Cataldis have everything from Boston to Worcester, including control of the ports, which they oh so graciously allow the other families to use for a fee. The Amattos run everything from Worcester to Springfield, and then there're the Farinas, who are in charge of Springfield to the border of New York. It's a system that's been in place since before my time, and as far as I could tell, it was working well for them.

Until Carlo Cataldi got greedy.

The Amattos have been having problems at the ports, shipments going missing and such, even though they pay a ridiculous amount to the Cataldis. Old Man Cataldi would say it's beyond their control and things happen, but we all know these issues are well within his purview, just like everyone knows they're most likely "missing" at the hands of Carlo. I don't know why Francesco allowed this bullshit, but seeing as the Amattos are the closest family to our territory in Boston, aside from the Cataldis, we've heard plenty of rumors about their escalating unhappiness with the way port business was being handled. The three families have seemed to have a sort of uneasy alliance for years, but with Carlo coming into power after his father's incarceration, those ties are shifting.

Naturally, my family circumvents the Boston Harbor completely, but that doesn't come without its own set of problems. It would be nice to have control of those ports and Mario Amatto just might be my ticket in.

"So, what's your grand plan?" The doubt in his voice isn't exactly subtle.

"I've been in talks with Mario Amatto. He's interested in an alliance."

"You think you can trust Mario any more than Cataldi?"

Another fair point, one that I've thought of myself, but Eoghan doesn't know the one detail that will cinch his loyalty.

I nod, keeping my eyes on the road. "He will. I'll have something of his that means more to him than any vendetta or whatever he has against Carlo."

Eoghan scoffs. "Oh yeah, what's that?"

"His daughter," I reply.

From the corner of my eye, I see Eoghan's gaze bore into the side of my head as I drive down the highway without a care in the world. Don't get me wrong, I have plenty to worry about where this crazy offer is concerned, but I'm not displaying any of that in front of my little brother.

"Come again? What are you going to do? Kidnap the poor girl? That's not what we do, Finn."

He's right and I would never dream of going there. I'm nothing like that piece-of-shit Carlo.

"I'm going to marry her."

Thankfully, we're close to my house right outside of the Boston city limits, so I won't have long to deal with the impending freak-out that's about to ensue in three, two...

"What the fuck do you mean you're going to marry Amatto's daughter? You have got to be fucking kidding me." Eoghan scrubs his hands over his face then opens and closes his mouth as though he's looking for the words to express what he didn't just yell in my ear.

"Can you lower your voice, brother? It's not like I can't hear you. I'm sitting right next to you."

"Are you shitting me right now, Finn? You just told me that you plan to marry Mario Amatto's daughter, and you what? Expect me to quietly congratulate you on what is probably one of the worst ideas you've ever had?" The volume of his voice rises with each word, right along with my irritation with his tone.

"Listen," I say as we pull up to my house. "Mom and Dad aren't aware of the proposal Amatto gave me, so I'd appreciate you keeping this to yourself."

I don't feel the need to explain my decision to my brother. My mother, on the other hand, is definitely going to have some very strong opinions on the subject.

"Who else knows?"

"Cillian. And now you."

I park in the long circular driveway in front of my house, and Eoghan shakes his head before opening the passenger door.

I live about thirty minutes outside of the city on nearly ten acres of land. The property has been in my family for generations. Years ago, I knocked down the old house that no one was living in and built a new one, which cost a pretty fucking penny. Especially with all the personal touches I've added, such as a spacious safe room and an underground gun range—and a soundproof basement. If I need to stay in the city, I have a penthouse, but this is my home.

I texted Cillian before leaving Shine and asked him to meet me at my house. We need to go over a few things. Fortunately for me, his car is already parked.

Good. At least there's someone else around to take the brunt of Eoghan's ire.

"Oh, I wouldn't dream of delivering the news to our mother. But you'd better make sure I'm in the room when you break it to her." The cheerful look in his eyes tells me how excited he is to watch my mom hand me my ass for even considering this and for keeping it from her. I may be the boss, but Eoghan and I are still brothers and have always reveled in the other getting in trouble with our parents.

Walking into the house, I head straight to my office

after texting Cillian to meet me and Eoghan there. A mahogany desk sits in front of a large window and the dark-green drapes are open to let in the natural sunlight. I let my mother design the room for me so she could feel like she contributed to my home in some way. I shouldn't be surprised that it looks so similar to my father's office, with the leather couch and tobacco-colored club chairs in front of the desk. I even let her convince me to cover the walls in wallpaper. I felt like a complete tool as I sat with my mother and combed through wallpaper samples, but I have to admit, this is one of my favorite rooms in the house. The bar cart set up in the corner, though? It might be my favorite detail of the room. I keep it well stocked for conversations such as this.

"What's going on?" Cillian asks when he makes his way in, wearing workout clothes and a fresh layer of sweat coating his face and shirt. Another thing I had put in was a state-of-the-art gym. Something the three of us have in common is our love for fighting, and we all despise losing, so building a space to keep us in peak physical shape was a must when I remodeled my home. Both Cillian and Eoghan are regular visitors to my house, and it isn't just to spend time with me; it's to use the equipment. Beats out anything in the city you'd have to pay a ridiculous fee for.

"Well, my brother just told me about his insane plan to marry a Mafia princess," Eoghan remarks, walking over to the bar in the corner of my office. He holds up the bottle of whiskey, and Cillian and I nod.

"Ah," Cillian says, sitting in front of my desk and accepting the glass from Eoghan. "Maybe this place could do with a woman's touch." My lieutenant smirks as he takes a sip from his glass.

"There will be no touching of anything. This is going to be a business arrangement. That's all," I say, rolling my eyes as I scrub my fingers through my hair.

Eoghan sits in the club chair next to Cillian and stares at me like I have two heads.

"Are you out of your mind? Word on the street is she isn't looking for anyone to make a housewife out of her. She's a ball-busting harpy if the rumors are true."

Cillian turns to my brother. "Word on the street? What fucking street? How would you know anything about Alessia Amatto?"

Eoghan shrugs. "I keep my ears open. Her dad is a player in our world."

"It doesn't matter what her reputation is. If her dad wants to come to an agreement for our mutual benefit, then she doesn't have much of a choice. The end goal is to push the Cataldis out and position our family and the Amattos where we want to be. Alessia will have to learn to accept the role she has to play in this. End of story."

My brother chuckles and sips his whiskey. "Yeah, we'll see about that."

CHAPTER TWO

ALESSIA

T HE MUFFLED POP COMING from my gun as I shoot at the paper target is almost as satisfying as when I hit a bull's-eye. That noise has come to symbolize power and dedication throughout the years. I'm a firm believer that *practice makes perfect*, and I've clocked a lot of hours here to become the markswoman I am today. Plus, there's nothing quite like blowing off a little steam at the gun range, or a lot of steam, as the case may be. When I think of the deal my father is trying to get me to go along with, my anger spikes and I raise the gun and shoot three more rounds. A wide smile spreads across my mouth when I see my aim is true and there're three holes in the head of the target.

"Alessia."

I turn to Enzo standing behind me and remove my noise-canceling earbuds before laying my gun on the table next to me.

"Yes?" My bodyguard holds his phone out to me.

I don't have to ask who's on the line, knowing full well that because I wasn't answering my phone, my father called Enzo to get ahold of me.

I roll my eyes and take the phone from Enzo's outstretched hand.

"Hello, Father."

"I see you're still angry with me," he says when he hears my annoyed tone. "Shooting didn't help?"

My father taught me to shoot after...well, after. He thought it would help me not only feel stronger and better able to defend myself if the need arose again, but he said it was a great stress reliever. He became one of my favorite people to go to the range with, always pushing me to do better and learn how to use a multitude of various guns. I didn't tell him I was coming here today, but he knows me well enough to know where to find me when I'm working out a problem and need to take the edge off. Drugs and alcohol never appealed to me. Shooting on the other hand? That's probably saved my sanity on more than one occasion.

"Have you decided to call this farce of a wedding off?" I chew the side of my lip as I lean back against the wall of the private shooting lane at my favorite range. Enzo stands just on the other side of the door, trying to give me privacy, but it's not as though he doesn't know exactly why we're here.

My father may be more progressive than any other made man out there, especially considering he's head of a powerful family, but some things he still holds true, like his right to sign a marriage contract on my behalf.

"Sweetheart, there is a lot riding on this union. You know it as well as I do. Your cooperation"—a snort of laughter escapes me—"will be the catalyst we need to bring down the Cataldis once and for all."

I bite the inside of my cheek, once again remembering why I'm considering this asinine idea in the first place. I know if I throw a big enough fit over being asked to marry Finnegan, my father will find another way. But uniting two powerful families would take care of all the problems we've been running into the last few years at the Boston ports, as well as various other businesses run by my father's men. It's perfectly within his right to choose a husband for me. When he brought up the idea to me a little over a week ago, I was dead set against it. He implored me to consider the deal, and I've spent every day since doing just that.

"I'm aware, Papa," I say, softening my tone. "But that doesn't change the fact that until a week ago, the Irish weren't exactly high on our Christmas card list."

Our families don't have many dealings with the Monaghans, but the few we've had are most likely responsible for several of my dad's gray hairs. There've been deals we've been cut out of, not to mention their casino has been steadily taking business from ours. I'm not stupid; my family makes money using beautiful call girls in the casinos to lure rich businessmen in. I don't necessarily love that aspect of the business, but it is what it is and sex sells. The Irish don't offer anything we don't, so it's always been a mystery as to why their tables are full every night of the week and ours seem to have more and more empty seats.

"Times are changing, Alessia, and we need to change with them. If partnering with the Irish is for the good of both of our organizations, then it's something we need to consider."

"I've done nothing but consider it since you brought it up."

"Finn wants an answer tonight, so I need you to stop thinking about it and make a decision."

"Why is he so desperate to have an unwilling wife?"

"Alessia," my father breathes out. "We need this deal as much as he does. If we have control of the ports, along with the Monaghans, that will change our business dealings and significantly expand our power and territory. The Cataldis are falling apart, and we need to strike before anyone else. With our combined efforts, we'd be unstoppable."

"And me being the Irishman's wife would ensure the Monaghans won't double cross us, yes, I know, Papa." It's not like this is the first time he's used that argument to convince me.

"My sources say he is a man of honor."

I outright laugh at my father's description of Finn.

"Really? Because my sources say he's a womanizing scoundrel."

Finn and his brother have a certain reputation in the Boston area that reaches all the way to New York. Honor is not a word I've heard used to describe him.

"Alessia, you can't believe idle gossip," my father admonishes. I imagine him waving his hand like he's brushing away my concerns. "He's a single man who hasn't had a wife to take care of. It's not like he's stepping out on his marriage."

One thing I've always admired about my father is his devotion and faithfulness to my mother. That's not the norm in our world, but my father has always believed a man's character is defined by his commitment to his vows made before God on his wedding day.

I let out a long sigh and stretch my neck, attempting to relieve the tension that's settled back in during this conversation.

"Listen, Papa. I need to go. I'm having lunch with Gemma in thirty minutes. We'll talk when I get home, yeah?"

"Okay, but I need to know if I'm inviting the Monaghan boy for dinner."

Only my father would refer to the head of the Irish mob as a boy.

"We'll talk when I get home. I love you."

"I love you too, *piccola demone*."

I hang up with a smile on my face at my father's old nickname for me. He's been calling me *little demon* since I was a young girl getting up to any mischief I could find.

Enzo walks in just after I disconnect the call, confirming he heard the conversation. Putting the noise-canceling earbuds back in my ear before picking up my pistol, I turn toward the fresh target Enzo set up for me.

Giving him a small smile of thanks, I face the target

and fire.

"You've been at the range," Gemma comments when she reaches our table at the little bistro fifteen minutes from where I go to shoot. It's a gorgeous spring day in the city, so I picked a table on the little outdoor patio surrounded by blooming flowers and ivy trailing up the columns of the veranda.

"How can you tell?" I ask, standing from my seat and leaning in to give her a hug.

We both sit and the waitress promptly makes her way over to our table to take Gemma's drink order. Her ice-blue eyes zero in on my glass of prosecco, and she lifts her brow. "I'll have the same," she says, pointing to my glass. The waitress smiles then hurries away.

"You always seem to sit a little taller when you've spent the morning shooting. Like the weight of the world isn't pressing on your shoulders."

"Am I that stressed out normally?" I ask with a laugh.

"It's not obvious to everyone else, but I know you too well—you can't hide it from me."

I smile at my best friend as the waitress returns with her glass of bubbly, and she takes a sip.

"So, why are we day drinking?" Gemma sets her glass on the table and pins me with her spill-it stare. It's not as intimidating as she thinks, at least not to me. To the world, she's a ball-busting beauty with long blonde hair, always perfectly styled in waves down to the middle of her back. When she turns her gaze on any man, they just about drop to their knees, wanting to give her the world. Or they run in the opposite direction because she's about to verbally cut them off at said knees. With her, it could really go either way, depending on her mood. To me, though, she's just Gemma, and I love her unconditionally, just like she loves me.

"I need to make a decision about the Irish proposal."

"The oh-so-romantic one that didn't involve a ring or even a question from the prospective groom?" Her disdain for what she considers an archaic tradition drips from every syllable.

"That would be the one," I reply, not wanting to get into all the details of why the proposal makes sense from a business standpoint, not that I could. I'd never talk to an outsider about my family's dealings. It's as much for her protection as it is mine.

We both attended Yale, me for a degree in finance and Gemma for marketing. She worked her ass off to be able to afford Yale, working nearly full time and applying for all the financial aid and any small scholarships she could. Coming from a single-mother household, she didn't have the opportunities afforded to me by my family's sizable bank account. She never allowed the stigma of growing up poor that some of the rich assholes in our college days tried to attach to her to discourage her in any way. Instead, it made her work that much harder. She didn't have any sort of backup plan or a rich daddy who was going to hand her a job after graduation. She fought tooth and nail for everything to make ends meet and soar to the top of her class. I've always admired her tenacity and the way she attacks every obstacle in front of her. That went a long way in her being the youngest head of marketing for a premier fashion house in Boston.

Gemma and I were assigned as roommates our freshman year, and after deciding dorm life wasn't for us, we rented a little apartment. She didn't recognize my last name because my father kept the Amatto name out of the press, unlike the Cataldis. When she first asked about the security I had trailing me between classes, I told her my family was well-off and my father was overprotective. She gave me what I've come to know as her signature I *know there's more to the story, but I'll let it slide* look, but she didn't pry further.

It wasn't until our second year that I admitted the truth: my father was head of a powerful Mafia family. It could have been the need to be honest with my friend, who had become as close to me as a sister, or it could have been the tequila. I guess we'll never know, but the next day when I remembered what I told her, I was petrified she'd look at me differently or be one of those weird Mafia-obsessed groupies I used to see around my brother before he passed. Instead, she made us a greasy breakfast and waved off my concerns with a flick of her slim wrist. "Alessia, there aren't many people who don't come from families with skeletons in their closets. I'm certainly not about to judge you for yours," she told me. Since then, I never felt the need to hide anything from her, even if I couldn't give her every detail about my life.

"Do you ever wish we were back in our apartment and the only things we had to worry about were studying and which party to go to on a Friday night?" I ask, suddenly nostalgic for a simpler time.

She tilts her head back and forth as she sips from her glass. "Sometimes, I suppose. But I'm not the one who has to settle into some arranged marriage for her family's sake."

I told Gemma about the proposal with Finn but didn't go into specific detail. I just explained uniting two powerful families would be beneficial for both of our organizations, and there's no tighter bond than marriage.

"I never imagined having to make this decision at twenty-eight," I begin. "I mean, it's not unusual in my world, but I don't know, I guess I thought I'd somehow escaped this particular fate."

Usually, these arrangements were made when the woman was much younger than I am. My father was content to let me use my degree and work alongside him at one of his real estate companies. I never thought he'd be pressuring me now, but then again, no one thought Francesco Cataldi would get sent to prison or that his son would be on the run after trying to take out an MC president and the US attorney who put his old man away.

"Then say no," she says. "I don't know what exactly you're going to gain from this, but if you're having reservations or you're scared—"

"I'm not afraid," I interject, knowing where her line of thinking is headed. The one and only serious relationship I had was with a man who *didn't* have the same distaste for violence against women as my father or as the Irish are rumored to possess. No one will ever hurt me like that again. I've spent hours in the gym and gun range to make sure of that.

Gemma's eyes soften, and she reaches for my hand. "I'm sorry. I shouldn't have brought it up. I just hate the thought of you tying yourself to a man because it'll help with some business deal or something. That's not a good reason to get married."

My reasons are definitely bigger than just a business deal, but without divulging the issues my family is having and why, I can't really explain it to her.

The waitress comes to take our order, and we settle into more neutral topics of discussion.

"So, who's your flavor of the week?" I ask, joking with Gemma about her love life. She never had a serious boyfriend in college, insisting it wasn't the time to be tied down to one man when there were so many to choose from. Her thinking has followed her well into her late twenties, and I don't see it changing anytime soon.

"Well...there's a new guy at that kickboxing gym down

the street from my apartment. Oh my God, Alessia." She sits back in her chair and dramatically fans herself. "You should see the abs on this guy. And the way he spars? So much intensity and precision. It's hot as hell."

Gemma used to join me and Enzo when we trained, and she developed quite the appetite for hand-to-hand combat. And the fighters she would spar with.

"Have you worked your charm on him yet?"

She laughs and shakes her head. "We went out for drinks last week, but I'm playing it cool."

"So, you didn't invite him back for a one-on-one demonstration of his *skills*?"

She clutches her imaginary pearls and gasps in feigned shock. "What kind of woman do you take me for?"

"The kind that isn't a buttoned-up prude like you're pretending to be?"

"Fair," she replies, and we share a knowing smile. "But no, there was no one-on-one anything. I don't know; I'd like to feel a connection for once. Maybe get to know a guy before I kick him out of bed the next morning. Maybe I wouldn't be so inclined to get rid of him if I actually like someone for their personality and not just the way they look in tight shorts."

"Don't knock those tight shorts, sister. There's nothing wrong with seeing the whole package before you *see the package*."

Gemma lets out a bark of laughter, scaring the waitress who sets our plates down in front of us.

"Scandalous talk from a married woman," she says, arching her brow.

"Not married yet. Also, not dead yet."

Gemma smiles and lifts her glass. "I'll cheers to that."

An hour later, Enzo is driving me home. I'm full and feel lighter than I did at the range. Though Gemma and I didn't talk more about my potential marriage, I feel better just having spent time with my best friend. She may not agree with the idea of me having to marry for the sake of family, but there's no doubt in my mind that she'll stand next to me and support me through it all.

Enzo parks the car around back and I head into the house through the kitchen entrance, grabbing a glass of water before making my way to my father's office. After two quick knocks, he calls for me to enter.

"How was lunch?" he asks, placing his readers on the desk in front of him.

It strikes me just now how much stress my father's been under for the last few years and how it's aged him. I suppose that could be attributed to the passage of time, but seeing him sitting behind his desk with exhaustion lining his face and dark smudges under his eyes, I'm reminded he won't be around forever. This life has taken its toll on the man who always seemed indestructible. But he's not. He's human, with worries, fears, and an unwavering need to do what's right for his family—the ones that live in this house and the ones that have been working for him since before I was born. The weight of that responsibility lies heavily on his shoulders, and it surprises me that this is the first time I'm seeing it so clearly.

"It was good." I sit on one of the leather club chairs in front of his oak desk, remembering when I was a little girl and my feet didn't touch the ground.

Old family pictures line the dark wood-paneled walls. My parents' extended families are back in Italy, and the photos proudly display our lineage. Though my father's immediate family has been here for several generations, my mother didn't come to the United States until after she met my father. He was visiting some of his cousins and saw my mother at the market early one morning. The way he tells the story, she was the most beautiful woman he'd ever laid eyes on, and the second she smiled at him, he was a goner. He came home from his vacation as a married man, and my grandfather was less than thrilled. He wanted my father to marry a daughter of one of the New York families in order to make an advantageous alliance. After five minutes with my mother, though, my grandfather was nearly as smitten with her as my dad. Lilliana Amatto has that way with people. It's something she's tried to instill in me. I have a feeling I've disappointed her more times than not on that front.

Letting out a quick huff of air, I look at my father. "Let's talk about the Irish."

One of my dad's bushy eyebrows quirks in question. "You've made your decision?"

My lips press together as I nod. "I'll agree to the

marriage." Once the words are out, it feels as though a ball of lead has dropped in my stomach, while my father looks relieved. "But we need to go over the contract before I walk down the aisle. I don't want any surprises once Finn thinks he has me where he wants me."

"Somehow, *piccola demone*, I have no doubt you'll keep him on his toes."

"We need Cataldi out of the way for good," I begin. "Then, when that happens, we need to have co-control over the ports. If Farina wants to use them, he can still pay the same fee he was paying to Francesco. Now that the old man is in prison and Carlo is in the wind, it's the perfect time to push in."

My father nods as he listens, giving me his full attention. It's something he's always been good about. I talk, and he listens—the respect between us goes both ways.

"Farina doesn't have the foothold the Monaghans do in Boston, and I need to know he's going to use that influence to protect our incoming and outgoing shipments as opposed to only caring about his business. No more disappearing merchandise." My family has been using ships to transport guns and cocaine for as long as I can remember. Lately, too many of those shipments have come up "missing" under Cataldi's supervision. "I also want a guarantee that there will be no human cargo running through the ports." Carlo had become particularly fond of that side of the underworld. I refuse to stand for it. If I'm willing to give up my freedom for this deal, I'll be damned if that continues under my watch.

"It's a nasty business I've never wanted to be a part of, either," my father states.

No one in this life is going to be nominated for sainthood anytime soon, but even with criminals, there are some lines you should never cross, and selling people to sick assholes is my hardest of lines. Carlo Cataldi doesn't have the same distaste for it as my father or myself. Sure, our organization deals in prostitution, but the women my father employs are there of their own free will and are well compensated for their time. No one is selling them to the highest bidder to do with as they please. If anyone hurts one of the girls, it's dealt with swiftly and violently.

"He's going to want a Catholic ceremony," my father states. "His mother is devout, and if I know anything about Irish boys, they never want to disappoint their mamas."

I nod in agreement. "That's fine, but I want it at St. Michael's. If I have to sit through a marriage mass, I'd feel better with it being at our church." I've been attending mass there since I was a baby. I'm sure my dad can make a sizable donation to the church to forego any of the premarriage counseling.

My dad notes it on the paper in front of him then raises his gaze to me. "We should discuss children."

My mouth goes dry with the thought. "Why?" It's a stupid question. Of course, there needs to be an agreement on having kids. Finn and I will be expected to do our part to carry on the family name.

"This isn't two people falling in love, getting married, and deciding to start a family type of situation, sweetheart. Nothing about this is typical, except in our life. Having a clause in regard to children is standard."

"How often do people agree not to have children?"

"I've never heard of it, but if the thought upsets you that much, I'll leave it out. The Irish don't usually put together marriage contracts like this, so he may not even notice."

"We're going into this lying already?"

"Not lying, just leaving out a clause they probably wouldn't have even thought about."

There was a time in my life when the idea of having kids was exciting, and there was a man I thought would be the father. Both of those fantasies were ripped from me in one night.

"Leave it out. If he says anything, then I'll consider it."

My father nods and sets his pen down. "Thank you for agreeing, Alessia. I know how hard this was for you."

It is hard, but the relief on my father's face is what makes me believe I made the right decision. I'm a woman in a world run by men. There isn't anything I can do to change that, even if my father allowed me to live my own life for as long as possible. I have an obligation to him and our family. But that doesn't mean I'll be a doormat, and heaven help my future husband if he thinks otherwise.

CHAPTER THREE

FINN

"**I**'M STILL NOT SURE about this," Cillian grumbles in the passenger seat as we head down the highway to meet my betrothed.

I'm getting fucking married. I roll my eyes at the thought.

"What's got your panties in a twist, Cill?"

Cillian lets out an irritated huff, shaking his head as though I asked one of the dumbest questions possible. "Where to begin? One, she's a spoiled Mafia princess—"

"I thought you liked the idea of me having a little *Suzy Homemaker* waiting by the hearth for me to come home."

I catch the hard side-eye he's giving me when I briefly glance in his direction.

"Second," he continues as if I hadn't spoken, "just because you marry the girl doesn't mean he's any more trustworthy. Who's to say Mario's not using her to fuck us over? Having her live in your house and 'accidentally' stumbling across certain files or overhearing conversations then running back to daddy dearest?"

"I don't keep anything at the house she could stumble across. Besides, how many men in the Mafia do you know of who use women to do their dirty work? I doubt Amatto is much different when it comes to his daughter. At least in that aspect. He's more interested in getting control of the ports."

"Which he's sharing with you. It's not a stretch to consider he'll try to muscle you out."

"That's where my marriage comes in. It's highly unlikely the man would be quick to screw us over if I have his daughter living in my home."

"I wouldn't bank on that. Our organizations have never really seen eye to eye, Finn. The way they conduct business and the way we do are miles apart. It seems reasonable his daughter is nothing but a bargaining chip to him. He doesn't want you taking over the ports on your own, and he's willing to give away his daughter because he knows you pose a threat to his power. He knows he can't take it by force. Seems to me he isn't interested in how his daughter feels or what happens to her at your hands, especially if he's that quick to ship her off."

"Jesus, Cillian. You make me sound like a monster." My hands tighten around the steering wheel as I become increasingly annoyed with Cillian's badgering on the subject.

"I know you, but he doesn't. The Italians have made no bones about their distaste for us. Now he's turning his daughter over to someone he thinks is dirt on his shoe, and we're supposed to trust he isn't planning on screwing us over?"

Everything Cillian is saying is true. But my family has been waiting to take out the Cataldis for as long as I can remember. With the old man being in prison and Carlo on the run, we're finally in a position, with the help of Amatto, to destroy them.

"Listen, I understand the history with the Cataldis and why you want them gone, but I wouldn't be a good lieutenant if I didn't bring up the very real possibility that this could blow up in your face."

My father made a vow to my mother at the funeral of her only sister. My parents believe she was murdered on the order of Francesco Cataldi for something as innocent as falling in love with the wrong man. Her son went missing that same night, and for years, my mother looked into the face of every blue-eyed, dark-haired boy for a resemblance to her sister. They couldn't find evidence, but considering the father of her child was Francesco's right-hand man, it made sense. Francesco was not the type of man to see that as anything less than a betrayal against him. My father promised my mother that he would make sure they paid for taking away her sister and her baby. So yeah, I'd say we have history. Back then, my father wasn't in the position to destroy him and his empire the way I am now. We have more money and more power than we did during my father's reign. The Cataldis, on the other hand, have been weakened. It's the perfect time to strike. We'll take them apart brick by brick and watch their kingdom crumble. Marrying the daughter of a power-hungry Italian is only one of the many moves I've been making.

Pulling up to the Amatto estate and seeing the giant house in front of me is exactly what I imagined it would look like, down to the gaudy fountain in the front of the house.

Cillian lets out a low whistle beside me as we stare at the three-story home in front of us.

"And here I was thinking your house was ridiculously huge," Cillian mutters.

"This place is like a fucking palace," I say, taking in the Italian palazzo-style home. Arches frame every window, and the dark stonework on the house showcases the vibrant green of the towering shrubs planted next to the house. The tall stone columns stretch from the marble steps to the sloped roof, and two guards walk from behind their considerable width toward our car. I didn't even see the fuckers when we pulled up, that's how wide the columns are.

Jesus fucking Christ, I feel like I'm in another country still ruled by medieval kings and queens instead of an estate outside of Worcester, Massachusetts.

Cillian rolls his window down as the guards approach, leaning down and looking inside the car.

"We're here to see Mario."

The guard straightens but keeps his hand on the gun holstered on his side. The other guard keeps his finger close to the trigger of the shotgun he grips in his hands.

Guard number two directs us where to park with the end of his shotgun and waits behind the car for us to exit.

"Warm welcome," my lieutenant comments as we follow the two men to the front door.

"Can't say I'm surprised."

Amatto doesn't like us too much. Hell, none of the Italian families do. They view us as nothing more than street hoodlums with no smarts, only brawn. At one point in history, that was true of the Irish mob, but things have changed across the East Coast. We got smarter and more organized. Instead of spending all our time fighting with other Irish families, we learned to coexist in our own territories. My family happens to control Boston but not the *Port* of Boston which has been held in the Cataldis tight grip.

Until now. this new alliance with Amatto will guarantee that.

Cillian and I walk through the arched doorway, and we're led through the massive foyer then down a short hallway to a sitting room with walls made of bookshelves and row upon row of old books lining the shelves. My mom would get a kick out of this place. She always tells Dad she wants him to build her a library in their house.

"Mr. Amatto will join you shortly," one of the nameless guards tells us.

Cillian looks around the space, walking up to one of the bookshelves and surveying its contents.

"Do you think this guy has read all of these?" he asks, eyeing the range of novels.

I shrug, not really interested in the reading habits of the Mafia don.

I take in the large space and the ornately carved wooden couches with thick leather cushions spaced throughout the room. One wall isn't covered in bookshelves; instead, it's painted with a mural that looks like something you'd find in the Sistine Chapel. Upon closer inspection, I realize it's a replica of the famous ceiling of the chapel. Jesus Christ, this man has his house decorated like he has money to burn. Everything is plush and expensive, including the books Cillian can't stop drooling over.

"These are mostly in Italian," he says, taking a book from the shelf and opening it.

"Yes, my father was a collector," I hear from the doorway of the library.

We turn toward the voice and see my future father-in-law standing tall with his wife by his side, her arm looped through his as they take us in.

Cillian returns the book to the shelf as the Amattos approach.

"So nice to meet you, Finnegan," Amatto's wife says in a faintly accented voice, welcoming me and Cillian to her home.

"You as well, Mrs. Amatto," I reply.

She waves her hand as a friendly smile graces her light-pink lips. "Please, call me Lilliana. We're going to be family soon."

I smile because I don't want to be rude to the woman, but the contract hasn't been signed. As much as Mario Amatto wants this deal to take place, I'm not about to be bowled over by him because he thinks I'm desperate for this alliance.

"Please have a seat. Alessia should be down shortly," Mario says. "Would you like a drink?"

Cillian and I sit on one of the lush leather couches while Mario fixes himself a scotch neat.

"Would love one, thank you. But I do prefer Irish whiskey."

"I'm afraid I only have scotch. I can ring one of my men to see if they can scrounge some up for you."

Leaning back on the couch, I wave my hand in his direction. "Don't go through any trouble. I'm sure what you're having is fine."

Yes, I'm sure the expensive scotch housed in a crystal decanter is perfectly delicious. I just wanted to make a point to remind him who he's dealing with. Not some smooth-talking Italian mafioso, but a no-bullshit Irishman who isn't going to put up with being steamrolled and isn't afraid to call him out if he tries.

"I'd love one too, Dad."

I look toward the doorway again and see the woman of the hour. Holy shit, the pictures I saw of Alessia Amatto did not do her justice. They must have been taken years ago because the pictures I saw were of a girl who looked far more innocent than the vixen standing before us.

Her dark hair is styled into soft waves that beg to be mussed up by my hands, and she's wearing a fitted red dress that shows off her trim waist and tightly holds to her rounded hips like it's a second skin. It's as though some higher being asked what I would find most attractive in a woman and then molded Alessia to my specifications.

While all of those thoughts are swirling in my head, I work damn hard to keep the mask of indifference I wear most days firmly in place. If I don't, I might start drooling over those curves and have a hell of a time *not* getting lost in the green eyes that hold fire and mischief behind a look of being the ice princess she's known for. It doesn't matter how attractive she is. I've never been one to come undone over a pretty face, and I'm not about to start now, no matter the visceral reaction I'm having to the stunning beauty before me.

"Alessia, come meet Finnegan and his man Cillian," her father says as he pours another glass of scotch.

Cillian and I stand from the couch, and Alessia walks straight to Cillian, leans in, and kisses both his cheeks. "So nice to meet you, Finnegan," she says, batting her thick eyelashes at my lieutenant.

I clear my throat. "I'm Finnegan, that's Cillian," I inform her with a smirk on my face. As if I don't know exactly what she's doing.

"Oh," she says with a light laugh and backs away from

my uncomfortable-looking lieutenant. "I'm so sorry. All you Irish boys look the same to me."

"Alessia," her mother admonishes. "Don't be rude to our guests. Finnegan is going to be your husband."

"Please, call me Finn," I say to Lilliana.

Alessia rolls her eyes, and a tinkling laugh follows. I shouldn't like the sound of it so much, especially considering she just tried to emasculate me and the entire male side of the Irish population.

"I was kidding, Mama. I'm sure Finn knows that." She shoots me a saccharine smile and tilts her head. "But the husband part hasn't been decided on, now has it?"

Mario hands Alessia a scotch, and she nods her thanks.

"Yes, yes, we'll discuss all of that after dinner, my dear. No need to keep the cook waiting." Mario holds his hand out for his wife and leads her out of the room.

Being the gentleman no one has ever accused me of being, I do the same with Alessia and place her hand in the crook of my arm.

"Sorry you don't have a companion this evening, Cillian. Next time, I'll be sure to have one of my cousins here," Alessia says.

"Will she have a hard time telling us apart like you pretended to? It might get awkward seeing one of your family members kiss your husband."

"I would never be jealous over a man. Besides, I'm sure by then I'll remember which of you is which." The smile she sends isn't cold, but it is challenging.

"Are you trying to make yourself as unappealing as possible to me, sweetheart?" I ask in a low voice.

"You know as well as I do, my face could be covered with hairy moles, and you would still find the idea of marriage to me enticing. It isn't me you're after, but the power my father can offer you."

I keep the surprised look off my face, but to realize she knows the parameters of this deal her father is offering takes me by surprise.

"We don't have to be enemies. That doesn't exactly make for a happy marriage."

Alessia's shrewd green eyes study me as she considers my statement. "We don't have to be friends either, and happiness is overrated."

She stops behind her chair, and I pull it out for her.

"That's your call, sweetie. Just remember, we're both getting something out of this deal and if you continue, I may not be so inclined to sign a marriage contract."

Fuck, I'm beginning to wonder if Cillian was on to something with his warning during the drive here. I always assumed Mafia princesses were raised to be meek and gentle, not whatever this is. Her comments aren't untrue or outright mean, more like she's a little resentful she's in this position to begin with.

We all have a seat at the large table adorned with a stunning centerpiece of fresh flowers and plates of meat and cheeses in front of us. Between the baroque wallpaper and ornate crystal chandelier, I'm beginning to sense a theme throughout the house, and it's one that screams old money. I'm not poor by any stretch of the imagination, but my family comes from humble beginnings. It's more than apparent the Amattos do not.

One of their staff members fills each of our glasses with red wine while we nibble on the assortment in front of us.

Alessia's mother takes the opportunity to regale the table with stories about what a sweet girl her daughter was growing up and how she loved to dance and sing and chase after her brother. I don't ask where Giovanni is. He died nearly ten years ago. So many rumors circulated over the cause of his death—he owed a rival family money and was shot when he refused to pay, a lovers' quarrel, maybe a secret relationship that ended badly. The rumors are endless. Mario remained quiet on the subject at the time, so stories ran rampant. I never delved into it myself since it didn't have anything to do with my family.

After the meat and cheeses are cleared, a delicious-smelling pasta is laid before us. Jesus. I would gain a hundred pounds in a year if I ate like this every day.

"My mother's recipe," Lilliana says.

I take a bite and groan in appreciation. "Absolutely delicious."

"I'll make sure Alessia has my old recipe book when she moves into your house."

A tight smile forms on my lips. "Well, according to Alessia, that hasn't been decided yet."

Mario waves his hand. "We'll discuss all of this after dinner. No need to worry about business when we're in the middle of our meal."

The look he shoots Alessia doesn't go unnoticed. It makes me wonder how much has actually already been decided on and if Alessia is aware of how badly her father wants this marriage to happen.

Our pasta plates are cleared, and servings of the most delicious-smelling veal are laid before each of us.

"Where did you go to college, Finn?" Alessia asks.

Cillian laughs before I can answer, and Mario narrows his eyes at his daughter.

"I didn't. There isn't much need for higher education in our line of work." I can tell she's trying to make me sound like an uneducated street punk. "My father taught me what I needed to know about the business. He took a trial-by-fire approach to my training."

"How did that work out for you?" she asks.

"Pretty well, considering I'm here to discuss marrying a spoiled Mafia princess because her father knows how powerful my family is. And the fact that, together, we'll very well be unstoppable." Cillian, Mario, and Lilliana's eyes ping-pong between Alessia and me.

"What good is a piece of paper when you have the respect of some of the most resourceful and dangerous criminals within the state? I had better things to do with my time than read a bunch of dusty books by dead guys," I continue before taking a bite of the mouthwatering veal in front of me. Damn, Mario's cook is a fucking genius with a slab of meat.

"Did you go to college, Alessia?" Cillian asks in an attempt to ease the tension at the table.

"I did." She sits straighter in her chair with a proud smile on her red lips. "Yale, then Wharton for my MBA."

"How is that working out for you?" I take a sip of wine and Alessia looks at me like she's trying to telepathically make me choke on it.

Most women in this life don't work a day in their lives, and I doubt she's any different. Sure, she can talk a big game with her fancy degrees, but does she really know how to play?

"Actually, Finn, Alessia's been a great help to my business. She's assisted my accountant and financial advisers in several more delicate business matters. She works for our real estate development company as well. She's quite knowledgeable when it comes to financial strategy." Mario smiles at his daughter.

"So you spent all that money to be a glorified accountant? Good to know I'm marrying a woman who can balance a checkbook." I'm being a dick. Actually, learning this about my soon-to-be wife is impressive, but like hell will I show her that.

"Well, like I said earlier, nothing is set in stone," Alessia says, taking a sip from her wineglass and shooting me a brittle smile.

Looks like I struck a nerve. Obviously if she went to Yale and Wharton, she's smart as hell and would probably have some fancy, high-paying corporate job if she weren't the daughter of Mario Amatto. But she needs to learn if she wants to take little digs at me, I'll bite back.

Cillian gives me a subtle kick under the table, and when I meet his eyes, they're imploring me to shut the fuck up. This marriage will cement my family and the Amattos as two of the most powerful organizations on the East Coast, and the look in Cillian's eyes is telling me I'm one word away from fucking it all up. That's fair, but damn, that girl is good at getting under my skin. It's no secret the Italians have always looked at us like we're dirt beneath their shoes. We aren't running some penny ante gang like the ones we've pushed out of Boston, but the Italians have never treated us with any kind of respect. That's been fine and dandy with me through the years. Let the assholes underestimate us. We've proven time and time again that we can hold our own. Which is why sometimes my mouth likes to run away with itself. Even if it's not the most opportune moment.

"Your family is Catholic, yes?" Lilliana asks, trying to direct the conversation into more neutral territory.

"Yes. My mother wouldn't allow us boys to miss a Sunday mass."

"I look forward to meeting her. I've always wanted Alessia to marry in the faith and raise children with the same beliefs she grew up with."

Alessia looks at her mother and her jaw tics with irritation. Looks like this isn't the first time Lilliana has mentioned children in her daughter's presence. Though I'm not opposed to having them if that's what she wants, kids aren't a deal breaker for me. My mother, on the other hand...

A member of the serving staff comes out to clear our plates and another lays the most delectable-looking cake in front of each of us.

"Tiramisu. It's our cook's specialty."

I take a bite, and the chocolate coffee flavor explodes on my tongue. Shit, maybe I should marry their cook instead of their ball-busting daughter.

"Does this recipe come with the marriage contract?" I ask, taking another bite of the decadent dessert.

"Sorry, it's her most guarded secret. But don't worry, I'm sure the contract will entice you more than the tiramisu," Mario replies.

I guess we'll see about that.

CHAPTER FOUR

ALESSIA

DINNER IS...NOT GOING WELL.

We made it through the first three courses. It was a little touch and go during the veal. But by the time dessert is served, I've decided to bite my tongue. Well, I should say the looks my father keeps shooting in my direction have made it clear he expects me to bite it.

When I walked into the library and saw Finn for the first time in person and dressed in what I'm sure is a custom black suit and crisp white shirt sans tie, I had to take a moment to compose myself. I've never been a slave to my baser desires, but that man oozes confidence and a certain swagger that used to be my kryptonite. It's gotten me into trouble in the past, and I'm not about to go into this marriage with him thinking he has the upper hand in any way, shape, or form, including him being aware that I find him impossibly attractive. All he had to do was turn those dark-blue eyes that held mischief and promise my way and a riot of butterflies took flight low in my belly. Then he stood, and I got the full view of all six foot two of the gorgeous man wearing a devil-may-care smirk. Could have been the wine at lunch, or it could have been my lack of a satisfying love life, or any love life, but something flared in me that I wasn't prepared for.

And I needed to shut it down fast.

The look on Finn's face when I "mistook" Cillian for him was priceless. He's obviously a man who knows the attention he garners from the female population, and he revels in it if the rumors are true. I've never been one to believe everything I hear about someone, but where there's smoke, there's fire. And my first instinct when I laid eyes on my future husband was there had to be truth to those rumors. It was in the way his presence took up the space. He stood tall and proud in the presence of my father, which most men don't do, but Finn was casual and confident, like being in the home of one of his toughest competitors wasn't anything more than a typical Tuesday night. I was intrigued and hated it, hence my sudden and visceral need to see the man knocked down a peg or two.

After the maid clears the dessert plates, my father suggests we head to the study for after-dinner cognac and cigars. My mother opts not to join us; she hates the smoke. Finn and Cillian thank her for the lovely meal. When the two men are saying their goodbyes to my mother, my father gently pulls me aside.

"What are you doing? Are you trying to make yourself as disagreeable as possible? I was under the impression you were on board with this marriage," he says in a low voice.

"I don't know what you mean, Papa," I reply with innocent, wide eyes. "I was just making conversation, trying to get to know the man better."

My father's brow quirks, and he gives me a flat look.

"Can you do that without insulting him?"

I smile sweetly. "Of course."

"Why don't I believe you?"

Kissing his cheek, I turn to the two men silently waiting to be shown to the study. It's not that I'm unwilling to partake in this unholy alliance, it's that if I don't set firm boundaries now, Finn is the type to walk all over me. I refuse to allow that to happen.

"Gentlemen, follow me."

Finn's eyes widen in surprise at the insinuation I'll be joining them. I may have the same distaste for cigar smoke as my mother, but I enjoy an after-dinner cognac, and I'll be damned if they discuss my future as Mrs. Monaghan without me in the room.

My father leads us to his study, and the entire time, Finn trails behind me. I've never been one to wax poetic about a man's gaze caressing my skin as I've read in so many books, but damn if I don't feel his eyes glued to me as I walk in front of him. I may or may not put a little extra sway in my hips as we enter the room.

"Please have a seat," my father instructs as his butler grabs the humidor box and offers a cigar to each of the men.

This is the only room in the house my mother allows him to smoke in and one of my favorites. Though I don't enjoy the smoke, the rich scent of cigars constantly hangs in the air. That scent will always remind me of my brother. He and I used to play hide-and-seek and he never failed to find me in here, ducked behind one of the couches or under the desk in the corner.

I make myself busy pouring drinks and hand a glass to my father, then Finn and Cillian, before I settle on the leather couch next to my father. We're facing each other across the low coffee table, the line between us clear until we sign a contract that binds our families together.

"Let's talk about the elephant in the room," Finn starts as I look around dramatically.

"I don't see an elephant," I say with fake confusion lacing my words.

His lips purse and my father mumbles something in Italian under his breath.

"You don't want this marriage," Finn says, leveling me with a look that dares me to lie.

"I want what's best for my family and the future of the business my father has built."

Finn puffs his cigar and leans back on the couch. "Same here," he says with that fucking irreverent smile.

"I also have reservations. Your organization is getting the better end of the deal, as far as I can see."

Finn chuckles and waves his hand for me to continue.

"You need my father's men to take control of the ports from Cataldi."

Finn's eyes flare for a moment when I speak so

frankly about business matters. Most families don't allow women to have a say or even any knowledge of what goes on behind the doors of these kinds of meetings. But I'm not most women, and my father has long since clued me in on the inner workings of his business.

"Same as your father needs ours. Anyone can fight for control, but neither your father nor I have made it to where we are by simply seizing that control. It's about keeping it, and quite frankly, neither of our organizations are in the position to keep it if Cataldi comes back for that particular fight," Finn counters.

It's no secret Carlo Cataldi has been missing since his run-in with a federal prosecutor and an MC president a few months ago. His father's conviction and Carlo's subsequent disappearance have thrown the Cataldi organization into a tailspin, every capo grabbing whatever they think they can and then some.

"Who do you think the men will take orders from? You or an Italian they've known their entire life?" I ask with a bite to my tone.

Finn lifts his chin, meeting my challenge. "That's all well and good for you, sweetheart, but where are you going to get the manpower to take over in the first place? They might be more inclined to listen to *your father*," he emphasizes his last two words, driving home the point that it's my father calling the shots, not me. "But it won't do much good if your men are cut down for trying."

The asshole has a point.

"The way I see it is we both need this deal. It's no secret it's expensive to have my shipments coming into ports so far from Boston. There're a lot of palms to grease from those ports to Boston. And it's also no secret that Cataldi has been bleeding the other families dry with his ever-increasing 'taxes' on shipments that aren't his. You could use other ports like I do, but it isn't going to solve any of our problems long term. We both need those ports, and I'd rather we create a united front for both of our families than fight Cataldi for power when he returns. If we're going to do this, now's the time. If not, then thank you for the meal and the fine Cuban." Finn snuffs out the cigar on the crystal ashtray to the side of him and leans forward, looking me in the eye, daring me to...actually, I can't quite tell. It's either wish him good night and good luck or marry him and unite our two families, becoming one of the most powerful organizations on the East Coast.

I've never been one to back down from a challenge.

"Look over the contract, Mr. Monaghan. If it meets your standard, we'll sign." I meet his challenging gaze with one of my own. A small smile ticks up the corner of his mouth, and he nods.

When my father hands him the contract, he reviews it quickly and hands it to Cillian, who does the same. The room is quiet as they go over the short document.

I catch my father's eyes, and he smiles, tipping his head down slightly in a nod of appreciation.

Cillian hands the contract back to Finn, who asks my father for a pen. He signs the paper with a flourish and smiles widely at me.

"Welcome to the family, Mrs. Monaghan."

My mother is a master at getting shopkeepers to bend over backward for her. It's been two days since having dinner with Finn, and I'm already wrapped in lace and silk, standing on a small platform in front of a huge mirror while a seamstress shoves pins into the expensive fabric, the needles poking dangerously close to my skin.

Gemma and my mother sit on a dark purple velvet couch, and from the reflection in the mirror, I see the tears in my mother's eyes.

"You look so beautiful," she says for the hundredth time, and I fight not to roll my eyes.

I love my mother and want her to have her moment seeing me in my wedding dress, but it's not as though this is some happy love connection that turned into a marriage proposal. This is a business transaction that's resulting in a marriage and a territory takeover. The only reason there's going to be an actual wedding in a church is because my mother wouldn't have it any other way, and from the sound of it, neither would Finn's.

In ten days' time, we're to be married at St. Michael's

in front of three hundred of our *closest* friends and family. Though we agreed it would be best to show the world and the other families that Finn and I are committed to this marriage, hence the lavish wedding in a church, I'm not looking forward to having to carry on this farce in front of so many people. I'm good at keeping a straight face in the company of my father's men, but to play a blushing bride is miles out of my comfort zone.

Gemma hands my mother another tissue from her bag and catches my eye in the mirror, trying not to laugh at the uncomfortable look on my face.

Since Gemma is aware of the fact this is business and not a love match, she didn't bother squealing with glee when I called and asked her to be my maid of honor. Instead, she told me she would stand with me, of course, and if I needed a quick escape, she could have a car running and waiting for me to jump in *Thelma and Louise* style. God, I love my best friend.

My mother wanted me to call five of my cousins to have them as bridesmaids, but I convinced her it would be a huge inconvenience to them, given the short notice. Of course, she argued, saying she could make it work, as made evident by the dress fitting in a wedding salon that had a six-month waiting list, but she finally relented. Barely.

"Mama, please don't cry. It's just a dress," I tell the teary woman dabbing the corners of her eyes with a tissue.

"I can't help it. You'll understand when you have a daughter of your own."

Much to my relief, Finn didn't bat an eye at there not being an heirs clause in the contract. The thought of being pregnant still terrifies me—even though it's been years since the night my brother found me bloodied and bruised at the hands of my ex after I'd told him I was pregnant. He didn't believe it was his for no other reason than he was a jealous asshole that swore the condoms he *usually* wore would have prevented the pregnancy. He accused me of trying to trap him into marriage. I miscarried that night in my brother's bed, too ashamed to tell my parents. Though my father eventually got the truth from me, I never told my mother what happened. Gemma knows, and the look of sympathy she gives me when she sees my mind play through the memory is too much for me to deal with. I turn my gaze to the woman who's just finishing with the pins.

"All right, Ms. Amatto, we're set here. I'll start on this today, and it shouldn't take more than three days to finish."

That's a fucking miracle if I've ever heard of one. A small part of me may have been hoping there was no way my dress would be sorted on such short notice, then I could postpone the wedding. There's no way to back out of the contract, not that I would do that to my father, but it would've been nice to have a few more days to let the idea that I was going to officially be a

Monaghan sink in. Doesn't really matter, though. It's happening whether I'm used to the idea or not.

"I don't have to be back to work for the rest of the day. How about the three of us have a nice lunch? Maybe you and I can try to get Alessia over there a little excited about her wedding. Does that sound good to you, Mrs. Amatto?"

The seamstress scrunches her brow at Gemma's suggestion, obviously confused as to why I wouldn't be excited about the "big day." She probably assumed I was knocked up, and that's why there was a rush to have this done so quickly.

I widen my eyes at Gemma, flick my gaze from my best friend to the seamstress, then back to Gemma. I see the moment it dawns on her that anyone dress shopping would be excited about their wedding and to not make it sound like I'm not. She shoots me an apologetic smile.

The shopkeeper may not know exactly who my father is, but it's common knowledge in Boston that he's a rich and powerful real estate developer. The last thing I want are rumors flying and the wrong person hearing them.

After one of the shop girls helps me out of the dress, the three of us head to my mother's favorite five-star restaurant. I figured it was the least I could do since my lack of cheer was dampening this entire event for her. She says the mushroom risotto is the best she's had in the States, and coming from a woman who grew up in Italy with a mother who could probably open her own five-star restaurant, that's high praise. I'm no stranger to dining at some of the most high-end restaurants in the city, but every time I walk in here and am hit in the face with beige *everything*, I'm grateful I never married some fancy uptight heir to his father's fortune. Not as though that was ever really an option. It's just all so *bland*. The walls, the tables, the people. I have a little laugh to myself when I think about coming here after picking out the wedding dress I'm going to wear to marry the head of the Irish mob. I'm sure if any of the ladies drinking their chardonnay at the tables surrounding us knew who we really were, they'd have an absolute conniption over their niçoise salad.

The waiter brings us our menus and a wine list. Instead of ordering a glass, we decide to share a bottle of prosecco. I also let the waiter know that as soon as this one is finished, we'll be ordering a second. It doesn't hurt to be prepared.

"I understand this isn't the most traditional way to start a marriage, sweetheart—"

"It's not unusual in our life, Mama," I say, cutting her off.

"No, it isn't, but that doesn't mean you can't have a happy marriage. It may not be starting off exactly how you envisioned, but as far as I can tell, there's no reason to believe Finn won't make a good husband."

It takes a monumental effort not to snort the sparkling wine through my nose. I can think of several reasons, the first being his reputation as a complete and unapologetic player. That doesn't sound like good husband material to me.

"I'm sure everything will be fine. It's not like he's going into this with expectations of a doting wife being at his beck and call." I made sure that was not the impression I made at dinner.

"Oh, I do hope you can find a way to hold your tongue, Alessia. If he thinks it's going to be a fight every time he walks through the door, there isn't anything stopping him from not coming home at all."

"One could hope," I mutter under my breath before taking another sip from my glass.

Though my mother doesn't catch my remark, Gemma does and almost chokes on the wine that's halfway down her throat.

My mother looks concerned while Gemma gets herself under control, and I watch her with an amused smirk.

"Sorry, wrong pipe," she says, taking a drink of the water in front of her. Her hand lifts to get the waiter's attention. "We should order. Mrs. Amatto, what are you having?"

I barely hold back my laughter as she quickly changes the subject.

"Are you meeting his family before the wedding?" Gemma asks after we order.

"We'll be having dinner with them tomorrow night, in fact," I reply, nodding to my mother.

"Well, that will be nice," she offers, but I look anything

but excited.

Being in Finn's company is disorienting. Hearing him moan when he tasted his food at dinner and the way he looked at me with a dare in his gaze before I agreed to sign the marriage contract stirred something in me. I detest men who have reputations like his, but there was something about the way he carried himself the other night that sparked some sort of challenge between us that I can't resist rising to. I'm used to men tiptoeing around me because of who my father is. Finn looked at me like he wanted to sink his teeth into me, and he was going to have a grand time doing it.

I lift my hand to signal to the waiter that we're ready for another bottle.

Finn Monaghan can keep that damn eye twinkle and his teeth to himself.

I'm surprised the former head of the Monaghan family doesn't live in a palatial estate like the one I grew up in. Don't get me wrong, his house is huge and behind a gate with an armed guard. But it's obvious when we pull up the driveway that Cormac and Maeve Monaghan have a house that's more of a home rather than the giant estate I grew up on. My father built an empire, and he wanted anyone who visited his home to see that. The Monaghans don't flaunt their wealth like my father does, even though I'm sure they're just as wealthy as my family.

Instead of a guard waiting on the front porch like at my house, we're greeted with the sight of an older couple, the woman with short blonde hair wearing a joyful smile on her face as we approach.

"Alessia, it's so good to meet you," she says, enveloping me in a hug.

When she pulls away, I give her a smile in return. "Nice to meet you as well, Mrs. Monaghan."

"Please call me Maeve. We don't stand on formalities."

Cormac forgoes the hug and holds out his hand instead. "Cormac Monaghan. Nice to meet you."

It's like looking at an older version of Finn with the same tall frame and commanding presence. Cormac has similar blue eyes, but Finn must get the stormy blue hue of his from his mom.

The couple introduces themselves to my parents as I wonder where the hell my future husband is.

"Come in, come in," Maeve tells my parents and me, opening the door to their home.

When we step inside, I see my earlier observations about their house are spot on. This house looks lived in and comfortable. Pictures of the family, some looking like they date back to the time when their relatives still lived in Ireland, cover every light-gray-painted wall. There's no rhyme or reason to the placement, just row after row of photographs of several generations of Monaghans.

"The boys are in the family room," Maeve says and waves for us to follow.

Yelling can be heard from where we stand. If I knew the woman better, I'd swear Maeve is not happy with the commotion by the way her shoulders seem to stiffen, even though she keeps a pleasant smile on her face. Entering the family room, I see my future husband. There's a man who is the spitting image of Maeve sitting beside him on a large couch that looks more comfortable than any piece of furniture we have in our house, and they're...playing a video game.

"You motherfucker," the blond man next to Finn complains. "That's cheating and you damn well know it."

Maeve doesn't waste a second and walks right behind the man and smacks him upside the head.

"Language, Eoghan. And turn off the damn game. Alessia and her parents are here." She shakes her head in disappointment when she looks at Finn. "I told you to meet us at the door, and instead, you're in here turning your brain to mush with your brother."

"Sorry, Mom." Finn stands and offers her a sheepish look. "But Eoghan was crying like a baby about how I never play him anymore because he's such a sore loser, and I didn't hear you."

"You're a damn liar," Eoghan says.

"Boy, if I have to tell you one more time to watch your mouth..." Maeve lets the threat trail off, and Eoghan shoots Finn a scathing glare.

"Sorry, Mom," the younger Monaghan concedes.

Finn walks around the couch and greets me with a kiss on both cheeks before saying hello to my mother and shaking my father's hand.

Eoghan approaches me with an outstretched hand and introduces himself. "Nice to meet you, Alessia. Listen, if at any point you want to run away with the more attractive brother who's a hell of a lot more fun than this sorry sack, you just let me know."

Finn walks up to Eoghan and smacks him on the back of the head, just like his mother did moments ago.

"Stop trying to flirt with my fiancée."

"What the hell is with this family and hitting me in the head today?" Eoghan says, rubbing his abused skull. "And I wasn't trying. I was simply letting her know she's got other options and doesn't have to be stuck with your boring ass for the rest of her life."

"From what I hear, your brother is anything but boring." Why am I bringing this up?

Finn's brows quirk up. "You've been checking up on me, sweetheart?" That damn smirk has made its appearance again.

"I like to know who I'm going into business with."

"Well, don't believe all the rumors unless, of course, they tell you I never leave any woman in my bed unsatisfied."

"You're getting a little ahead of yourself there, *sweetheart*. No one has said anything about me ever being in your bed. We're married on paper for the good of both of our families, not because I find you irresistible and can't wait to fall into a bed that countless women have been in before me."

Yes, I'm aware I'm being a bitch, but seriously? He's crossing so many lines no man would ever dream of crossing with me at the moment, and I don't find it particularly amusing or charming.

At least, that's what I'm telling myself.

"I wouldn't say *countless*," Finn counters, completely ignoring the rest of my statement.

I roll my eyes and turn away from Finn and Eoghan to face my parents and my future in-laws, who have walked outside to the patio. Thankfully, the French doors were left open, allowing the breeze to cool my heated skin. There's something about this man that lights a fire in the pit of my stomach, and I'm not entirely sure I hate it.

"You have a lovely home, Maeve. Thank you so much for inviting us," I say, walking outside to the seating area that overlooks an expansive backyard with a pool and an entire outdoor kitchen and bar setup.

Cormac rises from his seat and offers to pour me a glass of wine, which I accept with an appreciative smile. Finn and his brother join us outside with beers in their hands as though this is a relaxed dinner between old family friends instead of being the first time the Amattos and Monaghans have shared the same space without being heavily armed.

As I'm finishing my wine, a stout woman who looks to be in her sixties comes out to the patio and announces dinner is ready. Cormac is the first to stand, ushering my parents to the dining room as Maeve loops her arm through mine. "I know my boys can be a bit...much. But can I just say how happy I am to have a daughter after all the testosterone I've had to deal with for the last thirty or so years?"

I smile, wondering if she knows the context of my marriage to her son.

"It may not be what you had planned when you were a little girl, but Finn is a good man with a fierce heart, and I can tell you have the same." Her warm smile succeeds in putting me at ease, even though this situation is anything but comfortable. "Just a word of advice, if I may?"

I nod, and she leans in closer, as though we're sharing a secret. "Don't let him push you around. He's used to people following his orders, but I think we both know who's the real head of a family."

"You don't have to worry about that," I reply, mirroring the conspiratorial gleam in her eye.

"No, I don't suppose I will."

CHAPTER FIVE

FINN

A WEEK AND A half later, I'm standing in the small makeshift locker room in the basement of one of our bars we use for the fight nights Eoghan puts together. The room is sparse, with concrete floors and a metal bench sitting in front of a couple beat-to-hell lockers. It's not fancy, and the room smells like old mildew and sweat, but Eoghan says it adds to the authentic grittiness of these types of underground fights. I can't argue his logic considering they bring in a pretty penny for the family, and my brother thrives in this kind of environment. It's not often I participate in the fights, but with all this shit with Cataldi and my wedding, which is going to be taking place tomorrow, I need to blow off steam.

Usually, I spend this time mentally preparing myself for the ring in peace and quiet. Tonight, however, I don't get that luxury.

"All I'm trying to say is maybe getting in the ring the night before your wedding isn't the best idea." Eoghan has been trying to talk me out of fighting tonight, but bets have already been placed, and this type of crowd wouldn't take kindly to a last-minute cancelation.

"Cillian," my brother says, looking over at my lieutenant. "Help me out here."

Cillian looks to my brother, then me, and shakes his head. "You're on your own with this one. If he wants to fight, let him fight. He may as well get used to it since he's marrying Alessia."

My brother waves a dismissive hand, and I can't help the chuckle that escapes me.

"Mom is going to have a shit fit if you show up tomorrow with your pretty face busted up."

I shrug because, yes, I've thought about that, but no, I don't care. I need this.

"Honestly, Eoghan, out of everyone, I thought you'd understand my need to spill a little blood tonight." I finish taping my knuckles and test it by punching one hand into my palm then the other.

"It's not that I don't understand. It's that I don't want to hear it tomorrow when we show up to the church and you have a busted nose."

"Oh, come on. When was the last time anyone got a face shot on Finn?" Cillian asks.

"You two are impossible. And when did I become the voice of reason? Fuck you both for making me be the responsible one," Eoghan says, pointing a threatening finger between Cillian and me.

"It's really not a good look on you. You should probably stop trying," I tell my red-faced little brother. "It'll be fine."

Well, it *was* fine until round five when the giant Russian cage fighter landed an elbow to my eyebrow. It was a lucky-as-hell shot that had blood pouring from the cut and blinding me momentarily. I'd been mostly taking body shots, successfully guarding my face, and returning his sloppy blows with precise ones of my own. The guy relied on his strength and brawn, but I had him beat in skill. My confidence cost me, though, and now I'm sitting in a metal folding chair as Cillian butterfly bandages my fucking eyebrow.

"Could have been worse," Cillian says, wiping the excess blood from my brow.

"I should have seen it coming. He was going for the face in the first four rounds. He tired himself out so much, swinging hard and wide, I thought round five was going to be a cakewalk and I'd knock the guy out."

"Why didn't you go for the knockout earlier?"

I blow out a breath and chuckle at my stupidity. "I wanted to put on a good show."

"You got cocky."

"Sure as shit did." And now I have to face my mother with a busted eyebrow on my wedding day. As if the thought of tomorrow isn't stressful enough.

Cillian finishes and disposes of the bloody gauze he used to clean me up with. "Let's get a drink at the bar." He purposely slaps his hand on my bruised shoulder.

"Asshole," I mutter in his direction, but he just laughs and heads out of the room and up the stairs to the bar before I follow him.

The good thing about having these fights in the basement of a bar is the limitless supply of alcohol available upstairs. Since the fights are over for the night, everyone up here is either excited about their winnings and buying round after round for people, or they're drowning their sorrows over losing money and spending what they have left getting shit-faced. It's a win-win for business.

We make our way through the crowded space that's packed brick wall to brick wall with almost everyone who was downstairs watching the bloodshed take place. Thankfully, my brother always makes sure to reserve a corner table for us on fight nights. Not that it would matter when everyone here knows we own the place. I've made people give up their tables on busy nights like this for me on more than one occasion. Perks of being the boss.

Eoghan spends his time running the four bars we have in Boston and fight nights circulate between each of the four. It's always interesting to me the variety of people who come out for these nights. Some are your typical working-class crowd who enjoy boxing and are here for a good time. Others are dressed to the nines and reek of money, while others stink of the desperation of trying to feed their gambling addictions.

Eoghan runs a crew responsible for loaning the money to the sorry saps who don't know when to quit. That's part of how our family got started in this life. We were loan sharks and bootleggers who did what we had to do to survive. Then, when prohibition ended, we went into protection. My father wanted more for us and started the underground casino. When I came on board, I realized there was money being left on the table and started a little gunrunning business the Black Roses MC were happy to assist with. It brings in a pretty penny, and it'll be even more profitable when we gain control of the ports.

Cillian and I have a seat at the table, and Eoghan isn't far behind with a round of whiskeys.

He looks at me and shakes his head, a smile playing on his lips. "Mom's going to be pissed, brother."

I roll my eyes at the glee he takes in telling me that unnecessary observation.

"I tried to tell him," Cillian states.

"You most certainly did not," I say, looking at the man with a shit-eating grin sitting next to me. "You said if I want to fight, I should. And that I should get used to fighting, considering who I'm about to be married to."

"I was the one trying to keep you away from the ring tonight." Eoghan sits to the left of me, sipping his drink while still wearing an excited smile.

"Don't act like you aren't giddy as a schoolboy, knowing I'm going to get a ration from our mother tomorrow."

My brother smirks, and I want to wipe the smug smile off his face.

"Maybe I should give you a matching cut, Eoghan. Then she'll have two sets of ears to box."

"Now, why would you do that when I've gone through all the trouble of putting together this fine bachelor party for you?"

I look around the bar then back to my brother. "What bachelor party?"

"Exactly," he says, nodding at me. "You wouldn't let me plan anything for you, so we're stuck here drinking the same whiskey we do every night with the same people we see almost as often." He shakes his head in disappointment.

"When it's your turn to walk down the aisle, I'll make sure to throw you a damn bachelor party with all the strippers and alcohol you could possibly imagine."

Eoghan scoffs. "Like that'll ever happen. Marriage is for suckers."

"Or men trying to take over criminal empires," Cillian says with a smirk.

Ignoring my brother and lieutenant, I scan the crowd. I'm not looking for anyone in particular. It's just a habit of mine, making sure any and all possible threats are noticed and eliminated before they become a problem.

Eoghan is pouting in the corner, obviously wishing I'd taken him up on his offer to have a full-blown celebration tonight instead of sitting in one of our bars, but this is exactly where I'm comfortable. I don't need a *last night of freedom* celebration. As far as I'm concerned, the only thing that's going to change is I'll have a roommate with my last name.

A sexy as hell roommate that's sure to keep me on my

toes...but she'll never be in my bed.

It's obvious she isn't interested in mixing business with pleasure, which I fully think is for the best. Unfortunately, it doesn't answer the question of why; for the last week, I've been finding any excuse to call or text her. Asking her for little details about the wedding, which she doesn't know, just so she'll have to find out from Lilliana and get back to me. Or why I've been imagining her in my home and in the bed she's made clear she has no desire to be in. Three nights in a row, I've fisted my cock with thoughts of her painted-red lips tipped up at the corners while on her knees in front of me. Even in my fantasies, her eyes still held that glint of defiance, which I think made me come even harder. There has got to be something wrong with me. I'm inviting a woman who can't stand me into my home, into my sanctuary, and I'm getting off on her hating me.

My gaze must linger in one spot for too long. When I finally shake myself out of my thoughts of Alessia, a tall blonde with fake tits and a dress that leaves hardly anything to the imagination is walking over with a smile directed at me.

"Hey," she says. "I saw you fight tonight. Congratulations on the win. Can I buy you a drink to celebrate?"

I hold up my glass. "Already have one."

"Well," she says, sitting in the empty chair next to mine. "How about a different celebration? Somewhere not so crowded."

She leans in, a hair's breadth from my mouth. It would be nothing to lean over and take her lips in a bruising kiss, then take her to my brother's office and begin the "celebration" she has in mind. But her hair is too light, and the shade of red on her lips isn't the same one I can't seem to get out of my head. The shade worn by a woman who has obviously cast some unwanted, powerful spell over me. I shake my head and smile politely, telling the blonde, "Not tonight, sweetheart."

She shrugs a slim shoulder and licks her bottom lip in a move that's meant to look seductive but isn't doing a damn thing for me. "You sure?"

"While I appreciate the offer, I'm about to be a married man." I shoot her a smile in the hopes she isn't offended by my rejection, seeing as angry drunk women at a bar can be bad for business.

Her eyes trail up and down my body, and I'm getting the feeling she doesn't care one way or another about my marital status. "Lucky girl. Another time then."

Her nails scrape across my hand before she gets up and wanders off.

"Jesus," I mumble, taking a sip of my whiskey. "Does no one respect the bonds of marriage anymore?"

My brother and Cillian look at each other, then me, erupting in a fit of laughter.

Assholes.

"Finnegan Patrick Monaghan. Let me see your face." My mother storms into the dressing room at the church, eyeing me through the mirror while I straighten the tie that feels as though it's choking me.

Fucking Eoghan.

I turn and face my mother and she walks up to me, grabbing my chin and wrenching my head to the side, scrutinizing the cut and bruise above my eyebrow.

"Jesus, Mary, and Joseph," she grits out, letting her hand fall. "I would expect this from your brother, but seriously, Finn? Did you really need to fight the night before your wedding? And could you not have protected your face? You're better than that."

My mom shakes her head as I bark out a laugh. "Which has you more upset? The cut or that I let him get one in?"

"Honestly? I'm not sure." Her gaze softens as her blue eyes search mine. "Are you sure this is what you want?"

"A little late to call it off, don't you think?"

My mom was never fully on board with this plan. She's a good Catholic woman and tried to raise us the same, even with my father being the head of the *family* for so many years. She believes marriage is a sacred vow made before God that can't be broken. I don't know what would bother her more. If she knew about all the men I've sent to their deaths or if I got a divorce?

"It's not too late. When mass is over, and you're tied to Alessia for the rest of your natural life, then it would be too late."

I have the feeling my mom is under some misguided impression that I should be holding out for the love of my life or something. That's not something I've ever given thought to. I don't and never will harbor the idea that there's that one person in the world who you're destined to marry. My parents may feel that way about each other, but it's not realistic for me. What is, though, is making my family one of the most powerful on the East Coast. That's something I have control over, and I'll do whatever it takes to grab it, including marrying Alessia Amatto.

My mother stares into my eyes for a few moments, noting my silence before straightening my already perfect tie, then smiling widely at me.

"Well, I suppose it's time you walk an old lady to her seat then."

I look around the room with a slight frown. "What old lady?" I ask, then turn to her with a wink.

"Save the charm for your bride, son. You're going to need it." She laughs, and I take her arm, leading her out into the old Gothic-style church covered in blush-pink roses and white gauzy fabric to my father, sitting in the front pew.

My brother is standing off to the side of the altar, waiting for me to take my place with a shit-eating grin on his face.

I smile at the guests and lean over to whisper in my brother's ear. "You'll pay for that, asshole."

"Such language. And in the house of the Lord." He shakes his head, clicking his tongue.

I look around at the saint's faces in the stained-glass windows that line the long walls of the sanctuary. If they had a little brother like mine, they would surely understand and forgive the coarse language. Before I can tell him all the ways I'm going to pay him back for running to our mother, the music changes, and the doors at the back of the church open. Alessia told me Gemma, her best friend since college, was going to be the only person in her bridal party. This is the first time I've laid eyes on the woman walking out in a knee-length pastel-pink dress, and I notice my brother stand a bit straighter. I'll have to make sure to tell him she's off-limits, though that might make her more desirable to him. The last thing we need is Eoghan screwing around with the wrong person and creating any more tension for me or this deal.

When Gemma takes her place in the front, the music changes and everyone stands. I look at the doorway once more, and Alessia is there with her father. The air is knocked from my lungs. Goddamn, the woman is stunning. I'm glad everyone is looking at Alessia and not me, so I have a moment to compose myself. Her dress looks like she's been sewn into it, the intricate lace hugging every curve of her body until it reaches her knees then flares, creating a train that trails behind her. I catch her eye and smile, but she remains stoic as she walks up the long aisle.

I don't know why that bothers me like it does. This isn't real, at least not in the way two people getting married for love would be. But her air of indifference tugs at something in me. For a brief moment, I feel like a thief, stealing her moment to be a real bride, marrying someone she actually wants to spend the rest of her life with. Not someone she's marrying to gain power for her family. This is the life we live, though, and the commitment we've both made for our families. I've never been interested in marrying for love, but I can't help but wonder, as she glides toward me on her father's arm, if she had dreams of this day as a young woman. Maybe she feels as though she's missed out on her chance to have a real marriage with a wedding she's actually excited about. Not one she signed a contract for.

Alessia reaches me, and her father kisses her on the cheek before she turns toward me. Now that I can look her in the eye, there's no little girl with broken wedding dreams looking back at me. Instead, her green eyes are hard, and her shoulders are straight as she glares daggers at me. What the hell was going through my head when I felt a pang of regret only moments before? Alessia Amatto—well, Monaghan now—doesn't seem to possess one shred of girlish fantasies or dreams.

Throughout the entire ceremony she repeats the

words she's supposed to. She kneels and stands on cue, but there isn't one iota of sadness in any of it. There's no joy or love or happiness, not that I would have expected there to be. She's performing her duty and leaving emotions where they belong—far away from here. It's not like I'm all of a sudden thinking she's the most beautiful woman I've ever laid eyes on and am a lucky son of a bitch to be marrying her. It's not as though I thought she looked like an ethereal goddess with every word she spoke through her nude-colored lips. Lips that I'm excited to kiss even though I know it's fake, for show. No, those thoughts haven't crossed my mind once. And it's not as though her indifference unsettles me—frustrates me every time I look into her eyes and see not even a spark of emotion. Just an infuriating nothing.

When the wedding mass is finished and I've kissed her, feeling all the emotion of a fucking corpse from her, I smile wide and lean close to her ear.

"I liked the red lipstick better," I whisper and pull back with a happy grin on my face.

Alessia doesn't miss a beat and turns her fake-as-hell smile toward me. "Don't worry, I'll wear it to your funeral," she replies.

Any outside observer would think we were whispering words of love and devotion. I must be crazy, but there's a certain thrill in knowing my wife isn't afraid to speak her mind. She doesn't pretend to be the demure Mafia princess I mistakenly assumed she was.

Admittedly, I don't know her well, but she's sharp as a tack and tougher than many of the men I know. She doesn't cower to me or her father in a world where most women are expected to. She can stand in front of all these people and look like the blushing bride while whispering her plans for my death as sweetly as any other woman would express their affection for their new husband.

I'm obviously fucked in the head because I like it more than any reasonably sane man should.

Alessia and I have talked to nearly every guest at the reception that's being held in one of the premier hotels in Boston. I have to hand it to her mother, she puts together a nice wedding on short notice. The champagne silk draped across the ceiling gives the room an ethereal feel, along with the low lighting and tall centerpieces of white flowers at every table. It looks elegant and sweet, two things that scream *Lilliana*, which clues me in that Alessia probably had very little to do with the planning. My new wife is elegant, certainly, sweet, though? That would never be a word I'd use to describe my bride.

Alessia works the room as though she's been training for this her whole life. I admire her for the pleasant smile she's kept on her face the entire evening. She's a great little actress. I'm going to have to remember that.

It's important this marriage looks believable and unbreakable to the outside world. Several of Mario's associates are here, and we need to appear as a strong, unified front for anyone thinking they'll be challenging us in the days to come. The way I see it, the other Italian families are our biggest threat for the takeover of the ports in the coming weeks. If everyone thinks Alessia and I have a strong relationship, and by extension, her father and I have one as well, they'll be less inclined to challenge us. Family ties play an important part in this business, and now, two strong organizations are connected through marriage, fake as it may be.

After dinner, I spot my brother talking to Gemma at the temporary bar set up against a fabric-draped wall and an idea strikes. I head over to the round table filled with Alessia's cousins, whom she introduced me to earlier in the evening.

"Hello, ladies." They all turn their attention to me. "I don't suppose any of you can relate to having an annoying little brother or sister?"

The girls exchange cautious looks with each other, and I continue. "My brother over there needs to be put in his place, and I need some help doing it. Any takers?"

While the rest of the women glance at each other in confusion mixed with apprehension, one of the women leans forward. "What do you need?"

A smile stretches across my face, and I tell her my plan.

"Having fun, brother?" I ask, walking up to Eoghan and Gemma as they stand in front of the bar. I order myself a drink and take in the way the two of them are standing much too close to one another.

"There's the happy groom," he exclaims, shooting Gemma a wink.

"I was just telling your brother how it's amazing what Lilliana can do with one week and limitless spending," Gemma says, waving her hand around the ballroom.

"It's a talent, that's for sure," I reply. For a wedding based on a business deal and nothing else, Lilliana went all out. It makes me wonder who she had to pay off to score us this ballroom.

When Alessia's cousin walks up to my brother, I have to turn toward the bar so he doesn't see the smirk on my face.

"Hey, baby. I'm all set to go up to your room," Carla says, wrapping her arm around my brother's arm. "I told my dad I was staying at a friend's house. I'll just need a ride home in the morning because I have to babysit my little brother."

Through the mirror, I see the girl look at my brother with wide doe eyes while he looks like a deer caught in headlights.

"Umm, I'm sorry. I have no idea what you're talking about," he says, clearly uncomfortable, his gaze darting between Carla and Gemma.

"What do you mean? You told me ten minutes ago you had a suite here and asked if I wanted to come up and check it out."

Carla blinks rapidly, like she's trying to hold back tears, and I nearly lose it. It's everything I can do to swallow the whiskey I just sipped and not spit it all over the bartender.

""I'm going to go. You"—Gemma shoots my brother a disgusted look—"seem to have your hands full."

Gemma tosses her blonde hair over her shoulder and stomps off in the direction of her table.

When Carla unwraps herself from my brother's arm, she taps me on the shoulder, holding out her hand. "You owe me."

I pull the money clip from my pocket and slide out a crisp hundred, handing it to her with a shit-eating grin directed toward Eoghan.

"You fucking asshole," Eoghan growls as the girl walks back over to her table, waving the hundred.

"Told you I'd get you back," I say, handing him a fresh drink. "Stay away from Gemma. She's Alessia's best friend, and I don't need the headache."

"Ugh. You know I'm a sucker for a leggy blonde."

"I don't give a shit. The last thing I need is to smooth shit over when you inevitably fuck her and dump her."

"Marriage has made you boring."

"It's been four hours," I reply in a dry-as-hell tone.

"Oh, that's right. You've always been a boring asshole." Eoghan looks around the ballroom. "Speaking of marriage, your wife is over there looking rather uncomfortable for someone who's supposed to be a happy bride."

I find where his eyes have traveled to, and what I see causes my blood to boil.

CHAPTER SIX

ALESSIA

THE WEDDING WAS...A WEDDING. It's hard to be excited about getting married when you've had no time to get to know your groom, and the two of you barely tolerate each other at best. I would've been perfectly happy to have a small reception lunch, but my father and Finn decided it would be in our best interests to appear as a united front in the eyes of the other families. Nothing says united like a lavish party thrown by my family to welcome Finn and his family into ours. None of the Cataldis were invited, but the Farinas are here, much to my disgust. I wasn't surprised when my father invited them, but you could have knocked me over with a feather when my ex showed up instead of his father. Even I thought he wouldn't have the audacity after what he did to me, but wonders never cease. I should have known the devil of a man would show up to try to rattle me.

"You look lovely, Alessia," Orlando says, leaning down to kiss my cheek.

I flinch at his touch. Old habits die hard, as they say. "You have a lot of nerve walking in here. Careful,

Orlando, or you may not be walking out," I grit out through a fake smile, hoping my father is somewhere close and sees what's going on.

Orlando releases a dark chuckle and trails his cold fingertip down my arm. There was a time when one touch from him would light me on fire. Now, it turns my blood to ice, especially when I look into his cold brown gaze and recognize the evil behind his eyes.

"Oh, come on, Alessia. It was years ago. I was a hotheaded kid under a lot of stress. You know how my temper can be. And it's not like you ever had a kid, so you weren't pregnant after all. Tell me, what did you have to promise the Irish scum to get him to marry you? If you wanted a powerful man, we could have worked something out."

His hand is resting on my shoulder as though he has a right to touch me. I don't want to cause a scene, but I want him away from me even more.

"You make me sick, Orlando. I would rather marry Finn a thousand times—"

Before I can finish my sentence, Orlando's hand is knocked from my shoulder, replaced by a warm palm and a reassuring squeeze.

"Orlando Farina," my husband says in a dark tone. "I'm sorry your father couldn't make it, though I'm sure my beautiful bride was thankful for your company while I talked to my brother." He nods at Eoghan, who is standing at the bar with Cillian, neither of them wearing a smile as they shoot cold looks in my ex's direction. "I'm sure you'll understand it's been a long day, and Alessia and I are tired. We need to say our goodbyes."

Orlando looks at Finn with an irritated scowl. Though I can't see the man standing behind me, there's no missing the tension radiating from him.

"Goodbye, Orlando," Finn says in a low voice which leaves no room for argument. A small thrill runs up my spine. I must be losing my damn mind.

Orlando gives Finn a tight smile but doesn't look my way again as he slithers off and disappears into the crowd.

"I've never liked Orlando Farina," Finn says, taking his seat next to mine.

I don't reply because what is there really to say? He's an absolute piece of shit, and I'm afraid if my mouth opens right now, I'll scream. I haven't seen him face to face in nearly ten years, and I'd have been perfectly happy to never lay eyes on him again.

Gemma walks up to the table and looks behind her, then back at me. "Was that Orlando?"

When I nod in affirmation, Gemma looks ready to follow him out the door and shoot him between the eyes. She was never a fan of his, but I chalked it up to her being overprotective when we were in college. I wish I would have heeded her warning. Gemma was by my side in the aftermath of that horrible night and then after losing my brother to a "mugging." I never believed that fucking story, and neither did my father, especially knowing Gio beat Orlando to bloody hell for what he did to me only days prior to his death.

No one knew we were dating except Gemma and Enzo, who I made take a vow of silence. He's older and didn't want to involve our families right away. He said having the children of two powerful Mafia dons in a public relationship would put too much pressure on us as a new couple. Now I know it was so he could fuck around, but at the time, I thought it was romantic. Like *Romeo and Juliet* or some stupid shit. Of course, *Romeo and Juliet* was a tragedy, not unlike the ending of my relationship with Orlando.

Gemma looks at Finn and smiles. "Your brother is a pig," she tells him, and he barks out a loud laugh.

"You're not telling me anything I don't know."

When Finn's gaze turns to me, he studies the plastic smile I've tacked on. It's obvious he wants to ask questions about the little scene he walked in on, but thankfully, he lets it rest. "You about ready? I think I've done all the smiling and shaking hands I can stomach."

Sounds like Finn is about as much of a social butterfly as I am.

"Yes." I let out a sigh. "I'm ready to get out of this damn dress."

Finn's eyes sweep over me. "You look beautiful in it. I don't think I told you that."

"No, you only complained about my lipstick."

He shrugs. "What can I say? Red's my favorite color."

"You don't strike me as the type to have one."

"I never did before." He pauses before shaking his

head a bit. "But you do look stunning, Alessia."

It's a strangely tender moment, well, tender for us, and I don't know what to say in response. Do I tell him I've never seen a man fill out a tux the way he does? Or say when his lips brushed mine at the end of the ceremony, I felt it down to the tips of my toes? Those things may be true, but there's a reason I don't let gorgeous men cloud my judgment anymore. And that reason had better be leaving this damn building after getting the brush-off from me and my husband.

Gemma leans over to hug me, and before letting go, she whispers, "If you want me to poison Orlando for you, I would do it in a heartbeat, you know that, right?"

"Where on earth would you get poison?"

"I have my ways."

I chuckle as I pull away from her embrace. While my best friend never met a challenge she couldn't face head-on, I'm pretty sure poisoning my ex is beyond her capabilities.

"I'll call you tomorrow," I tell her before turning to my new husband. "Let's at least say goodbye to our parents." My mother would probably have a conniption if we just up and left.

Finn stands, taking my hand in his as we make our way to his parents and say good night before finding mine at their table, laughing with a couple of my aunts and uncles.

My parents stand, and my mother holds me in her arms. "You made a beautiful bride, sweetheart. Even if it wasn't the groom of your dreams, I hope it was at least a wedding you loved."

My mother put in so much work in a short amount of time, and I'm grateful to her for it. Was it the wedding of my dreams? No. But it was the wedding of hers, and seeing her happy makes me happy.

"I loved it, Mama. Thank you so much."

When it's my father's turn to hug me, he leans in to whisper to me. "I saw Orlando talking to you. I'm sorry I didn't get there in time. I never imagined he'd have the gall to show up in his father's place."

"It's okay, Papa. Finn took care of it."

I kiss his cheek and step back next to Finn.

"Good night. Lilliana, thank you for a wonderful evening." Finn shakes my father's hand, then hugs my mother before leading me out of the ballroom to the elevators.

When we step inside the mirrored elevator, Finn swipes his key card to allow us to access the penthouse level of the hotel.

"Fancy," I tell him. "I hope it has two rooms."

"Ah. What every groom longs to hear on his wedding night." He shoots me a smirk. "Don't worry, princess. There're two rooms."

I show no outward sign that I'm relieved he didn't assume that just because we're married now, he's entitled to my body. But inside my chest, the pressure lessens.

"Is Orlando Farina going to be a problem?" he asks,

staring me in the face as we ascend to our floor.

"Hopefully not, but don't be surprised if he has designs on port control as well."

"That's not what I was talking about."

I didn't think it was, but I'm not about to tell him my sad story. Instead, I point to the small bandage on his face. "Is whoever gave you that cut above your eye going to be a problem?"

Finn laughs and shakes his head. "No. But nice deflection."

His lip is quirked in a half smile as the doors to the suite open, and he waves his arm, motioning for me to exit the elevator.

"You're not going to carry me over the threshold, husband? This marriage is already a disappointment."

"Alessia, you and I both know you'd rip my balls off if I tried."

I shrug and make my way past the large marble table with a bottle of chilled champagne and a note, probably from the hotel, congratulating us on our nuptials. The suite is dimly lit, and I head to the large window overlooking the city.

"It's almost a shame we're only here for the night," I say, taking in the view of the Boston Harbor.

Through the reflection of the window, my eyes are fixed on Finn walking up behind me to look out the window. He looks like a powerful ruler gazing over his kingdom. I suppose it won't be much longer until it's all under his control. Well, *our* control.

Though it pains me, I have to admit we make a good-looking couple. He certainly knows how to wear a tux well, with the tie hanging loosely around his neck and the first couple buttons undone at his neck. A sudden urge to taste the skin there takes me by surprise. My husband is attractive, there's no denying it, but mixing business with pleasure has always been a hard no for me. I was involved with a man in this life before, and I have no intention of ever going there again.

My next realization hits me like a brick to the head. My mother helped me get this dress on. There are about a thousand tiny buttons up the back, and unless I want to cut myself out of it, I'm going to need help.

"I have a little problem," I admit to Finn, and his dark-blue gaze slides to me. I swipe my hair over my shoulder, exposing the long row of buttons I have no way of reaching.

Finn nods in understanding, and his long fingers begin to deftly push each button through the fabric. I watch him concentrate, and when the first several have been undone, I feel the front of my dress loosen.

"That should be enough," I tell him when he's halfway down the row.

He stops, but his hand remains on the next button, staring at the exposed skin. Our gazes collide through the reflection of the large window. He holds my stare as he undoes the next one, then the next, as though daring me to stop him. Or daring me not to. My breath stalls in my lungs, but I make no move to pull away. I'm caught in the trance of his heated stare and can't seem to find the wherewithal to break free.

Another button is undone.

Then another.

The featherlight touch of Finn's knuckles begins to travel up my spine, sending goose bumps over my entire body.

Just as I'm about to turn to face the man causing the riot of butterflies to take flight in my belly, the shrill sound of Finn's phone sounds through the silent hotel suite.

His eyes drop, but I don't miss the way he tightly clenches his jaw when he pulls his phone from his pocket.

"Yeah," he answers, walking away from me.

Holy shit. What the hell am I doing? Only a few seconds before whatever that was, I was telling myself there was no way in hell I'd ever get involved with another man in the mob. Then, the first time he touches me, I practically melt at his feet. It's maddening and frightening how quickly I can throw my resolve out the window with the simple touch of his skin against mine.

Before he ends the call, I take hurried steps into one of the bedrooms, praying it's the one my mother had my things sent to earlier in the day. My bag is sitting on the bed, and relief flows through me. The last thing I want to do is walk to the other bedroom on the opposite end of the suite and have to face Finn again. Moving to close the door, my head lifts, and our gazes meet for a brief moment before I shut the door, locking it for good measure.

Finn is gone when I wake up the next morning. He had some business to take care of. At least that's what he wrote on the note he left on the table with a breakfast meant for four instead of just me.

As I sit on one of the white leather sofas in the suite and nibble on the fresh fruit left on the breakfast bar, thoughts of last night run through my head. It scares me to think how easily I let my attraction to Finn run away with itself. His gentle touch while he undid the buttons on my wedding dress nearly knocked over every defensive wall I'd spent the last several years building. It's not that I haven't dated in the years since Orlando, but it's never been a man from this world. It's been handsome, rich men who come from good families that I've met at one gala or another. My father has always made it a point to front himself as a wealthy real estate developer, and part of that role means I've had to endure several charity functions throughout the years. The men I met there were nice enough and never suspected my family made their money by less than legal means. Not the kind of men who carry a 9mm on their hip every time they leave the house or who are more likely to walk through the door with blood splatter on their sleeve rather than a bouquet of flowers. If they come home at all.

Maybe for a brief moment last night, I saw something different in Finn's eyes. There was a moment of insecurity, of indecision, when he was touching me. As though he was holding his breath, waiting to see what I would do. That certainly isn't par for the course with men in this life. They take and take until you have nothing left, without care or hesitation. They also don't order what looks to be everything on the breakfast menu because they aren't sure what you like. And they don't leave notes letting you know why they aren't here. Nothing has been what I expected, and that does absolutely nothing to calm my nerves.

My phone dings with a text from Enzo, jolting me from my thoughts.

Enzo: *What time would you like to leave?*

Me: *Give me thirty minutes. Have you eaten? I have a ton of food up here.*

Enzo: *Mr. Monaghan took care of breakfast for the men. I'll have the car waiting out front.*

Today is the day I move into Finn's house. Since everything with our marriage was fast-tracked, I wasn't able to schedule a move until this morning, which worked out fine for appearance's sake. I am a good Catholic girl, after all.

Walking into the bedroom where I slept alone last night, my wedding dress catches my eye. It would probably look odd to walk through the lobby of the hotel with it slung over my shoulder, but I don't recall there being a bag in here other than the luggage that was in my room. I pull out my phone again to text Enzo.

Me: *I need a large garment bag for my dress sent up, please.*

Enzo: *Mr. Monaghan informed me that his mother would be by in the next hour to collect your dress.*

That's an odd thing for a man in Finn's position to consider. Pulling up his name on my phone screen, I decide to call him.

"Hello, dear," he answers on the second ring, making me smile with the overly enthusiastic tone in his voice.

"Good morning. Thank you for ordering breakfast before you left."

"It was no problem. I was about to call you and let you know my mother is coming by to take care of your dress. Your parents went back to their house last night, and your mother realized she didn't leave the bag for you."

"I wasn't aware our mothers had each other's numbers."

Finn chuckles deeply into the phone. I like that sound. *Dammit.*

"My mom offered to take care of it for us."

"She really doesn't need to. I can have Enzo send one up."

"She insisted on helping. I find it's best to let her do those little things rather than arguing with her."

"Is she going to check to see if we slept in the same bed while she's here?"

Finn laughs wholeheartedly, and I find I like that sound just as much. "No, dear wife. I doubt our parents are under the illusion that because we're married, we are so overcome with romantic notions that we're suddenly in love and ready to give them grandchildren."

"That wasn't in the contract," I remind him.

"It didn't need to be, Alessia. I know how those contracts work with other families. If you didn't have it in there, I assumed there was a reason. Your body is your own. I always thought that clause was outdated and rather barbaric. Wouldn't you agree?"

Of course I do. That's why I purposely left it out. But I didn't think he knew so much about marriage contracts or considered a clause to determine when and how many times the woman was to become pregnant as antiquated as I do.

"Well, tell her thank you for me. Or maybe I'll call my mother to tell her, since I don't have her number."

"When you get home, I'll make sure to give it to you. I'm assuming you'll be leaving the suite soon?"

"Enzo will be here shortly to take me back to my parents' so I can pack a few things. Then I'll be at your house early this afternoon."

"Our house, Alessia. And I'll be home by then."

Our house.

"Okay. See you then," I reply and disconnect the call.

I've had about all I can take of Finn's sweeter side. It's

disconcerting, and after last night, that's the last thing I need.

The low growl coming from the cat carrier next to me in the back seat has Enzo looking a bit nervous.

"Are you sure Finn is going to be okay with your pet?"

A laugh escapes me at his derisive tone when referring to my black Bombay cat, Lucian. Enzo is many things, but a cat person is not one of them.

"He said I can bring anything I want to the house. And Lucian will be fine once he settles in."

"*Fine* is not a word I would use to describe the furball," Enzo grumbles.

Our last year of college, Gemma and I found Lucian living on scraps behind our building. He was a pathetic little thing, and I simply didn't have the heart to leave him there. Enzo did not agree with my decision.

I roll my eyes and peer into my cat's angry yellow stare while he lets out another unhappy growl. Okay, maybe it'll take more than a few days for Lucian to come to terms with living in a new home.

Pulling up to the guard gate, one of Finn's men waves us through. This is the first time I've seen his house. It's a huge two-story, modern transitional home with gray brickwork running up to meet each tall peaked A-line section of the black-shingled roof. Lush green shrubbery lines his circular driveway. The house reminds me of the children's story, *The Three Little Pigs* and the one who built his house out of brick so the Big Bad Wolf couldn't blow it down. Smart pig.

I don't know what I was expecting, but this isn't it. In all the years my father and the other families had discussed the Irish and their brash tactics, it never occurred to me they would live in homes on a huge estate with guards and so much beauty surrounding them.

What did you expect, Alessia, some hovel in the middle of nowhere?

I grab the cat carrier and get out of the car as Enzo takes my bags from the back of the large SUV.

When I walk up the front steps, Eoghan opens the door for me.

"I saw you pull in. Finn is just freshening up," he says, which makes me wonder what took him from the hotel suite this morning, but I don't ask.

He eyes the carrier in my hand with a wide grin. "Oh, this is going to be great."

Eoghan ushers me into the house, and Finn meets me in the foyer with a smile and damp hair, fresh out of the shower.

"Welcome home, dear," he exclaims as I bend down and open the door to free Lucian from his little prison. He darts out of the carrier and past Finn's leg, causing the tall Irishman to jump back into the table in the center of his foyer, nearly sending the large vase holding a bouquet of white calla lilies to the floor.

"What the hell is that?" Finn yelps, grabbing the vase before it smashes to the ground.

"That's Lucian. He's really very sweet once he feels comfortable," I reply.

Enzo lets out a quiet chuckle and tries to hide it with a cough, but I don't miss it. I narrow my eyes at him, and Finn looks from my bodyguard then back to me. He didn't miss the laugh, either.

"I get the feeling not everyone feels the same about the demon cat as you do, wife," he says as he straightens his white button-down shirt.

Eoghan can't contain his laughter and is having a hard time catching his breath every time he looks at Finn's face.

"This is too good. You always hated cats and the institution of marriage, and now you're married to a cat lady."

"Hey," I bark at Eoghan. "One cat doesn't make me a cat lady." I turn to my husband. "And you told me I could bring anything I wanted to the house."

Finn nods and lets out a slow breath. "I have a feeling this is one of those times in marriage that I hear people talk about where, no matter what I say, you're going to get your way."

I smile. "Get used to it, husband. If you wanted a meek and compliant housewife, you married into the wrong family."

A grin tilts the corner of Finn's mouth as he grabs the

empty carrier.

"Oh, I definitely married into the right one." He tilts his head toward the staircase, signaling for me to follow.

"Come on. I'll show you to your room. I'm sure Lucifer—"

"Lucian," I correct.

"Right. I'm sure Lucian will warm up to me in no time."

"You'll be one big, happy cat family," Eoghan says, doubling over in laughter again.

Happy may be a stretch, but one thing is certain—like it or not, we are family now.

CHAPTER SEVEN

FINN

I'T'S BEEN TWO WEEKS since Alessia and her damn cat moved in. I've never been a big fan of cats in general, but I'm convinced there's something wrong with this one. Any time I get within five feet of him, he lets out a disturbing growl I didn't know cats made. It's unsettling, to say the least. Thankfully, he hasn't destroyed anything in the house, but he likes to hide under furniture and dart out between my legs, scaring the hell out of me.

At least the damn cat is paying me some attention. Alessia is even more standoffish than she was before we got married. I thought something shifted after our wedding night. It had for me. When I undid the buttons on her dress and stared at the smooth skin on her back that reminded me of the satiny texture of a rose petal, I couldn't *not* touch her. There was a driving need coming from somewhere deep inside me. Maybe it was the whiskey making me bold, or maybe it was simply her, my wife, who now finds any excuse to avoid me.

Granted, I've been busy. The casino is busier than ever, and we just lost our casino host. That was the phone call that came in on our wedding night. If stealing from me wasn't enough to end his life, pulling me away from that moment with my wife would have cemented his place in hell. Why anyone would think they can steal from my family and get away with a slap on the wrist is beyond me. After a week of watching his every move like a fucking hawk, Cillian finally caught him red-handed. To say I was in a terrible mood the first week Alessia was living here is an understatement. Now, I'm short an employee, and we're still trying to determine if anyone was helping the thief. So far, we haven't found anything, but I've been going through the financial records of every single one of my employees. To top it off, we still don't know where Cataldi is hiding, and we've been running into some pushback at the docks.

She seemed happy with her room, which I had an interior designer come in and decorate for her. The dark reds I suggested confused the hell out of the decorator, but it reminded me of the color of the dress she wore the first night I met her. The damn dress that I haven't been able to get off my mind.

The one night I was home at a reasonable time for dinner, she'd been out with Gemma, so I ate by myself in the kitchen. While I was cutting into my perfectly prepared steak, it dawned on me I had no idea how she spends her days or evenings. I see her most mornings while I get my coffee and breakfast, but as soon as Alessia finishes eating, she heads to her room, and I lock myself in my office or go to the casino.

In an attempt to thaw this ice wall that's formed between us, I told her if she'd like to do any redecorating to let one of my staff know and they would make sure she had a credit card for my account. She looked at me like I was the stupidest man on the planet. She stomped away, mumbling something about spending my money and decorating a house was all men like me thought women were good for. I thought making this house her own would have made her a tad happy, but apparently, I missed the mark. It's as though I'm living with the quietest houseguest in the world instead of the fiery Italian woman I met a few short weeks ago. And surprising to me, I hate it.

Walking through the hallway to the state-of-the-art gym on the first floor, I notice the door is cracked open and hear grunting and heavy breathing coming from inside the room. Cillian and my brother aren't here, and if one of my men wants to use the facilities, they usually send me a text.

I quietly make my way to the door and push it in slightly so I can get a look at what the hell is going on in my house.

"Stop dropping your right shoulder before you throw a punch. You may as well be waving a neon sign telling your opponent what your next move is," Enzo instructs.

The man is in workout shorts and a T-shirt, which is the most casual I've ever seen him.

"I'm not dropping shit," Alessia barks out.

"Let's take a break."

Enzo steps out of the way and it's the first time I've seen Alessia in three days. Sweat is pouring from her face to her chest, dampening the tight tank top she's wearing. By the looks of it, they've been going at it for some time. Seeing her flushed cheeks shining with sweat has my mind wandering to images of her I've been fantasizing about nearly every night when I get home exhausted and in need of a release. The fact that she trains is a more than pleasant surprise and gives me an idea of how I can get to know my new wife.

"Let's go again," she tells Enzo as she sets her water bottle on the floor.

Her bodyguard raises his hands with the punch mitts, and they get back to work on her strikes. Her form is near perfect, but Enzo is right about her shoulder.

"You're dropping your shoulder," I say, swinging the door open and stepping into the room.

Alessia jumps, clearly unaware that I was standing at the door watching her. Enzo, on the other hand, shoots me a smirk like he knew the entire time. Good quality to have in a bodyguard. She insisted he stay with her even though I told her we have guards of our own. She refused my suggestion, and her father agreed to it. If it makes her feel more comfortable being here with one of her own, I'm not about to take that away from her.

Alessia collects herself and stands straight, irritation flaring in her eyes. "I didn't realize you were an expert in boxing."

"I wouldn't call myself an expert," I say, my mouth

tilting in a small smile. "But I have eyes, and Enzo is correct."

"By all means, then." Alessia waves her arm as though saying the stage is mine. "Show me how it's done."

I hold out my hand to Enzo for the punch mitts, and he hands them over, still wearing the smirk.

"She's not a fan of being told she's not perfect," he stage-whispers, and Alessia scoffs.

"I had no idea," I reply in a droll tone as I fasten the mitts to my hands.

When I turn toward my wife, she's trying to look bored and unaffected, but I see the challenge flare in her gaze.

I hold my hands up. "Begin."

Her first few punches are perfect, but I can tell she's concentrating too hard. I nod my head, acknowledging she's doing well, which relaxes her enough for her to get a little cocky, and she drops that shoulder again.

"Right there," I say before she throws another punch. "You got sloppy because you thought you had the upper hand."

Alessia plants her mitted fists on her hips. "Ugh, you're as bad as Enzo."

I laugh because her irritation with me and her bodyguard is cute. She *really* doesn't like being corrected.

"Do you work out every day?" Again, I have no idea what she does with her time, and that unsettles me.

"Most," she replies.

"Good. I'll meet you here every morning at the same time. We'll work out together."

"I don't know..." She doesn't look excited about my offer in the least.

"I think it would be a great addition to your training for Mr. Monaghan to join us," Enzo supplies.

"It's settled," I say, even though she hasn't agreed. "See you tomorrow, dear." I plaster a happy smile on my face as I return the mitts to Enzo.

"I thought you came in to work out?" Alessia asks.

"I think I'm going to go for a run instead."

And then take a cold shower.

The run did me some good, but it didn't clear my thoughts of Alessia at all. My shower, which wasn't cold, involved me fisting my cock with thoughts of my wife in her tight tank covered in sweat and shorts that left little to the imagination. After, I called my brother to have him put me on the schedule for a fight tonight. Then, I made a call to my man inside the Cataldi organization to have him meet me at the bar. It's not uncommon for men in any of the three Italian families in Massachusetts to come to a fight every now and then, so there's no reason to believe it would raise any suspicion.

The basement is packed wall to wall with people when I get there. As soon as I see the ring set up in the middle of the large, brightly lit space, I breathe a little easier. This is exactly what I need tonight. I shake hands with a couple of regulars and keep an eye out for my cousin, who I have placed in the Cataldi organization. When I spot him, a sense of relief washes through me. It's important for us to have face-to-face meetings every once in a while. I want Luca to remember he has family who cares about him, and his time being my mole in the Cataldi family is important to me and mine, even if no one except me, him, and Cillian knows about our family ties—or that he's still alive.

"Luca," I say when he approaches, and I hold out my hand, shaking his like I would with any other person here tonight. "Any word?" I ask, looking around the room and keeping a friendly smile on my face.

"None. Seems Carlo has vanished into the wind. I doubt he'll stay hidden for long though. If there's one thing I've learned about the man throughout my years there, it's that he thrives on control, and with the old man in prison, it's his to take."

When Carlo's father went to prison on RICO charges, it was a prime opportunity for Carlo to take over the family. But his pride got in the way, and he wanted to settle a score with the US attorney who put his father away and the MC that was protecting her when his usual intimidation tactics didn't work. The dumb fuck thought he could get away with kidnapping the couple, killing the Black Roses MC president then selling his woman into the skin trade. Thankfully, Luca was in the right place at the right time and overheard where they were holding the couple. Needless to say, the plan blew up in Carlo's face, but he still managed to get away like the snake he is.

"I think Farina might have something to do with it."

"Really." I raise my brows in surprise. "What makes you say that?"

"Whispers and innuendo. Nothing concrete."

Luca has been one of the bodyguards with the Cataldis since my men shot the capo he was serving under and the rest of his crew. We were hoping Carlo would have decided to give Luca a shot with his own crew since the one he was with handled the skin trade for Carlo, but instead, he threw Luca in the house to guard his family before he made a decision where to put him next. I can tell he's been getting restless with keeping the charade, but until we have a lock on Carlo and can dismantle his organization, Luca needs to keep up the ruse a bit longer.

"Keep your eyes and ears open. I thought with the moves I made on the port, it would have brought Carlo out of hiding, but none of my men have heard anything about him."

Luca nods and looks at the ring. "You going in tonight?"

"Yup," I answer, taking a sip from the water bottle in my hand. I never drink before a fight. Afterward, on the other hand, is an entirely different story.

"I heard you got married. Congratulations," my cousin

offers.

I tilt my head from side to side, trying to alleviate the tension in my neck. Luca must sense the dip in my mood, and his mouth quirks up in a knowing smile.

"Ah, not the happy union everyone seems to believe, then." His gaze swings to the ring then back to me. "Good luck." The way his eyes dance with laughter tells me it's not the fight he's referring to.

When Luca turns and melts back into the crowd, I go in search of my brother. Naturally, I find him chatting up a tall blonde at the little bar we have down here.

He sees me approach and excuses himself from the woman.

"You're in luck. The Russian wanted a fight, but I didn't have anyone in his weight class willing to go up against him. You game?"

Once upon a time, I entertained the idea of doing a little business with one of the Russian families from New York. It would have caused some issues with the Italians out that way, but they assured me they would be able to handle anything the Italians threw at us. I didn't get a good feeling from them, though, and I've put those plans on the back burner. Of course, once they found out my brother ran the illegal fight nights in Boston, they wanted in. I guess New York had enough of the shit they'd inevitably start after the fights had been called. So far, we've had no such problems, but any time they come in for a fight, we bring in extra men, just in case.

"I'm up for it," I reply.

"Was that one of Cataldi's men you were talking to earlier?" my brother asks nonchalantly, but I see the question in his gaze.

"He's just here for the fight. Wanted me to know that he doesn't want any problems."

"Hmm." Eoghan doesn't say anything else about Luca being here on his own. I'm grateful for that. It's not that I relish the idea of keeping secrets from my brother, but Luca and I decided when we started this little operation that the fewer people who know, the better. If he was ever found out, no one would be able to get any information from my brother because he doesn't know anything. We've gone to great lengths to ensure no one in my family or the Cataldis were aware of his true identity, except Cillian, but that was just in case anything happened to me—which isn't a far-fetched notion—he would have someone to warn him and get him out if need be. Plus, my brother is a bit of a hothead and a mama's boy. I don't know if it would be possible for him to keep the fact that her only sister's son isn't actually dead like we were all led to believe. It's a long, convoluted story even I had a hard time wrapping my head around—not to mention believing—when Luca contacted me all those years ago.

"Go get ready, and I'll call you out when it's time."

I head to the makeshift locker room and change before Cillian meets me inside.

"Blowing off steam?" he asks as I'm taping up my knuckles.

"Something like that." I flex my hands, testing the tape. Hell yes, I'm blowing off steam. He's not married to one of the most tempting and infuriating women on the planet. "I thought you were at the casino tonight?" Without a casino host, Cillian has been filling in.

"I have one of my guys covering for a few hours. When Eoghan told me you were fighting the Russian, I couldn't very well *not* show up."

Cillian has always been at my side when I've had dealings with the Russians. His laid-back demeanor seems to relax just about everyone, but the man has a keen eye and shrewd instincts. He can sniff bullshit from half a mile away and has a sixth sense for when shit's about to hit the fan.

"The Russians have been here a few times. They've kept level heads."

"You say that like it's not my job to make sure we get ahead of any shit they might start."

"Fair," I acknowledge.

"Last time you needed a fight to blow off steam, it was because you were getting married the next day. Am I correct in assuming the reason for the fight tonight is because of your wife?"

"Living with Alessia has been...quiet."

Confusion knits his brow. "That's a good thing, right?"

I tilt my head back and forth and flex my hands once again in the tape. "I thought it would be, but these last couple weeks, she's mostly kept to herself. I don't know. It's a little weird, to be honest. I was ready for a fight, for her to come in and try to take over my space, but we hardly see each other."

"Most men would kill for that," Cillian jokes.

"We had a...moment the night we got married, but since then, it's as though she's been avoiding me."

"Maybe your touch with the ladies is wearing off." Cillian shrugs, and I have the distinct urge to punch him in his smug face.

"Asshole."

My brother opens the door before I can list all the reasons Cillian is wrong about me losing anything.

"Ready?" Eoghan asks, and I stand from the bench, twisting my arms before I grab my gloves.

"Let's do it."

The three of us walk out to the crowded room, and the energy coming from the crowd spurs me on. Cillian helps me secure my gloves and I step into the ring, getting a look at my opponent. This isn't the first time I've seen Dmitri fight, so I'm somewhat prepared for what's to come. The man is a fucking beast covered in tattoos and has a permanent scowl etched on his face.

My brother announces us, and the Russian and I tap gloves before separating. When the bell dings, he's immediately on the move. Damn, this guy has a lot of skill behind his brawn, and he's giving me a run for my money right off the bat. For every blow I throw, he returns combos with just as much force. This is going to be a close match, but I can tell the way to win will be to tire him out. He's using too much energy already, probably trying to get an early knockout so he can go home with the honor of beating the head of the Monaghan family. I get in a quick jab to his temple before he swings, but his fist goes wide and he stumbles to the side. My eyes shoot up for the briefest of moments and catch a man in the crowd grabbing a woman roughly by the arm. When she swings around, the angry look slashed across her face is all too familiar.

Probably because it's my fucking wife.

Our eyes lock for one second before the Russian blocks her from my vision and sends his powerful fist flying at my face. I dodge it at the last second and send an uppercut into his jaw, knocking the giant out cold.

Alessia is staring at me, shock and fear warring for dominance in her gaze. I give nothing away as I point my gloved fist at her then to the hallway leading to the locker room.

What the hell is she doing here?

CHAPTER EIGHT
ALESSIA

I SHOULD HAVE NEVER let Gemma convince me to come to some underground illegal boxing match, but the guy she met at her gym apparently wanted to come check it out, so here we are.

My nerves are high. I know the Monaghans own the bar above the basement, but Finn is likely at the casino like he's been every night the last two weeks. She wanted a night out, and I had nothing better to do, so I agreed to come with her. Enzo is with me because we learned a long time ago that it was easier to tell him where we were going rather than have him sullen and angry with me the next day for putting myself in unnecessary, risky situations. Nothing worse than having to deal with a brooding bodyguard all damn day. Plus, he threatened to tell my father if we snuck off without him when we were in college. I suppose now he'd go tattle to my husband.

My husband.

It's still strange to think about Finn that way. When he saw Enzo and I sparring earlier today, I was more than a little surprised he offered to train together instead of laughing outright. There isn't a single woman I know in our life who likes to fight or has any of the training I do. Most men want their wives soft and pliant, not loudmouths that throw a mean right hook, even if they apparently drop their shoulder. The memory of the way he intently studied my form when he put on the mitts still makes my heart race faster than normal. He watched me and pointed out where I was making the mistake. Most men would have condescendingly patted me on the head before handing me their credit card so I could spend my time doing something "fun" like shopping or getting my hair done. Instead, Finn made plans to train with me.

Our marriage certainly isn't what I was expecting.

"Honey, you need to loosen up," Gemma says, pulling me through the crowd to the bar sitting against the concrete wall.

The first fight of the night finished before we got here, but we saw them cleaning the blood from the ring. The crowd is lining up with several of the bookmakers throughout the room to place bets on the next bloody match. I'd be lying if I said I wasn't worried about Eoghan or Finn catching us here tonight, but what would either of them do? It's not like I'm some sort of prisoner in Finn's house. And it's not as though I'm running off on him to hang out with my best friend. The man is never there. He obviously doesn't care about where I spend my time, so why should I care if he finds out I came here tonight? That doesn't mean I'm not keeping an eye out for my husband or his brother though.

Gemma and I are standing in line to get a drink from the small bar set up down here, with Enzo keeping a respectable distance. He's fine with allowing us to have our fun, but he makes sure we're safe while doing it.

With drinks in hand, Gemma spots her crush from the gym and waves. We begin making our way to him and the group he's with when I hear a familiar voice on the microphone.

"Ladies and gentlemen, you're in for a surprise tonight. We have none other than the man, the myth, the boss of Boston. Finnegan Monaghan."

The crowd goes wild as my head jerks toward the ring, and I see my husband step into it with Cillian next to him, helping him tie his gloves.

So many thoughts run through my head as I stand stock-still in the middle of the crowd. Gemma is saying something to me as Eoghan announces the other fighter. Some Russian guy I'm not familiar with. I don't catch his name, too shocked to hear anything but the blood rushing in my ears.

The bell dings and the men circle each other while getting a feel for the other's fighting movements. Finn lands a couple blows, but his opponent lands just as many. These two are pretty evenly matched. The way Finn moves with the confidence of a trained fighter has me remembering earlier today when I scoffed at the idea that he knew better than Enzo or me when we were working out. *He obviously does know better,* I think to myself as I watch him dance around the Russian. I'm equally in awe of his skill as I am irritated as hell I didn't know about his underground fighting. The cut above his brow on our wedding day makes perfect sense now. Maybe if I would have asked, he would have told me where it came from, but I didn't. I didn't care to get to know much about my husband before we were married. I thought I'd known everything necessary, considering this is only a business arrangement.

I catch Enzo's eye as he stands a few feet from where Gemma and I are. I'm not sure if we should stay or not. Maybe there's a reason he doesn't want me to know this part of him, or maybe...hell, I don't know, but I'm suddenly feeling very out of place being down here watching Finn trade blows with his opponent when he didn't invite me here or even tell me this is something he does.

Turning toward Gemma, I signal to the door. She nods and picks up on the fact I want to leave. I need to process this turn of events.

On our way to where Enzo is standing, we pass a group of overly obnoxious men hollering at the fighters in the ring.

One of them grabs me by the arm. "Where are you off to? Let me buy you a drink."

I try to dislodge my arm from his grip, but he yanks me toward him. I turn around to tell the man that, in no uncertain terms, he can fuck right off. Before the words leave my mouth, my gaze collides with Finn's. Our eyes lock for barely a second, but he immediately takes in the scene. Finn's eyes glaze over in a cold fury that makes my stomach plummet. In the next moment, Enzo has his arms around the man holding my arm, shoving him away, but my stare doesn't leave Finn's. The Russian blocks my view of him, and before I can gather my thoughts, Finn sends a powerful uppercut into his jaw, knocking the man out cold. I'm tempted to run, not knowing if he's pissed about someone grabbing me or if he's pissed I'm here. Before I can make my feet move, Finn focuses the entirety of his fierce gaze on me and points from me to the hallway, signaling where he wants me to go.

"Oh shit, Alessia. What do you want to do?" Gemma asks, looking between Finn and me. There's no doubt in my mind that if I said we need to get the hell out of here, she'd grab my hand and make a run for it with me.

"Mrs. Monaghan, interesting seeing you here," I hear a voice call behind me.

Shit.

I turn and come face to face with Cillian. Well, I suppose there's no use trying to make a mad dash toward the door now. I doubt I'd get more than five feet without one of his men stopping me.

"I think Finn would like a word," he says, a small smirk playing on his lips.

I straighten my spine and lift my chin, staring him dead in the eye. I don't give a shit if I'm somewhere I shouldn't be. Or that I've discovered some secret my husband is trying to keep from me for God knows what reason. I'm Alessia Amatto, and no one will make me feel like I don't belong anywhere I choose to be.

"I'm sure he does." I turn to my best friend, who is busy shooting daggers at Finn's lieutenant. Of course, Cillian is completely nonplussed by Gemma's attitude. In fact, I think I see a hint of a smile on his face as he stares right back at her.

Her brow arches before she turns to me with a question in her eyes. *Stay or run?* she's silently asking me. Only my best friend would think we could outrun the Irish mob in the basement of one of their own bars.

"I'll call you tomorrow," I say and give her a quick hug before turning toward Cillian. May as well follow him now. No use putting off the argument my husband and I are about to have if the cold look in Finn's eyes is anything to go by.

I reach the locker room moments before my husband. When he walks in, we stare at each other for a brief moment, neither of us saying a word.

"What the hell possessed you to walk into an underground fighting ring?" he asks in a deceptively calm tone.

"There're plenty of other women here, Finn. Why shouldn't I be here too?"

"Those other women aren't my wife, Alessia."

I work my jaw back and forth, the weight of his words falling heavily on my guarded heart. "I see." *Boy, do I see.* "I didn't realize I was walking into where you met with your fucking *goomah*." The explosion of anger that comes out as I yell at him surprises even me.

It's not that I didn't know men in Finn's position usually have a few mistresses, especially knowing what I do about him. It just wasn't something I was expecting to care about. But fuck do I care. Maybe my heart isn't as impenetrable as I thought.

"My what?" he asks, confusion creasing his brow.

Before I can answer, there's a quick knock at the door, followed by Eoghan peeking his head inside.

"You might want to come out for this, brother."

Finn takes a deep breath and looks from me to his brother, anger radiating from him.

"Stay here," he commands before walking out and slamming the door behind him. I raise both middle fingers to the door and let out a scream of sheer annoyance. This is such bullshit. How dare he assume I'm going to stay in this little room that smells of sweat and muscle cream just because he demanded it? I don't have to actually do anything he tells me.

My phone dings with a text alert, and I see Gemma's name flash on the screen.

Gemma: *You okay? Enzo put me in a cab and told me I need to go home, but the driver is waiting around the corner. Do you want to make a run for it?*

See? Always ready to be my partner in crime.

Me: *I'm fine. Just confused and extremely fucking pissed. I think Finn is more worried about my running* into his girlfriend than anything else.

Gemma: *That slimy asshole!*

Me: *It is what it is.*

And that's the fucking truth. If Finn wants to have a hundred girlfriends, no one is going to think any less of him.

Gemma: *What do you want me to do? Stay or go?*

The urge to tell her I'll meet her outside and we'll get the hell out of here is strong. I'm so fucking tempted to go to the most expensive bar in downtown Boston and order bottle after bottle of champagne courtesy of Finn and the credit card he gave me last week to redecorate his house. I still can't believe he suggested that, but if there's one thing that's paramount in this life and in this deal we made, it's to present a united front. So, as much as I would love to run out of this room, my upbringing and loyalty to my family won't allow it.

Me: *Go. I'll call you tomorrow.*

I put my phone back in my purse and look around the space. I spot Finn's clothes hanging in an old beat-to-shit locker. For no other reason except for the fact I must be a glutton for punishment, I walk over to his suit and run my hands down the sleeve. One thing I can certainly appreciate about the man is he knows how to dress well. The fabric of his jacket is soft and feels as expensive as I'm sure it is. I lower my face to the fabric and inhale, trying to place the rich, masculine scent that I've come to associate with the man who pisses me off to no end. Cedarwood maybe? My eye catches on something shiny next to his wallet and keys sitting on the little shelf in the locker. It's his wedding ring. Of fucking course. I wonder if he takes it off every time he goes to the casino—if that's even where he's been spending his time.

I grab the thick gold band and examine it in my hand. This little thing really means nothing. Flashes of my future run through my mind. Me being bored and home by myself. The fake smiles I'll have to wear in front of our families for the rest of our lives. Me losing bits and pieces of myself because of the image I'm meant to maintain in front of the world. I knew going in that this was business and there were things I was going to have to turn a blind eye to. It's how this world works. But I wasn't prepared to have it thrown in my face like it is tonight.

Well, fuck that.

If our vows mean nothing to him, then the loyalty I've been raised to have toward my marriage and our image means nothing to me.

I march out of the small room where Finn demanded I wait for him and into the large, brightly lit basement where a few people still linger about. I spot my husband walking in from a side door, shaking out his hand. He heads to the bar and signals for the bartender. The young woman loads a towel with ice and hands it to him before a woman with long blonde hair and a short-as-hell dress runs over to him and takes his hand, examining his knuckles.

And I see fucking red.

I march over to him and throw the gold band at his face.

"Fuck you. You don't dictate what I do or where I spend my time," I spit at him.

The blonde playing nursemaid turns to me with a sour look on her face.

"Excuse you. Who the hell do you think you are?"

Before I can think better of it or consider the consequences of my actions, my fist goes flying straight to the girl's nose. She stumbles back on her high heels, her hands immediately clutching her nose, which now has blood pouring out of it and down the front of her gaudy-as-hell dress.

"I'm his wife."

"You're fucking insane," she screeches and runs toward the stairs leading up to the bar.

Finn stands to his full height, towering over me.

"I think it's time to go, Alessia."

"I don't have to go anywhere with you," I spit back.

I turn and see Enzo walking in through the door Finn did just moments ago. My husband locks eyes with my bodyguard and tilts his chin to the door Gemma and I entered the basement through.

"Enzo will take you home. I'm grabbing my things and I'll meet you there."

"I already told you—"

Finn leans down and puts his face level with mine. "Do not argue with me," he says through clenched teeth. "Go home with Enzo."

He turns around and heads to the locker room, leaving me staring after him with my jaw hanging open.

"Come on. The car is out front," my bodyguard informs me.

Enzo leads me out of the basement and people stare as I walk by. I pay them no mind and allow Enzo to walk in front of me with my head held high.

The entire ride home, my hand is throbbing. When we turn onto the private road leading to Finn's house, I notice headlights behind us. Finn must have been flooring it to catch up to us.

After Enzo opens the door for me, I step out, determined to make it to my room and lock the door before my asshole of a husband even steps foot in the house.

"Just so you know," Enzo starts, "he hurt his hand beating the man's face into a bloody mess."

"What man?" I saw him fight. He knocked the Russian out cold before he demanded I meet him in the locker room.

"The man who grabbed you. Told him he'd better think twice before touching what doesn't belong to him."

I scoff. "I don't belong to Finn."

Enzo simply nods as Finn stops behind my car and throws his into park.

He steps out wearing slacks and his white dress shirt is only half done up, his jacket slung over his arm.

"We need to talk," he growls before slamming his car door.

"I don't need to do anything you tell me," I shoot back, my voice full of defiance as I stomp up the stairs and open the door. I attempt to slam it in his face, but the man is quick and stops it from closing with his booted foot.

"That wasn't a request, Alessia. Get your ass in the kitchen."

There has never been a time in my life when I was so fucking angry I felt like my head was about to explode from pure rage. I've heard people talk about being that angry. I've even been worried watching the vein in the side of my father's temple pulse when he was mad, but never in my life have I felt the kind of white-hot rage I do at this moment.

Instead of ignoring him and going to my room, I stomp after him and stop in the dimly lit kitchen, watching as he pulls out the ice tray from the glossy black refrigerator. He tosses it on the white marble countertops with a jarring clatter in the otherwise silent space then grabs two bags from the drawer, setting them next to the trays. He loudly slams the drawer shut before filling the bags with ice. If he doesn't have any sense of self-preservation then who am I to save him from this argument? He has yet to acknowledge my presence in the kitchen, instead tending to his swollen hand, and I've had just about enough of being ignored when he was the one who demanded I follow him in here.

I slap both of my hands on the center island dividing us. "I won't have you throwing your whores in front of my face."

His gaze flicks to mine before moving back to the bags. "Is that what *goomah* means?"

My mouth stays clamped shut in a firm line instead of answering. Unfortunately, the daggers I'm staring at him aren't actually ripping him to shreds where he stands.

"You were somewhere you shouldn't have been without checking with me or even telling me you were going to one of my establishments."

"I didn't realize I needed your permission to leave the house in the first place. Why don't you tell me all the places I'm not allowed to go. I'll make a little list and tack it to *your* forehead!"

"So violent," he says, handing me the ice pack. I stare at it and then him.

"Take it." He shakes the bag a couple times. "I know your hand hurts like a bitch."

Begrudgingly, I grab the baggie from him because he's right. Breaking that bitch's nose hurt like hell without boxing gloves.

"We need to get a few things straight." Finn leans back against the counter with his arms crossed over his broad chest. To any other person, he looks cool and calm, as though we were about to have a discussion about the weather. To me, though, I see a powerful man who is keeping his fury contained just below the surface.

Here goes. This is the part he tells me he can do whatever the hell he wants, and I have no say in the matter. Well, fuck him. If he can do whatever he pleases, then so can I.

"I do not go there to meet my mistresses. I go to the fights to relieve stress."

"If that's not where you meet your mistresses, then what was one of them doing there? They obviously know more about where you spend your time than I do. Otherwise, why would she be there?"

"I'd met that woman before we got married."

"I don't care where or when you meet your mistress, Finn." I throw my hands in the air with frustration. Does he honestly think that's the important detail here? "Let me be very clear. If you think you can screw around with anyone you want, then so can I. I won't be one of those women who stays locked in the house and makes you a nice home-cooked meal while you walk in smelling like cheap perfume. I'll have my own life, and if you want to fuck around, then I will too."

Finn's eyes turn dark with anger, and the calm facade he kept in place is about to crack right down the middle. Fear lances through me for a moment, worried I just crossed a very serious line. Hell, I know I did. I jumped straight over it, flipping him off as I went.

He walks around the kitchen island and holds my defiant stare with a determined one of his own.

"Let's get a few things straight." I open my mouth to interrupt, and he slams his hand over it before I can get a word out. "You will not talk over me. One, that girl is not my mistress. I've never touched her or any woman since you and I said our vows. I don't care if they were made for a business arrangement. They still mean something, and I don't take that shit lightly. Two, the reason I didn't want you at the fight wasn't so you wouldn't run into a sidepiece that, once again, doesn't exist. It was because it's a dangerous place, and if anything happened to you there, I would never fucking forgive myself. I can't control what other women do, but that is not the place for you or Gemma to spend your time. And three." He leans closer and his voice drops to an ominous tone I've yet to hear from him. "If you ever so much as entertain the thought of having any sort of extramarital affair, wife, I will find the man who has an obvious death wish and make myself his fairy *fucking* godmother. I will carve the skin from any part of his body that touched you and force him to watch as I dissolve it in acid over and over before I slit his fucking throat."

My breath stills in my chest as I stare into his eyes, seeing he means every word, every threat.

"Am I clear?"

I nod and he removes his hand from my mouth.

"Good. Now, about the Suzy Homemaker comment," he begins, and my head spins at the ease with which he changes the subject from committing gruesome acts of violence to me being a housewife. "I never thought of you as the housewife type."

I give him a flat look.

"Okay," he says on a chuckle. "When I got to know you a little, I could tell that it didn't interest you. You're in need of something to do, and I happen to be in need of a casino host."

I narrow my gaze and study Finn for a few moments. "What happened to the last one?"

"They were caught skimming."

So they're dead.

"I've never worked in my father's casinos. I don't know the first thing about it."

"No, but I've seen you be friendly and charming when you want to be. And I don't have to worry about you stealing from me."

I mull over his offer. It would give me something to do, and it beats the hell out of being home alone and bored every night.

"I'll think about it," I reply.

Finn nods. "Okay."

There's a beat of awkward silence in the kitchen now that both of our tempers have fizzled out.

I put the ice on the counter and look Finn in the eye. "Thanks for the ice pack and the job offer."

He nods but doesn't say anything. The air between us is charged, and I'm still a frazzled jumble of emotions.

I turn to leave the kitchen, but before I reach the doorway, he calls after me.

"That was a good punch. You didn't drop your shoulder."

I chuckle and turn my head.

"I guess you knew what you were talking about earlier after all."

Finn shrugs with a boyish grin. It's not one I've seen before, and goddammit if it doesn't do some very inconvenient and unwanted things to my body.

Fuck.

I think I want to sleep with my husband.

CHAPTER NINE

FINN

BEING THAT CLOSE TO Alessia while she read me the riot act to make sure I knew where she stood in this marriage had my blood pumping more than any fight ever has. She was completely off base with her assumptions about me and other women or what I expect of her out of this marriage, but the fact she fought so hard with me about it sent heated thrills through my body. And when she punched that woman who was trying to fuss all over me after she saw the state my hand was in? Fuck, it was all I could do not to throw her over my shoulder and lock us in the dressing room of that fucking basement.

The thirty seconds it took me to put my clothes back on before getting in my car and driving to our house was hell with the hard-on I was sporting. Over the last few weeks, she's been a very polite ghost at home, but tonight she was the goddamn firecracker I saw glimpses of before our wedding. It was intoxicating.

Now I'm standing in my kitchen, nursing a whiskey, and trying like hell to convince myself it's not the right time to go upstairs and break her damn door down.

I'm so fucked.

I pull out my phone to text Cillian about the change in casino employment. It will take the task from him and give him more time to focus on other things I need, like finding Carlo Cataldi and also making sure things run smoothly at the docks. Alessia was never going to be happy staying home and doing nothing with her days and nights, but I didn't know what the hell to do with her. It's not like I've ever had a wife to deal with.

Me: *Alessia is taking over as casino host.*

I see the three dots pop up on and then off the screen a few times before he finally sends his reply.

Cillian: *If that's what you think is best.*

I don't bother responding because regardless of what he thinks or whether I think it's what's best, it's what's going to happen. Obviously, the idea of her being at the casino around men who are drinking heavily and used to getting whatever they want isn't where I'd prefer her to be, but it's the safest option within my organization. It's heavily guarded, and I'll probably add a few more just to make myself feel better. It's not like I could have her out running the docks. Actually, she'd probably handle business like a boss down there and bust the skulls of anyone who dared to question her.

I laugh at the vision of her punching that woman again. Yeah, she'd have no problem getting everyone in line, especially with the weight of my organization and her father's behind her.

And the blood is rushing to my cock again.

I'm not going to lie. It's a little odd for me to find my wife's violent nature the absolute fucking turn-on that I do. I always thought I needed someone soft, someone to smooth my sharp edges. I was sure as shit wrong about that. Alessia's fire gets my blood heated faster and hotter than the thought of any other woman.

And that's a problem.

I wasn't meant to have feelings for my wife. I was meant to have her as a backup if Mario got any bright ideas about double-crossing me. This attraction is a distraction that's rather inconvenient, especially considering she's sleeping one floor up. Or maybe she isn't sleeping. Maybe she's waiting to see if I'll come knocking on her door tonight. There was no mistaking the way her pupils dilated when I held my hand over her mouth or the way she leaned just *that* much closer when our chests were barely touching. What if I had slid my hand lower and held her pretty little neck in my grasp? What if I would have slid it farther still? I can't help but wonder how far she would have let me take it or if the temptation of being so close had her panties wet.

Knock it off, fucker. You're just torturing yourself at this point.

After downing the rest of my whiskey, I head up the stairs to my room. When I pass the door of Alessia's bedroom, I stop for a moment. What would come out of my mouth if I knocked and she opened her door? Would she invite me in or slam it in my face? It could really go either way with her.

Inhaling a deep breath, I close my eyes and shake myself out of these stupid questions that are sure to plague me the rest of the night. Instead of knocking, I decide to shut myself in my room, head to my bathroom, and turn the shower on. Seems another cold shower is needed in order to get through this night.

When I step inside my gym in the morning, I spot Enzo throwing some combinations at the bag hanging from the ceiling. Alessia still hasn't come down, but I am early and thought I'd warm up before our scheduled training session. I'm not sure if she's still willing to work out with me after last night, but seeing Enzo relieves some of the worry.

"Mr. Monaghan," Enzo says, stepping back from the bag. "Alessia will be down shortly. Thought I'd get started."

"I had the same idea. And please, call me Finn."

Enzo nods and begins his routine again.

"About last night," I begin. "What possessed you to think it was a good idea to bring Alessia and Gemma to the fights? You have to know how dangerous places like that can be for women who come alone."

He stops punching the bag and turns to face me. "Have you tried telling Alessia she couldn't do something? Because I have, and it didn't work out for me. She'll go on her own if I don't agree. I realized a long time ago it was safer for her if I didn't try to stop her from doing something and instead did my job as her bodyguard, Mr. Monaghan."

I nod a few times, completely understanding why he would have taken that approach. "I just told you to call me Finn."

"Well, I figured it was because you didn't think I was going to argue with you. But I work for Alessia and Mr. Amatto, and I take my orders from them. I don't mean you any disrespect, and I didn't want you to think I was being too informal when—"

"When you told me to shove it up my ass?" I finish for him.

Enzo chuckles. "I wasn't going to put it like that."

"No, I don't suppose you would've. Thank you for looking out for her."

"It's my job, Mr.—"

"Finn," I correct. "And I'm glad she has you. She obviously trusts you, and that means I trust you, too."

Enzo nods and turns back to the bag, but I'm not done. There really isn't anyone I can ask about Alessia, considering we've never run in the same circles. Besides, what's a little small talk since we're the only ones in here this early?

"You've been with her a long time?"

"Since she was in high school," he pants out, never breaking his concentration.

"She must have been a handful in college. That's where she met Gemma, right?"

Enzo nods but keeps working the bag.

"She have a lot of admirers in college? How did they handle it when they found out her dad was head of a Mafia family?"

"Jesus Christ, Finn. Stop trying to interrogate my bodyguard," Alessia says as she walks into the room with three cups of disgusting-looking green juice in her hands. "Here," she hands me one and Enzo the other.

I lean down to smell the concoction before wrinkling my nose.

"Don't be a baby. It's good for you, and it doesn't taste that bad," Alessia huffs.

Enzo and I share a look that says it's definitely going to taste *that* bad. We raise our glasses in a toast, and the three of us chug the contents of the glasses.

Holy shit, it tastes worse than I thought it would. Enzo's face is nearly the color of the disgusting liquid, and Alessia is wearing a satisfied smile on her face.

"It tastes like fucking gym socks and lemon," I say, trying not to gag.

Alessia rolls her eyes and collects the empty glasses, setting them on one of the benches.

"How's your hand?" I ask, watching her flex it a few times before grabbing her gloves.

"A little sore."

"We don't have to do bag work today," I tell her.

"Afraid of hurting yours more?" She points to my

bruised knuckles.

"This is nothing," I tell her.

"Then stop trying to make excuses for me to get out of training today and put on those mitts." Her tone leaves no room for argument as she points to the pads on the bench.

"Yes, ma'am."

An hour later, Alessia is covered in sweat, but she never once complained about her hand hurting. I'm learning more and more about my wife as we work out. The biggest revelation being that she's more competitive than I gave her credit for. Every punch and combo I throw, she's right behind me, doing the same. She doesn't tell us she needs a break or needs to fix her hair or whatever excuse a woman might use to stop. She's also really fucking good. I see where she could improve and point it out a few times. Instead of saying it's too difficult or complaining about how long we've been going at it, she nods and tries harder, never giving up until whatever correction I make becomes natural. Alessia's quick wit and tough shell have always impressed me, but her tenacity and determination are making me respect her that much more. My wife is a triple threat.

I am so fucked.

"Alright, I have to tap out," I say while she continues to work with Enzo.

"Already?" she asks. "Is your hand bothering you?" The mock concern in her voice doesn't go unnoticed, but I ignore it.

"Be ready to leave here at five. I want to show you around the casino and talk about what you can expect before we get busy. There's a high-roller poker game tonight that we host once a month. You'll need to study up on the players."

"I didn't agree to work for you yet."

"You and I both know sitting home all night isn't your speed. I need the help and you need something to do. It's a win-win."

Her jaw works back and forth as she considers her decision. "Fine. I'll be ready."

"I'll leave you to it then." I gather my towel and the cups, trying like hell to keep the victorious grin off my face before heading out the door.

"How's your hand really?" Enzo asks right before the door latches.

"Hurts like a bitch," Alessia responds.

"We could have stopped or worked on legs today."

"It's as though you don't even know me, Enzo. You really think I'm going to sit around icing my hand while Finn works out with the same injury? Not on your life."

"You're a very stubborn woman, Alessia."

"Would you expect anything less?"

I hear Enzo chuckle and my mouth tilts in a smile as well.

"Good point. You about ready to call it a day?"

"Fifteen more minutes."

I walk away from the door to get ready for my meeting

with Cillian, wearing a smile the entire way to my bedroom.

That woman is something else.

It's five minutes to five, and I'm waiting patiently at the bottom of the stairs for Alessia. I want to give her enough time to get a feel for the casino before being pulled into a million different directions. I plan to stay the entire night and work from my office there. It's not that I don't trust my decision. I know she'll make a great host, but I don't want her to feel like I'm throwing her to the wolves on her first night there.

Enzo will also be on the floor with Alessia as her personal guard. Though the clientele isn't as rowdy as the ones that come to the fights, it still brings me peace of mind to know that his only responsibility is to be there looking after her safety.

Finally, Alessia appears at the top of the stairs, and I swear to God, it's like one of those stupid teen movies I caught my brother watching with a girlfriend when he was in high school. She walks down the curved staircase, and I'm instantly enthralled by her red lips and the smooth skin of her long, tanned legs.

The dress reminds me of the one she was wearing the first night we met. Instead, this one is black, but it hugs her just as well as the red I loved seeing her in.

I'm half tempted to have her go upstairs and change simply because I don't want the eyes of every man in the place all over her tonight. It would be an impossible feat for any red-blooded man to accomplish. Plus, I already hear her telling me to fuck off if I dared ask.

"Ready?" she asks, but I'm stuck staring at those damn red lips to register that I'm still holding her coat over my arm.

"Finn, what the hell's wrong with you?"

That snaps me to attention, and I hold her jacket open so she can slide her arms in. When she pulls her hair from the collar, a whiff of something flowery and light hits my nose. The temptation to bury my face in her long, dark waves is strong, but instead, I take a step back and open the front door.

"Your chariot awaits," I say, holding my arm toward my car that Enzo has started.

She looks at me and quirks her brow. "Why are you acting so weird?"

She's right. Since I saw her walk down the stairs, my brain went a little haywire. I don't have an answer for her, so I simply shrug and walk with her down the stairs and open the car door.

On the way to the casino, I work to get my head on straight and focus on the binder I had Cillian put together for Alessia. It's filled with short bios and preferences of the men that are going to be playing in the poker game tonight and a few of the other regulars that spend a shit ton of money in our establishment on a regular basis. Alessia studies each preference sheet and nods, making little notes when I mention something that isn't on there.

"What about the girls?" she asks. "There's nothing in here about any of their preferences for the escorts."

I specifically had Cillian leave that out. I'm not sure why since that's something a good host would know about the high-end clients, but we have a house madam that takes care of those needs should one of the players request some time with one of our girls.

"That's handled separately," I tell her.

She studies me for a moment then shrugs. "Seems like something I should be aware of, but it's your casino."

Enzo parks the car in a private garage reserved for staff. It's one of the small ways I show my appreciation for their time and discretion working for my family. Parking in Boston can be a pain in the ass, and this way, they never have to worry about finding a spot or someone messing with their car while they're here.

The casino is beneath one of the most exclusive and high-end bars in Boston, owned by my family. Our name is nowhere near any licensing for this place. If some cop or FBI agent looked into the owner of this establishment, it would lead them to several different shell companies ending up in the Cayman Islands. Some creative paperwork and some generous deposits in the bank accounts of a few city officials were all it took to get the licensing needed to open the doors. This is a members-only establishment, which offers some anonymity to our clients when they enter. The upper level where the bar is has a speakeasy feel to it, a nod to my family's past of running the biggest bootlegging operation in Boston during prohibition. But the real action happens a level below.

Alessia looks around the bar with the deep-emerald-green wallpaper and rich, dark oak accents that match the low ceiling. Several tables are scattered around the main floor, with more private tables lining the walls.

I nod to the bartender on duty, who is getting everything set up for opening, before walking down a short hallway to a door that blends perfectly with the wall. Alessia watches with interest as I move the picture of my grandparents to the side, revealing a small keypad.

"Everyone has their own code, including staff, so we know who's entered and when."

"Fancy," she remarks with a small tilt to her red lips.

I enter my code and push the door in, revealing another staircase. When we get to the bottom, it opens into a small alcove where we'll have a security guard and one of the girls greeting guests upon arrival.

"You'll be up here at the beginning of the night and greeting everyone when they come in. All guests are required to leave any of their weapons in one of the several lockboxes we have for them."

"That must go over well."

I look her in the eye with a smirk playing on my lips.

"No one argues with me."

Alessia hums but doesn't say anything.

Thick curtains hang from the ceiling, partitioning off the alcove from the rest of the casino. When I open them, the impressed look in Alessia's eyes sends pride shooting through me. I've worked hard at taking the back room gambling den my grandfather started and turned it into a high-class casino you would find at the finest resorts in Vegas or Atlantic City.

It's not often I get to see someone's expression when they first enter, and Alessia's reaction doesn't disappoint as she takes in the expansive underground space with dark wood and felt-lined blackjack and poker tables. I wanted it to have a similar feeling to the bar upstairs—classy and expensive. We have a few roulette wheels and craps tables set up throughout. Everything is the same high-end quality you would find in any legitimate casino, minus the tired-looking dealers and straight-off-the-street gamblers in jeans and T-shirts. We require a strict dress code in the casino, not that we've ever had to enforce it. Our clientele comes here for an experience they won't find in any of the smoky, backroom gambling halls that are in so many of the dive bars in Boston.

"It's beautiful, Finn," she says, looking at me with a small grin. "I'm impressed."

"Not the back-alley thugs you've always assumed we were?"

Alessia laughs. "No. I'd say this is definitely a step

above what I imagined. I almost feel underdressed."

My gaze travels over her, and I shake my head. "Trust me. No one would ever say that."

A light blush covers Alessia's cheeks, and I clear my throat of the words that are stuck there. I want to tell her that she's one of the most stunning creatures I've ever laid eyes on. That she looks too good in that dress, and I want to see what she's wearing underneath. Instead, I tilt my head, signaling for her to follow me to the other side of the room where there's another set of thick drapes separating the three offices we have down here from the floor.

I point to the one on the left. "That will be yours." Then I point to the one on the right. "And that's for security."

"What about that one?" she asks, pointing to the door at the end of the hallway.

"That's my office."

I open the door to the security office, and low and behold, there's Cillian going through footage from a few nights ago.

"I thought I'd find you here," I say as he pauses the recording and looks in our direction.

"Alessia, good to see you," he says, standing and holding out his hand.

She takes it with a professional smile, already slipping into her role. "You too, Cillian."

"I'm going to show her to her office and get her set up. Meet me in mine," I tell my lieutenant.

He nods and turns back to the monitors, restarting the recording he was studying when we walked in.

Alessia and I cross the hall, and I open the door to her office. We've cleared it out after that rat bastard was caught stealing. The space is bare, with gray walls and nothing but a desk and file cabinet. I probably should have had someone come in and at least set her up with a plant or some shit.

"You can decorate however you like," I tell her as she sets her bag on the desk.

"I doubt I'll be in here much," she replies, sitting on the chair behind her desk and wincing. "But I'll probably at least get a new office chair."

I smile at her distaste for the cheap office furniture. "Whatever you want, princess."

She sends me a glare and rolls her eyes.

Making my way over to the file cabinet, I open it and signal for her to stand next to me. "In here, you'll find everything you'll need about all our clients. It's similar to what I had you go over in the car but more in-depth. I like for each member to feel like they're the most important patron we have, which means knowing their wives, mistresses, and kids' names. Shit, even their dog's name, if we can get that information."

"Finn, I've pretty much been preparing for this my entire life. Who do you think was at my father's side at every dinner party or charity function? Trust me, my mother has been training me since I was old enough to carry a conversation."

She grabs a stack of folders and sits at her desk, opening the first one. "Are you going to stand there and stare at me all night or get to your own work?"

I smile and shake my head. "There's a phone in the top drawer of your desk with all the numbers you'll need while you're here. Keep it on you when you're on the floor in case anyone needs to get hold of you. If you have any questions, Cillian or I can answer them. I'll be in my office if you need me."

"Just come get me when the doors open," she replies without looking up from her file.

Getting the distinct impression I've been dismissed, I head to my office, where Cillian is waiting patiently for me. It's similar to the one I had set up for Alessia. I don't keep my personal items here, all that stuff is at my home office, but I do keep a picture of me and my brother when we were kids with my dad and grandfather.

"Three generations of Monaghan men," my grandfather said proudly that day. He died not too long after the photo was taken, but he'd made a huge impression on my brother and me. He made sure we understood the importance of keeping family close and the loyalty we need to have to each other above all else.

"Alessia's set up?" Cillian asks as I have a seat in my dark leather chair. I'll need to order one like this for Alessia's office.

"Yup. Did you find anything on the security footage?" Since finding out our last host was stealing from us, I had Cillian reviewing the cameras, going back the last several weeks to see if he saw anything remotely suspicious from the dealers down to the coat check girl.

"Nothing. He may not have been working with anyone."

"I want to make sure. I'll be damned if anyone here thinks they can steal from me and get away with it."

Cillian nods. "Hence offering the job to your wife?"

"You don't seem thrilled with the idea, Cillian. Something you want to say?" I lean back in my chair and cock my head to the side, waiting for his reply.

"Nothing I haven't said before. You take a lot of risks keeping her close to your business when this little arrangement is so new."

He had similar reservations before we married, and I feel the same way now as I did then.

"She's not going to fuck me over, Cill. Her family has just as much to lose as we do."

Cillian shrugs but isn't finished. "Alessia is a beautiful woman." I nod because I already know this. "You sure it's a good idea having her here with all the rich assholes? It's entirely possible they'll mistake her for one of the girls and get a little handsy."

"If anyone has a problem with her not being for sale, they can come find me. I expect everyone within these walls to treat her with the same respect they treat me."

"Expectations and actuality are two different things, Finn."

"Then I'll handle it like I handled that punk at the fights last night. If the men who walk through those doors care about walking out with all of their limbs attached, they'll be damn careful not to disrespect what's mine."

Cillian gives me a flat look and exhales. "I hope to fuck this doesn't blow up in our faces."

CHAPTER TEN

ALESSIA

T HE FIRST NIGHT AFTER working at the casino, Finn nearly had to carry me to bed. These late nights are a far cry from what I'm used to, but at least it's something to do rather than twiddling my thumbs every day. And I like it. So far, the clientele has been pleasant, even if a few of them have cast me suspicious glances from time to time. It'll take some getting used to for a lot of the old-school Irish men to see one of the Amattos in their space, let alone working in one of their establishments.

I've been there every night for the last week. Finn told me to take the evening off tonight, saying he didn't want me getting burned out at the start. I tried to argue a little, but honestly, it was halfhearted at best. I just need a little time to adjust to my new schedule. Either that or Finn was tired of having to lead a zombie up to bed every night. He leaves me at my bedroom door and says a polite good night before heading to his room.

Every. Damn. Night.

There was a fire in him the night of the fights I haven't seen since. It seems the only time he gets in my space is when we're arguing. Otherwise, he's a perfectly respectable stranger. I liked him in my space the other night. Maybe a little too much. When he covered my mouth with his hand so I wouldn't interrupt him, I felt something more than fury toward his domineering attitude. A lot more. Having him that close, that intense, it shook me. It made me uncomfortable, then it made me have to change my panties when I got to my room. What the hell is wrong with me? I'm not attracted to men like Finn. Men who demand to be listened to like that, who have no problem invading my personal space to command my attention. I hate that, in fact. So why did I have a sudden and intense urge to press myself into his heated body and shut him up by slamming my mouth to his?

Scrubbing my hands over my face then groaning at the ceiling, I sit up from my bed and check the time on my phone. It's nearly ten in the morning. I'll admit, it was a touch daunting, seeing the red walls, cream duvet, and massive cream-colored tufted leather headboard when I first walked into this room a few weeks ago. I don't think I've seen such bold colors painted on a bedroom wall before, but considering red is my favorite color, I quite like the space. Good thing, considering this is my new home.

Even though Finn and I haven't been getting back from the casino until around four a.m., we've still been training in his gym every day. Aside from boxing, I've found my husband is skilled in Muay Thai and Tae

Kwon Do. Come to find out, when Enzo was a kid, he envisioned himself as a UFC fighter, so those two have been sparring at the end of our training sessions for fun. There's something about watching Finn trying to incapacitate Enzo that has enthralled me on more than one occasion when I was meant to be stretching and cooling down. The look of fierce determination and focus Finn wore was more than a little distracting and did little to slow my racing heart rate from our workout. Damn that man for being so tempting and completely wrong for me. Not that there would be any chance of finding a man that was right for me. He made it very clear what his stance on marriage and fidelity are.

Trusting men like Finn can be dangerous, especially to my heart. It's one thing to say you find the idea of infidelity offensive, but it's another to go your entire life married to one woman and never fall into the bed of another. Especially a man who's as powerful as Finn, who surely has women throwing themselves at him, with or without the band of gold he wears. Hell, there are plenty of women out there who find it a challenge. I don't have much faith in the declaration he made in regard to cheating. But even I'll admit, an entire lifetime is a long-ass time to go without sex. And the way Finn makes me feel when he doesn't think I notice him watching me makes the idea of having a platonic marriage with him nearly unbearable. The only problem is knowing I have to keep my heart guarded at all times, and sex tends to muddy the waters. But when my mind wanders to him sweaty and breathless in the gym or the night of our wedding when he was helping me with the buttons of my dress, my reasons for wanting the walls seem to be less and less pressing.

"Get it together, Alessia," I say out loud to my cat, who is pawing at my blanket, trying to get me out of bed to go feed him.

"Fine, you win." I scratch his head and throw the covers off me.

Throwing on a robe over my nightgown, I walk down the stairs and into the kitchen. Finn hasn't made it down yet, if the lack of coffee brewing is any indication. I start the pot and decide to make us a light breakfast before our workout. As I'm finishing cutting the fruit, Finn walks into the kitchen in nothing but a pair of running shorts, his naked chest that's smattered with a bit of hair on full display. My husband works out a lot, and I see the hours he's put in in every ripple of muscle on his defined chest, all the way to his toned abs, straight down to the top of his shorts, where a deep, chiseled V-cut muscle dives under the waistband.

You will not stare. You will not drool, I tell myself as my heart rate kicks up several notches.

"Good morning." His voice is husky, and his hair is still mussed from sleep. "You made breakfast?"

"It's nothing fancy. Just some fruit and yogurt before we head to the gym," I reply, putting a spoon in his bowl and sliding it across the island.

"Looks better than the sludge you made us drink the

other day."

"God, you're such a baby. How about, *Thank you, Alessia, for caring about my well-being and eating habits instead of lacing the energy drinks I'm constantly pouring into my body with arsenic?* You realize how unhealthy those things are, right?" Turning toward the coffeepot, I pull down two mugs, barely resisting the temptation to throw one at his head.

As I'm pouring my coffee, I feel the heat from his nearly naked body radiate into my back, with nothing but my thin robe and nightgown separating us.

"Thank you for not murdering me, Alessia." His voice is low, and I feel the vibration of his chest as he chuckles.

Everything stops. My breath, my heart, my awareness of what the hell is going on around me. The only thing I feel is the warmth against my back and the minty scent of Finn's freshly brushed teeth as he holds himself still behind me.

"Shit," I say when I look down and realize I've overfilled my mug and there's coffee dripping from the counter onto the gray marbled tile and my bare feet.

Damn distracting man.

Finn takes a step back, and I can finally take a breath before grabbing the paper towel and cleaning up the mess.

"I was thinking we could go for a run instead of the gym this morning. Test your endurance."

"My endurance is fine, but I wouldn't mind some

outdoor exercise," I reply, tossing the soiled paper towels in the trash.

I turn and find him leaning against the island with the bowl of fruit and yogurt in his hands and his legs crossed as he shovels a spoonful into his mouth. What is it about this man looking so casual and at ease while he eats his breakfast that's an absolute turn-on? I'm used to seeing him as the boss, commanding his employees or grappling with Enzo. This relaxed version of him eating fruit and yogurt as I sip my coffee on the other side of the kitchen is new to me. It strikes me that though we work out together and have been married for a full month, this is the first time I've seen him up close and personal without a shirt. There was the night at the fights, but I was so blinded by rage I didn't have the chance to appreciate the exquisite physique of my husband. In the gym, he wears a rash guard. The only time we'd run into each other before we started our workouts, he was on the way to or from the casino or wherever he was spending his time away from the house, dressed in his usual attire of a suit without a tie.

"What made you get a tattoo there?" I ask, pointing to the Celtic trinity knot inked over his heart, trying to make it seem as though the reason I'm studying the hard planes of his chest and defined abs is that I'm admiring his tattoo.

His smirk is a dead giveaway. He knows that's not what had my attention captivated for so long.

"Lost a bet."

"Really?" It's not uncommon for anyone to have tattoos these days. Honestly, I'm surprised he doesn't have more.

"No, not really. My brother has the same one. Though I was quite drunk when I got it." Finn chuckles at the memory.

"Why don't you have more?"

"I never thought of anything I'd want inked into my skin for the rest of my life."

"Too much of a commitment?"

He doesn't answer. And I'm not actually referring to tattoos either. Nothing I've heard about the man would indicate he's interested in any sort of commitment, tattoos or otherwise.

"What does it mean?"

"The Celtic knot?" he asks, and I nod. "There're different meanings for different people. I like the idea of it representing the idea of past, present and future. I honor my past, live in the present, and am always looking toward the future. Or something along those lines. Like I said, there was a lot of whiskey involved."

A laugh escapes him before he shakes his head a bit, clearing his thoughts. "I'll be down in ten minutes for our run."

I nod in his direction and finish my coffee. "I'll meet you at the door."

Finn stares at me like he wants to say something but doesn't know how.

"The commitment comment...I want you to know

it's not that I'm opposed. I've just never had anything I wanted to keep forever." So he picked up on the innuendo of my question. Nice to know my husband is as smart as people give him credit for.

He looks down at his bare feet and nods, signaling he's said all he has to say on the matter. "See you in ten."

Finn turns and leaves the kitchen, leaving me to completely overthink everything.

When we step outside into the chilly spring air, I'm no closer to figuring out what he was talking about in the kitchen. Did he not have any intention of staying in this marriage forever? I suppose if he wanted a divorce, there's no stopping him. Once his own organization is strong enough and the rival families have been taken care of, he won't need my father. Therefore, he won't need to stay married. We've both made it clear this marriage is no more than a business arrangement.

We finish stretching and begin a light jog over a well-used path.

"Let's loop around the property and down to the river then back. It's about a three-mile run," Finn says.

"Easy." I concentrate on my breathing, enjoying the scenery. "I had no idea how beautiful it is out here." I take in the giant oak trees along the path, full of green leaves now that spring is finally here.

"You should join me on runs more often," he replies.

"Maybe if you invited me, I would." Okay, so maybe not in the beginning, but in the last week since that fight night, I would have jumped at the chance to get to know him a bit better.

Finn is silent for a few moments. "I'm sorry. I'm not used to someone living with me. When my brother or Cillian are here, they're just sort of always there. It wasn't intentional to make you feel unwelcome."

"I never said you made me feel that way." Not entirely, at least.

He raises his brows in my direction but doesn't argue as we continue our run.

"Okay, I didn't necessarily feel at home these last couple weeks, but that's hardly your fault." I can accept that I could've made more of an effort, even if it pains me.

"I told you to redecorate." And we're back to that. It's infuriating that a man would assume because I'm a woman, shopping would be the way to my heart.

"Telling me I have an unlimited budget so I can shop until my little heart's content isn't exactly the way to make me feel at home."

"There're plenty of women who would see it differently." Would it be too much to trip him and watch him fall flat on his face?

"You didn't marry those women, did you?"

"I'm beginning to realize you aren't like most women I've ever met, Alessia."

"I'm not sure whether or not to take that as a compliment."

Finn smiles but doesn't comment. The trail leads us to the river flowing wildly through the back of the property. As a clap of thunder sounds overhead, both of us look up and notice the clouds that were just peeking over the horizon when we began our jog have moved directly overhead. And now they've decided it would be the perfect time to open and dump buckets of rain on us.

"Ah!" I yell as the cold rain pours over my heated flesh. "Fucking spring storms."

Finn points to a little weather-worn boat house at the river's edge a short distance from where we're standing.

"I'll race you," he calls as he takes off in a sprint to the small shelter.

"Asshole," I mumble as I bolt after him.

Finn beats me to the boathouse with a triumphant smile on his face.

"You cheated." My balled fists rest on my hips as I cast a glare in his direction.

"Of course I did," he laughs out. "I never said it was going to be a fair race."

I look around the small wooden structure, with a rowboat on a lift so it's not resting in the water.

"Do you row?" I ask.

Finn shakes his head. "No. This place is left over from when my family was in the bootlegging business." He has a seat on one of the old wooden benches as he catches his breath. "My family has owned this property since before my dad was born. They used the river to transport whiskey."

"I didn't realize your family had owned the property that long." I sit next to him as the raindrops splash violently against the roof and the river.

"Longer," Finn begins. "My great, great—hell, there might be another great in there—grandfather came over during the potato famine in Ireland. They started as farmers and thieves."

"Quite the combination," I joke.

Finn shrugs. "They fought for everything they had, and when others couldn't survive without some help, they did what they could, and sometimes that was by less than legal means."

"So...philanthropy and thievery."

"Survival," he replies. "Back then, the community of Irish immigrants who settled here looked at my family as their leaders in a sense. Then came prohibition and that's where we really made a name for ourselves. Of course, that ended, and we had to learn to adapt and change."

"I'd say you've done a good job, considering you haven't been pushed out yet."

"Your father and I are alike in that, I think. We've both worked to get where we are and work hard to stay here without sacrificing part of ourselves to do it."

I think about that for a few minutes, and for some reason, the thought angers me. No, my father and Finn didn't have to sacrifice themselves, but I did. I sacrificed my freedom and plans for a different future.

"That's easy for you to say, isn't it?" I stand from the bench and walk to the other side of the boathouse to try to get some space from Finn in this small building. "You're not the one who gave up their future to make sure this war with Cataldi ended in our favor. You're not the one who was married off to unite two powerful families."

"Hey, there's a ring on my finger too, Alessia," Finn replies. "I'm in this marriage, same as you. You think I wanted a bride who barely looks at me, who barely tolerates my presence? I did what I had to do because, without this marriage and show of a united front, he was going to force us all out, so the only family standing in Massachusetts was his. We *all* agreed we couldn't let that happen. No one forced you."

I let out a humorless burst of laughter. "No, I wasn't forced. I was told if we didn't get married, none of us would survive this war. You're so right, Finn. You gave up just as much as I did." It would be impossible for him to miss the caustic sarcasm dripping from my words. "I never had a choice. I was born a girl into a man's world, and there's nothing I'm good for besides keeping my husband happy and popping out a couple kids."

"Whoa, I've never asked that of you."

I open my mouth to argue, but he cuts me off. "If you bring up redecorating or shopping one more time, I swear to God, Alessia." Finn stands from the bench and stares at me. "I thought I was doing something nice. I have no idea what the fuck I'm doing here, either. But I sure as shit never wanted you to feel like some second-class citizen who holds no power. There's nothing about having that kind of wife that appeals to me in the slightest."

"Oh really? Then you'd be the first. Men in this life don't like their women to have power, as though it would make them look like less of a man. They certainly don't want them to have opinions or lives outside of whatever their husbands deem safe and respectable. You can't honestly expect me to believe you're any different."

"The hell I can't!" he yells, and points an angry finger at me. "Don't fucking compare me to the men in your world, Alessia. You're in mine now, and let me tell you, it's a hell of a lot different. If you would have decided not to sign that contract, I would have figured something else out. I would still be out there fighting because I'll never bow to that piece of shit, Cataldi. We decided this was the best course of action." He waves the same finger between the two of us. "You, me, and your father. I sure as hell never pressured you into it. In fact, it was your father who contacted me. I wasn't a hundred percent on board until that first dinner at your house." Finn is standing directly in front of me, his eyes holding so much anger, but there's hurt there, too. As though I'd made the worst comparison when I talked about the type of men I was used to dealing with in my world.

He inhales a deep breath and lets it out slowly through his nose, seemingly trying to calm himself before he continues. "When I laid eyes on you, everything changed. You weren't the shrinking violet or standoffish princess everyone thought you were. I could see the fire and the strength in your eyes. I could practically taste the defiance in every word you spoke. It fucking captivated me from the first moment you opened your red lips and spoke to me. I was hooked. That's why I signed that contract. Not to clip your wings or make you subservient to me, but I knew that night I wanted you next to me." He takes one step closer, then another, until barely millimeters separate us. "I wanted you in my life and, goddammit, in my bed. You fucking consumed me before I had a chance to save myself, and even if I could, I wouldn't change a damn thing. I would tie you to me because I'm a selfish bastard."

His breaths are coming out in hot pants against my cool flesh. He talks about me consuming him, but in this moment, all I feel, hear, or taste is him. Instead of doing the sensible thing that the voice in the back of my mind is telling me—take a step back and regroup—I grab him by the front of his wet shirt and slam my mouth to his. Thunder claps in the distance as though the sky is saying *finally, you're taking what you want.* Or it's warning me that I've just made a grave error in judgment by allowing this man to break through my walls and take a part of myself I swore no one would ever have again.

Finn pulls away, his gaze spearing into me. "Be certain this is what you want, Alessia. If we do this, you're mine, and I won't promise to let you go if you change your mind." His gravelly words dance across my lips.

"Don't insult me, Finn." I clutch his shirt tighter in my grasp. "I'm perfectly capable of escaping you if I want to."

A smile tilts the corner of his lips. "I better make damn sure you never want to, then."

When he slams his mouth to mine, the kiss takes on a life of its own, pulling us both into a thick haze of lust that neither of us can control, not that we would want to.

His hands are everywhere, running down my sides and over my ass as he pulls me tighter against his body, his hard cock digging into me. I loop my arms around his shoulders before he lifts me and slams my back into the wall. The boat house creaks, and I break the kiss, tilting my head to the side to give his mouth access to my neck. The feel of his lips and tongue trailing wet kisses along my neck, biting and tasting my sensitive flesh, is spurring me on. Needy moans erupt from somewhere deep within me. I've never felt so desperate for release in my entire life as my hips wriggle around, trying to find purchase on anything to sate this intense desire consuming me.

"Does my wife need to come?"

We seem to have gone from zero to a hundred in the span of the last few minutes, but really, we've been dancing around this inevitably for the last couple weeks.

"God, yes," I moan out, wanting nothing more than to feel him slide inside of me.

He sets me down on my feet and spins me around.

"Hands on the wall," he commands. "This is going to be quick, but I don't think I can make it back to our house without feeling your tight pussy strangle me first."

"I'm hearing a lot of talk and not seeing any action," I tease, grinding my ass back into him.

The deep chuckle I feel more than hear over my heavy panting sends shivers racing down my spine. Finn's hands move to the waist of my shorts, and he yanks them down, baring my naked flesh to him.

"You're so fucking wet for me," he says, trailing his finger through my center.

"Finn, please."

"Please what? Please fill you with my fingers and play with your clit until you come? Or please slide my cock inside you while you scream my name? You have to choose," he whispers hotly against my ear.

"Fuck. I want your cock inside me," I beg. It should surprise me how easily he got me to this point, maybe even scare me a little, but goddammit, all I care about right now is Finn relieving the ache in my core.

He doesn't make me wait long and pulls his own shorts lower before lining himself up at my entrance and slamming into me in one thrust.

We both let out a cry of pleasure with the first thrust, and each after that is punctuated with another moan or a curse falling from his lips. My nails dig into the old wood, sure to leave deep grooves.

"Fuck, Alessia, you feel so damn good," he pants into my ear as he leans over my back, covering me with his chest. He stands straight and slows his thrusts but still reaches so, so deep. "Fuck, baby. You should see how well you take me. Your pussy looks so good swallowing my cock."

I moan loudly. His filthy words, along with his pumping in and out of me, are quickly taking me to the precipice.

"Harder, Finn. Make me come."

He doesn't disappoint as his fingers tangle in my hair under the ponytail that sits askew, and he grips the strands firmly in his fist.

His hips begin moving at an almost punishing pace, throwing me over the edge I was just teetering on. I fall into absolute bliss as my orgasm crashes through me. My entire body feels as though it's going to explode into tiny little pieces, but he doesn't slow as I scream out in pleasure. My vision goes hazy around the edges before he thrusts hard once more, tightening his grip on my hip, and bellows out his own release. Hearing my husband come undone may have just become my favorite sound to fall from his lips.

We both still, panting as we each try to catch our breaths. Finn finally releases my hair from his grasp and runs his fingers down the slick skin of my back before leaning over and kissing me right behind the ear.

"It's a good thing we don't have to work tonight, wife. That was just a little taste."

He bends down and pulls my shorts back up my trembling legs, and I wince at the feel of his release between my thighs.

"I need you to hurry your cute little ass back to the house because I've had plenty of time to fantasize about all the places and ways I want to take you, so if you plan to leave the house in the next week, we'd better get started."

Sweet Jesus, what am I getting myself into?

CHAPTER ELEVEN

FINN

WHEN WE MAKE IT back to the house, I send a text to my security team that no one is to come into the house until I tell them otherwise. The jog back home was fucking torturous. Every damn time I thought about the way Alessia's ass jiggled when I slammed into her from behind, the memory had the blood rushing to my cock. Thank God she's a fast fucking runner because I was moments away from saying fuck it and pulling her behind a tree so I could sink inside her again.

"Get upstairs. We need a shower, then I need to eat your pussy until you come on my face," I tell her as she slips through the doorway.

"You have a way with words, husband," she replies with sarcasm heavy in her tone.

"I have a way with my tongue too, wife." My hand comes down on her delectable ass, and she yelps in surprise. Her gaze meets mine, and she gives me that death stare that turned me the fuck on the first time I saw it at her parents' house. This time, though, there's something else in her eyes. It's desire and excitement and maybe a little apprehension, as if she doesn't know what to expect with this new turn of events. That makes two of us, but I figure the answers will come eventually. The only thing that matters to me in this particular moment is seeing her spread out on my sheets, wearing nothing as I take my time getting to know every inch of her body. I wasn't fucking kidding when I said I had a multitude of fantasies about every which way I was going to have her. The first is going to be in my shower with me on my knees eating her wet cunt.

We head up the stairs, and Alessia turns toward her door and begins to walk inside before I grasp her arm and whirl her around.

"Where the hell are you going?" I ask.

"To take a shower?" Her confusion would be cute if I wasn't so damn wound up.

"You're going to the wrong room. When I said shower, I meant my shower. When I say bed, I mean my bed, and when I say I'm going to play out every fucking fantasy I've had of you these last weeks, I mean that too."

"Finn, all of my shampoo and things are in my shower already." Her reasoning for wanting to go to her shower doesn't deter me in the least.

"I have all that shit in my shower, Alessia."

She opens her mouth to protest, so I do the only sensible thing I can think of and bend at the waist, wrapping my arms around her thighs before I throw her over my shoulder.

"Finn! Are you fucking insane?" she screeches.

"You should have listened to me," I reply as my hand

lays a resounding slap against her ass.

I take several long strides into my room, slamming the door before I carry her to my shower and deposit her inside.

"You're such a fucking caveman," she huffs out.

"Role-play. I like it." My lips quirk up in a smirk as I throw her a wink.

Alessia glares at me, but there's no real heat behind it. She looks around the large shower stall with dual heads and dark-gray tile, mimicking river rock. Her eyes widen when she spots bottles of the same shampoo and conditioner she uses on the shelf. Then her gaze travels to mine, a question in her expression.

"I like the way your hair smells," is all I say before kneeling in front of her and tapping her foot. She lifts it, and I take off her running shoe and her sock before I move to her other foot and do the same.

"That's not stalkerish at all," she jokes, but when I stand to my full height and rip my shirt over my head, any further words or arguments she has die on her lips. It's similar to the look she gave me this morning in the kitchen, and I fucking preen like a goddamn peacock under her appreciative stare.

"Your turn." I point to her shirt, and the little minx tilts her lips in a small smile before lifting it over her head, bra and all, and throwing her top over my head.

This is the first moment I've seen my wife fully topless. My eyes drink up her round breasts and all the smooth tan skin on display. I no longer have to imagine what color her perfect dusty-rose nipples are that are pointed into tight buds, begging for my mouth.

I grab Alessia around the waist, slamming her body to mine and feeling all of her curves against my naked chest. My hand loops in her hair, and I yank her head back, tipping her head up so I can smash my mouth to hers. The kiss is raw and desperate, our tongues battling for dominance. Her small hands claw at my back, and she digs her nails into my skin, which elicits a low growl from deep within my chest.

Fuck, I love a woman who gives as good as she gets.

I slap my hand on the shower valve and turn it on. Alessia lets out a squeak as cold water pours over us, but it quickly heats to the perfect temperature.

My lips trail down the column of her long neck, biting and sucking on the wet skin. My mouth finds her hard nipple, and I release the grip I have on her hair before plumping her breast in my hand and biting down hard on the bud in my mouth. Alessia lets out a loud moan as her fingers dig into my scalp, pulling the short strands. Her skin is sweet and warm from the steam of the shower, and a feral groan escapes me as I feast on her full tits. Fuck, I've thought about this, pleasured myself with images of this very thing over and over, but no matter how many times I imagined us in this position, it's nothing compared to the real thing.

"That feels so good, Finn."

A smile crosses my lips and I look up to find her eyes on me. Sinking to my knees, I trail both hands down her flat stomach to the waist of her shorts and roll them over her ass and down her toned legs. She lifts one foot at a time so I can remove the offending material completely before tossing it outside the shower stall.

What I see in front of me has my mouth watering for a taste. Her pussy is glistening with her arousal and my release from earlier. I bury my face between her legs and part her lower lips with my tongue, her taste flooding my mouth.

Alessia squeals and pulls on my hair. "Let me clean up first."

I growl and glare up at her. "If you're worried about that shit, I'm obviously not doing this right."

I grab her hips and push her back to the shower wall before throwing a leg over my shoulder, opening her up to me. My lips and tongue attack her clit, and I spear two fingers inside her, then curl them, running them over the bundle of nerves inside of her as my tongue flicks her swollen clit at a punishing pace.

Moans and curses fall from her lips as she yanks on my hair, but she's no longer concerned with the bullshit she was saying before about needing to clean herself for me. Why the fuck should she? I plan on eating her out and coming inside her repeatedly for the rest of the day and night, and I'm not going to stop for a fucking shower every time.

It doesn't take long before my wife's slick walls begin to tremble and tighten around my fingers.

"Fuck, don't stop," she says as though she needs to tell

me. What kind of clueless men has she been with in the past? Clearly, she's been with men who can't tell when she's about to come. Fucking pathetic.

Her pussy clamps down around my fingers, and she lets out an ear-piercing scream that echoes off the shower walls. It's fucking music to my ears.

My fingers slow, but my tongue keeps at her as she comes down from her orgasm. I stand and grab her by the back of her head and smash my mouth to hers again, shoving my tongue inside so she can taste herself.

"There will never be a time when I won't want your taste in my mouth or all over my face. I don't give a shit if I've just come inside you, or if you haven't showered after a workout, or any other bullshit some asshole told you. I will eat you out any time, day or night, and I'll love every second of it. Understood?"

"How do you make me want to kiss you and punch the hell out of you at the same time?" she asks, and I smile wide.

"It's my Irish charm."

Alessia rolls her eyes and looks down at my drenched shorts and my cock begging for an escape. Her hand moves to the waistband, but I catch her wrist and bring it to my mouth, kissing her pulse point.

"Let's finish our shower. The next time I bury myself inside you, I want to have a little more space and a hell of a lot more time."

The little pout that turns down the edges of Alessia's mouth is fucking adorable, but it doesn't change my mind. I shuck my sopping wet shorts and throw them outside the shower. Pouring a generous amount of Alessia's shampoo into my hand, I instruct her to tilt her head back so I can wash her hair. She has a look of surprise on her face but does as I ask. I can't really blame her. This is the first time I've washed a woman's hair, but there's something instinctual in me that calls for me to take care of my wife's needs. I'm not going to look too closely at it, though. Today isn't the day for introspection, as far as I'm concerned.

When I finish with her hair, I quickly wash my own as she grabs a bottle of body wash and rubs the lather over my body, paying special attention to my still-hard cock.

"Vixen," I growl, and she laughs, shrugging her shoulder.

We finish our shower, and before she can step out of the bathroom, I pick her up and throw her on the black silk sheets of my bed. Alessia lets out a squeak of surprise then gives me a flat, unamused look.

"You don't know what that defiant look does to me, Alessia." I kneel on the California King mattress and spread her legs wide. "Every time I'd see that look in your eyes these last few weeks, it was all I could do not to throw you down on the closest flat surface and fuck you until your eyes rolled back in your head."

"You should have tried. I may have surprised you," she says with an impish grin.

I let out a bark of laughter. "Yeah, you ripping my dick off would have surprised the shit out of me alright." And

I certainly wasn't going to take that chance.

Alessia looks at the heavy appendage jutting straight toward her. "You should try it now."

"Grab the headboard and hold on tight." Her arms quickly lift to the dark wooden slat behind her, and I grab her hip with one hand, using my other to line my cock up with her center and push into her tight heat.

"Fuck. Your pussy was made to take me." I look down at where we're connected then back to her face. Her eyes are half-lidded as her breaths come out in short pants in time with every one of my thrusts inside her.

With one hand holding her hip, I bring my other to her mouth and she parts her lips, allowing me to push a finger inside. Her tongue swirls around the digit as she releases a moan. I remove my finger from her mouth and press it to her clit, rubbing furiously.

"That's it, baby. Come on my dick. I want to feel you fucking strangle me with your pussy."

I'm pushing into her at a brutal pace as sweat drips from my brow and down my temples.

"Oh, God. Fuck. I'm going to come," she yells, and I feel her tighten before she lets out a high-pitched scream. I look at her eyes, and sure enough, they're rolled back as wave after wave hits her. Seeing her so swept away in her orgasm and the way she tightly pulses around me tips me over the edge, and I release myself deep within her on a roar. Jesus fucking Christ, I've never had a woman make me come so hard and so fast in my entire life.

It takes several long moments to catch my breath before I pull myself from her body and watch our combined releases leak from her pussy. I've never had sex without a condom, so I never understood the satisfaction the sight in front of me would bring. Although, I highly doubt I would feel this way about anyone other than my wife splayed out in front of me, looking thoroughly fucked and completely sated. Prowling up her body, I lower my mouth to hers for a deep kiss as she wraps her arms around my damp back.

"Come here," I command, rolling to my back and taking her with me so she's draped over my chest.

"We're going to take a nap, then you're going to sit on my face so I can eat you out again before I fuck you from behind."

"Jesus Christ, Finn. You're so damn bossy." Alessia releases a tired chuckle but doesn't object to my plan.

"I told you I had every intention of living out every one of my fantasies. Now rest up. You're going to need your energy."

She tries to lift her body from mine, surely so she can tell me to go fuck myself, but I tighten my grip around her waist, and she settles.

"Brute," she says with a huff.

"You fucking like it."

She doesn't say anything, and I peer down at her. Her eyes are closed while a small smile plays on her lips.

Yeah, she isn't going anywhere.

The rest of the day passes in a blur of sex, insults from my lovely wife, and more sex.

We finally make it downstairs around eight at night to scrounge up some food. The house is quiet, not surprising since I told my men we weren't to be disturbed. Even my phone wasn't ringing off the hook, which is a damn miracle in and of itself.

Alessia grabs a bunch of ingredients from the fridge and pantry so we can throw together some sandwiches. She makes one for herself and takes a big bite.

"You're not going to make one for your husband?" I ask, watching her lick the mustard from the corner of her mouth. Goddamn, I need her to do that with my cock.

"You have two hands."

"You know," I start as I take some bread from the bag and place it on my plate. "You were a lot less mouthy in my fantasies."

Alessia shrugs and swallows her mouthful. "That's your problem. It's not like you didn't have a good idea of who you married on our wedding day. What about me says I'm the *cook for my man* type?"

"I'll give you that, but a sandwich is hardly cooking. I assumed I was marrying a proper Italian woman who liked to cook."

"That's what you get for assuming. You married an Italian woman who likes to eat. The cooking we left to the staff or my mother."

"Is it too late to change my mind?"

Alessia narrows her eyes and glares at me. "Depends. Do you like having your dick attached to your body?"

"I'm fond of it there. And so are you."

I lean over and risk a kiss from the annoyed woman in front of me. She obliges, and it only takes seconds for me to forget about my growling stomach. I turn her back to the counter and lift her, setting her down and stepping between her spread legs before she wraps her limbs around me, never breaking the kiss.

Just as I'm about to rip her shirt down the middle so I can see her tits bounce in my face, my fucking phone starts vibrating on the marble counter next to me.

I look down and see Cillian's name flash on the screen. Dammit. I'd love to ignore the call and continue with my plan for Alessia's body and this countertop, but Cillian doesn't generally call unless it's important.

"Yeah," I answer after the second ring.

"We have some movement on Cataldi. Thought you might want to know. One of our contacts saw him downtown, heading into a strip club."

"Fuck. Did they see him leave or know if he's still in there?"

"Says they haven't seen him leave yet."

"Okay. I'll meet you at your place."

I disconnect the call and look at my wife.

"You have to go," she says. I don't miss the disappointment in her voice. I'd be lying if I said it didn't bring me a small sense of delight, knowing she doesn't want me to leave.

"Yeah. Cillian got a tip about Cataldi. Hopefully I won't be home too late."

Alessia quirks her brow and tilts her head to the side.

"Okay, hopefully I'll be home before sunrise."

She nods and pushes me back a step so she can hop off the counter.

"Do me a favor," I say, looping my arm around her waist and pulling her flush against my chest. "Sleep in my bed tonight."

"You won't even be there," she replies.

"No, but I want to think of you there." I lean down for a soft kiss.

Alessia nods and looks me in the eye. "Then you have to do me a favor."

I nod and smile at my little dealmaker of a wife.

"Don't die tonight."

"Death wouldn't be so cruel as to take me the first night I finally get to sink between your thighs."

Alessia rolls her green eyes and smacks my chest. "God, save the lines."

"For who? I'm a married man now."

"Lucky me," she says with sarcasm dripping from each syllable.

"No, baby. Lucky me."

After meeting at Cillian's place, we get in one car and drive to the club Carlo was known to frequent, parking out front. It's one of the few that doesn't have any affiliation with the Italians or our family.

"Did you talk to your guy?" I ask Cillian, not wanting to be sitting in this small sedan all night while my wife is waiting for me in my bed. If she's still asleep when I get home, maybe I'll take it upon myself to move all her things into my bedroom. I'm sure she'll appreciate that. *Yeah right.*

"It's not a guy."

"Wait. We're relying on the word of a stripper?"

"Don't be a dick, Finn. Yes, we're relying on the word of a stripper. She's a nice girl, and you sound like a judgmental asshole."

"Sorry, I just didn't realize you made friends at strip clubs. Most men don't come here for coffee and a chat."

"Shut the fuck up. Let's go in and see if we spot him. I don't want to sit in a car all night with your ass."

We'd decided to dress in casual clothes and baseball caps to look like any other Joe Schmo ready for some fun.

"Fine by me," I tell my lieutenant, and we head in.

The dark club is packed, so we take a table toward the back of the building. I order two drinks from the waitress, who has to lean in close to hear me over the thumping bass of the music blaring from the speakers.

"How's married life?" Cillian asks, scanning the club.

A grin spreads across my face before I can answer.

"You fucked her." He isn't asking a question, and his tone has my hackles rising.

"Cillian, I'm going to say this one time—watch your tone when it comes to Alessia. She's my wife, and she will be given respect."

Cillian stares at me wordlessly for a beat then nods. "Fine." He takes a sip of his beer the waitress dropped off and continues scanning the crowd. "She know you're at a strip club?"

I sit back casually in my seat, keeping my ball cap low across my forehead. "I didn't tell her, but she'd understand. She knows how important it is to find Cataldi."

"Yeah. Wives are always understanding of their husbands watching a bunch of naked women dance around."

I roll my eyes but keep my posture as casual as possible.

One of the bleach-blonde dancers comes over to our table and trails her hand over my shoulder and down my chest, stopping before she reaches my belt.

"How about a private dance, honey? Your friend can come too if he wants."

Her fingers tease the waist of my pants, and I gently remove her hand from my body.

"Maybe later," I say, not meaning it in the least, but not wanting her telling the other girls we aren't interested. It's strange that the best way to call attention to yourself in a club like this isn't getting a lap dance but turning one down.

"Okay, I'll be back. Maybe I'll bring a friend with me."

I smile, and she saunters off in her sky-high heels.

"How long do you think we should stay?" I ask Cillian.

"If we don't spot him in the next couple hours, we'll head to the casino, and I'll pull up some footage from around the club. My source left for the night, but she didn't see him leave."

Cillian has a decent computer setup at his place. But I sank a shit ton of money into the one at the club, and I may have had a talented hacker friend of mine come in and open a few back doors that get me into the BPD camera feeds. I don't want to start banging on doors, but I don't want to sit here all night either. The problem with this club not being affiliated with our organization is we don't have the same allowances afforded to us. They wouldn't hesitate to call the cops if I made a scene.

"Fucking Cataldi. I can't wait till we get rid of this guy. He's seriously fucking with my plans," I mumble.

Cillian just sips his beer and leans farther back in his chair.

Looks like I'm in for a long night with the wet blanket sitting next to me.

CHAPTER TWELVE

ALESSIA

FINN DIDN'T COME HOME last night, and there was no text or missed call from him to tell me he was staying out all night. When I woke this morning and felt the cold sheets on his side of the bed, my heart sank into my stomach. *Don't overthink this, Alessia.*

My brain is saying one thing, but the memories I have of late nights waiting for Orlando to come home after telling me to meet him at his apartment flip through my head like a movie reel. So many nights wasted waiting for a man who found a better offer at some bar or strip joint he was at. Of him always coming home and being surprised to find me in his apartment because he was so high or drunk he'd forgotten we'd made plans. I should have left, should have stopped returning his calls, but I was barely nineteen and so, so naive. Every time he promised nothing happened, I believed him. He said all the right things and when I pushed back, he found a way to make me think I was the crazy one for not believing him. When that stopped working, he resorted to other measures to keep me quiet and under his thumb.

I wasn't a stupid girl by any stretch, but Orlando had

a way with words and apologies. Fucking prick.

My phone rings, jarring me out of my memories.

Grabbing it from the bedside table, I see Gemma's name flash on the screen.

"Hey," I answer, not trying to hide my maudlin mood from my best friend.

"Uh-oh. What's going on?"

I haven't really talked to Gemma about the attraction that had been developing for my husband over the last few weeks. Gemma isn't the type to cast judgment, but I was still a little embarrassed. I've spent the last ten years swearing off any man who was a part of this world, only to start falling for the first one I spoke more than three sentences to outside of the occasional party my parents had with the rest of the families. Not only that, but this was supposed to be a business arrangement, not a love match. Hell, Finn and I barely knew each other when we said our vows. But he was right when he said there was some spark there the first time we met, even though I didn't want to admit it to myself.

"I think I made a huge mistake," I grumble into the phone.

"You're going to have to be a little more specific, sweetie."

"I slept with him," I whisper.

"With Finn?"

"Of course. Who else would we be talking about?"

"Well, sorry, Alessia. But last time we talked about him, I thought we were still on the 'he's the scourge of the earth' page. I didn't realize we flipped to the 'he's hot as sin, and I let him rock my body' page. Give a girl a second to catch up, yeah?"

A laugh escapes me at the indignant tone in her voice, and I scrub a hand over my face, letting out a low groan.

"Shit, Gemma. I don't know what I was thinking."

"I have a pretty good idea. Your husband is gorgeous with a body and smile to match. I'm honestly surprised you held out this long."

"He's the head of a criminal organization. The exact type of man I told myself I was never going to get involved with again."

She hums into the phone, and I can practically hear her gears turning. "True, but that doesn't mean he's anything like your ex. When that asshole at the fights put his hands on you, he handled it like any self-respecting man would."

"That just says he's possessive, not that he cares. Orlando would have done the same thing if he saw someone touching what was his."

"Did he blame you for it later? Did he say you must have been flirting with him? Because Orlando sure as hell would have done that."

"No. He was upset that we went there because it wasn't the safest situation."

"It wasn't one of my best ideas, so I can't fault him there."

The day after the fight, when I talked to Gemma, she apologized for suggesting we go. Neither of us had been to an underground fight, so she didn't know what to expect. Plus, the guy she went there to see apparently spent the evening doing lines of coke with his buddies at the bar they went to afterward, which is a huge turnoff for her. Gemma is all about staying in control at all times, and there's nothing that can get out of control faster than being around a bunch of people high on coke.

"But he didn't come home last night and that is definitely something Orlando did," I grumble.

"What did he say when he left?"

I can't tell her exactly what he said because the less Gemma knows about our business, the safer it is for her. "He had some business to take care of," is all I tell her.

"Do you have reason to believe he's lying? Aside from you believing every powerful man in your world is an adulterer, that is?"

"I mean, no...I know why he left and how important it was. And he did say when we got home from the fights that he isn't a cheater and that he takes our marriage vows seriously."

Then, yesterday, he said a lot of other things that would make me believe he wasn't interested in having other women. But that could very well have been all talk. People say shit they don't mean in the throes of passion all the time.

"So, he told you he's not a cheater and he left last night because some important business came up, which, let's be honest, isn't out of the realm of possibility considering his business isn't exactly a nine-to-five gig."

"When you say it like that..."

"Honestly, Alessia, I think you might be looking for trouble that isn't there." She pauses, either to gather her thoughts or because she knows whatever is about to come out of her mouth is going to annoy me. Not that it matters; she'll tell me whatever's on her mind regardless of if she thinks I won't like it. "Don't get me wrong, I understand your hesitation. You've never been one to separate sex and feelings, so of course you're going to have some big feelings, especially when it comes to sleeping with your husband. And I completely understand avoiding any relationships with men from your world. Believe me, I get that, but not every man is the same. Can you honestly say you think Finn is anything like Orlando? Finn still takes his mother to brunch every Sunday after church for Chrissake."

"I feel like you shouldn't be talking about church and using the Lord's name in vain in the same sentence."

Gemma laughs loudly into the phone, and I smile. "You can kiss my sacrilegious ass, Mrs. Monaghan."

That's the first time since our wedding someone used my married name. Even at the casino, people call me Alessia. I didn't want to put on airs with the other employees or clientele. Of course, they all know Finn and I are married, but making everyone refer to me as Mrs. Monaghan seemed a bit much.

"Honey, I think you need to talk with him. Draw some

boundaries. Let him know if he's out all night to give you a heads-up. What's the worst he's going to say?"

The worst would be he'd laugh at me and tell me it's none of my business where he spends his time or with whom. Men like Finn aren't used to answering to anyone, let alone their wives. We may have had a day of amazing sex, and he may have been saying all the right things, but how well can I trust that? Trust him?

"Maybe I'll try it," I concede.

"Oh, I know a brush-off when I hear one." Gemma chuckles into the phone. "Okay, I was actually calling because we haven't had lunch since you started working at the casino and I miss my bestie." After a few more minutes of chatting and planning a lunch date for next week, I hang up and decide to get my ass out of Finn's bed and make some coffee. Lucian is staring at me from the foot of the bed, probably wondering when I'm going to get my lazy ass up and feed him. I send a text to Enzo, letting him know to come an hour earlier for a workout since I'm up early anyway, and I'd like to take a trip to my favorite gun range. Nothing like shooting several rounds for a couple hours to center my whirling thoughts.

After feeding my cat, I'm standing in the kitchen at the espresso machine, a wedding gift from my mother, when the back door opens and in walks my husband. He looks tired, but the second his eyes land on me, they brighten. I give him a small smile but don't move. When he comes up behind me, he nuzzles his face into my neck.

"You going to make me one, wife?"

"Again, you have two hands and are perfectly capable of making your own."

A small growl leaves his throat. "Mmm, that mouth. It fucking gets me hard every damn time." He punctuates his statement by grinding his hips into my ass.

My head turns slightly to look him in the eye when I spot flecks of glitter on his cheek. I turn my body halfway in his arms, which are still pinning me to the counter, and see it on his neck as well.

"I'm surprised you can still get it up after the night you've apparently had."

I buck my hips back hard, forcing him away from me, and he lets out a grunt of pain.

"Jesus Christ, woman. What the hell was that for?"

"Oh, I don't know maybe the fact that you stayed out all night without a simple text letting me know you weren't coming home."

"I'm sor—"

"Or maybe when you do, you have glitter all over your body like you've been fucking some cheap whore in the back of a strip club!"

I've seen this little scene play out one too many times in my life with Orlando. I'll be damned if I put myself through it again.

Finn's hand goes to his neck, and he wipes it before looking at his hand. "For fuck's sake."

He marches over to the kitchen sink, grabbing a paper

towel and wetting it, then rubbing it over his neck.

"Don't fucking bother. I already saw it."

"Alessia, I swear on everything, this is not what it looks like."

I scoff and shake my head, my lip curled in disgust. "Yeah, I've heard that one before."

Finn holds up both palms in a surrendering gesture. "Okay, I know that's what any man in my position would say. I swear, I wasn't fucking any whores, but I was at a strip club."

My mouth opens and closes like a fucking fish, not believing he's so brazenly admitting to it. "I don't know if I should be mad you went or thankful you're actually being honest about something."

"Hey," he barks. "I've never lied to you."

"The hell you haven't! All that bullshit you spewed at the boathouse yesterday and in this very house, this very kitchen, only hours ago. Then you take off to a strip club and have the audacity to have a dancer's glitter still on you when you come home," I yell; deciding mad is definitely the emotion I'm going with.

"First off." Finn forcefully tosses the damp towel into the trash then leans against the counter, clutching the edge of the counter so tight his knuckles are turning white. "I meant every word I said to you yesterday and every day before that. Including the words I said when we took our vows, which I believe I've already made clear. Secondly, I will not be standing in *my* kitchen and be compared to another man who you obviously had a bad experience with, Alessia. I am my own fucking man, and I don't lie or cheat. Period. If you had let me finish, I would have told you that Cillian has a friend who works in a club and saw Carlo Cataldi there. She knew Cillian was looking for him, so she called to let him know. He went into a back room before we got there and didn't come out again. Once we were certain he'd left and we missed him, we went to the casino and watched hours of boring-ass camera footage. We were searching for anyone we knew that he could've been meeting with or any clues as to where he's been hiding or who's been hiding him. I did not get a lap dance or anything of the sort, even though I was asked a few times, which is where the glitter is probably from. Dancers tend to get a little handsy when they're trying to convince you to drop that kind of cash."

Finn is breathing hard as he pushes off the counter opposite me and steps forward. This time I allow him into my personal space, though I'm still unsure if it's the best idea. "I didn't call because I didn't think of it, and you have every right to be upset about that. This is just as new to me as it is to you. Obviously, I need to consider that you were worried—"

"I wasn't worried," I say, cutting him off. I was, but like hell am I going to admit that to him.

His lips quirk in a smile as he backs me against the counter again, caging me between his arms but not touching me yet.

"Fine. I need to consider that you have feelings that

have nothing to do with you worrying about me being out all night. I'll try to do better in the future. But you need to remember who you married, wife. And it isn't some piece-of-shit capo with something to prove to his buddies by going and getting his dick sucked at strip joints instead of doing everything in his power to get home to you."

I lift my chin and stare my husband in the eye. "Fine. I'll work on it."

He nods and has that fucking smirk on his face. "Fine."

As soon as he leans down to swipe a kiss on my mouth, a throat clears behind him.

"Am I interrupting?" Enzo asks with his gym bag in his hand.

"Yes," Finn says at the same time I tell him no.

Enzo looks between us, and I duck under Finn's arm, needing a touch of space.

"Good news. Finn's back in time for a workout," I say, looking between both men.

Even though it's obvious my husband is exhausted, I plan on making this training session as brutal for him as possible. I may believe him about the strip club thing, but that doesn't mean he doesn't deserve a little torture for the no-call, no-show situation.

My lips are in a thin line as I stare at my husband, waiting for him to say something, probably having a pretty good idea I'm doing this on purpose.

"Fine," he breathes out. "Let me get changed really quick."

"Fine," I parrot back. "It'll give me a chance to make a smoothie for you."

"Can't wait," he replies in a flat tone before he nods at Enzo on his way out of the kitchen.

"Alright. I get you're mad at him, but why do I have to drink that disgusting concoction," Enzo complains when Finn's out of earshot.

"Because it's good for you. Jesus, do any of the men in this house listen to me?" I say the last part more to myself as I pull out the ingredients and make three smoothies.

Two with extra garlic.

Finn finally joins us in the gym. After showering, of course.

"I thought we could work on some jiu-jitsu today. We've been doing all upper body. Do you have any experience in it?" I ask my husband.

"A little. When Eoghan and I were kids, my parents had us try just about every martial arts practice they could find. Eoghan is better at it than I am. Don't tell him I said that, though."

We stretch out to warm up our muscles then get to it. I will say Finn isn't bad, but I can tell he hasn't practiced these kinds of moves in a long time. He has several pounds on me, so obviously, his size gives him an advantage. But I have years of training on him, so I make up for the size difference in skill. Still, I work for every pin I get.

And boy, I am working hard for it. At first, I could tell he wasn't totally on board with trying to pin me, afraid he was going to hurt me. I, on the other hand, have no such reservations. When I tangled our legs and flipped him on his back, pinning him to the mat, there was a flare of pride and something else in his eyes. I saw it several times after the boathouse yesterday. Excitement and lust run through his gaze every time we're on the mat, tangled in each other. But unlike yesterday, he has a snowball's chance in hell of taking this any further. Finn responds to touch like no man I've ever met before, so I decide I'm going to torture the hell out of him with it. Even though having his weight pressing into me and hearing the heavy pants and grunts coming from him is having an effect on certain parts of my anatomy, I'm more determined to teach him a lesson than I'm willing to give in to temptation. Okay, so maybe the warring emotions are neck and neck, but that doesn't change my focus.

After an hour of grappling, Enzo lets me know we have an appointment at the gun range.

"Sorry to cut this short, but we have to go," I tell my husband.

The look of disappointment on Finn's face sends glee and a feeling of victory through me. He was hoping all the sweating and rolling around would lead to something else.

Not today, pal.

"We have a range here, you know," he says in a lame attempt to keep me home.

I discovered it the first week I lived here and used it a few times. It's a nice range and far more convenient than driving an hour to the one I used to go to nearly every day. But that's not the point I'm making today.

"I know. I like this one better. Don't worry; I'll make it back in time to meet you before work tonight."

He lets out a breath and nods. "Fine. I'll see you later. I'll take a nap while you're gone."

"You do that." I bound up to him and give him a quick kiss on the lips then step back before he can take it any further. A girl can only take so much before she breaks, and I'm determined to make him sweat it out a little longer.

When Enzo and I get in the car, he looks at me and shakes his head. "Does that little workout slash torture session have anything to do with what I walked in on earlier?"

"Maybe. I'm just making sure he's well aware of who he's married to. Every action has consequences. Especially when you piss off your wife."

"If he didn't get the point before, I'm sure he does now."

I smile but decide not to comment further.

The casino is busier than I've ever seen it before. Several high rollers are here at the same time, and I don't think I've smiled so much for so long in my entire life. I've had to make sure everyone's favorite liquor is stocked and ready, even going so far as to send one of the security guards out for a couple more high-end bottles Finn doesn't keep stocked regularly. When one of the men was disappointed his favorite dealer wasn't in tonight, I called her and offered to double her nightly wage to come in and deal for him. Finn said this is unusual, and normally, they let us know ahead of time when they're coming in, but things like this can happen. I can tell he was impressed with how I handled the situation, not running to him with every little issue that popped up.

It's about two in the morning, and it looks like things are starting to wind down. Thank God.

"I need to see you in your office," Finn says in my ear. "Now."

Shit. Did someone complain? Or did that one asshole run to Finn upset because there wasn't room at his favorite table, and I couldn't ask another customer to move? God, these rich pricks are like children when they don't get their way.

I follow him to my office, and he opens the door, letting me go in before him.

"Have a seat," he says, loosening his tie.

I sit behind my desk in the new chair that appeared my second night at the casino, but he makes no move to sit in a chair. Instead, he closes the door and stands in front of it, his dark gaze boring into mine.

"What is it?" I ask, swallowing past the growing lump in my throat.

Finn doesn't answer but reaches behind him and locks the handle. He stalks toward me and around my desk before spinning my chair so I'm facing him as he towers over me.

"You are spectacular." Finn leans down and takes my lips in an open-mouthed kiss. "Watching you handle business like a fucking professional made me so damn proud tonight." He kisses my neck, licking and taking tiny nibbles up and down the column. "But I couldn't wait another second to taste your pussy, wife."

He kneels before me and grabs the back of my neck in one hand before lifting my dress and ripping the thin lace panties from my body, then crushing my mouth in a fevered kiss.

"I'm still mad at you," I argue, pulling back, but there's no heat behind my words.

"Then let me make it up to you."

He lifts me from the chair and sets me on the edge of my desk. When I pull my dress up to my waist, he smirks.

"Yeah, you're really mad."

"Shut up." I grab the back of his head and pull it closer

to my center. I can be mad and need him to get me off at the same time. That's totally reasonable.

Finn wastes no time before he dives two fingers into my core and begins licking my clit like a madman. I throw my head back and let out a long moan at the sensation of having his mouth where I absolutely ache for him. He doesn't stop his ministrations as he takes the hand squeezing my thigh and moves it up to my mouth, covering it to keep my noises quiet.

It's all too much, the desire and anger mixing, his head between my legs and his palm covering my mouth. When he curls his fingers inside me and finds the little bundle of nerves he seems to be so fucking in tune with, I come unraveled, biting his palm as the orgasm rips through me. Finn groans with the bite of pain I deliver, and I think I found out something new about my husband.

His tongue slows, following me down from the peak. When my shivers have subsided and he's wrung every bit of pleasure he can from my body, he leans back and puts his two fingers in his mouth, groaning at my taste coating them.

Finn stands and shoves the pair of destroyed panties that were sitting on my desk into his pocket.

"Goddammit. I don't have another pair here," I gripe. I guess it's time to bring some extras just in case my husband gets that destructive urge again.

"That's fine. We aren't staying," he replies, running his hands through his hair to tame the wild strands I was just yanking as though they were the only thing keeping me grounded.

"We still have guests," I point out, standing from the desk and straightening my dress.

"Cillian is here. He'll handle the next couple hours for you. I'm taking you home so I can fuck you in our bed. Your little stunt today showed me something I didn't know about you."

Of fucking course he knew what I was doing. "Yeah, what's that?"

"You're bendy as fuck, wife, and I've been imagining all the different ways I get to fuck you now."

This man looks like he's going to try to break me.

Challenge accepted.

CHAPTER THIRTEEN
FINN

T HE WEEK FLIES BY in a flurry of sex with my wife, working at the casino, and more sex with my wife. Routine has always made me itchy, but this is one I have no problem falling into. Makes me wonder why I never opted to have a serious relationship in the past. Oh yeah, because no other woman could hold a candle to my fiery, vivacious wife, who is currently punching the hell out of a bag in our gym.

God, she's magnificent. I've never met a woman who can match me in all areas of my life, but the way she attacks everything in front of her is so in line with how I've lived. Alessia and I were cut from the same cloth. She's stubborn as hell and never backs down from a fight or a challenge. She has a knack for putting people at ease, but she holds her boundaries with grace and elegance instead of brute force as I do. I'm finding that not only is my wife one of the sexiest women I've ever laid eyes on, but her strength, intelligence and wit match her beauty.

"What are you staring at?" she asks as I stand on the other side of the gym, mesmerized by the sweat dripping down the front of her tank top into her cleavage. Fuck, I want to trace my tongue through there.

"You're still dropping your right shoulder."

"The hell I am." She lets out a huff of annoyance and turns back to the bag, muttering, "Fuck you and your right shoulder bullshit," while she puts even more force behind each punch.

She wasn't, but messing with Alessia is one of the highlights of my day. I love the line she gets between her brows when she's annoyed by me, then takes out her frustrations in other ways. Those fucking green smoothies she makes Enzo and I drink have gotten progressively fouler. I swear, I'm practically sweating garlic from my pores at this point.

My phone lights up on the bench and I see my brother's name on the screen. I set down the weights I was working with and grab the phone before walking out of the gym.

"Hey," I greet.

"Hey yourself. How's the little wife?"

"Kicking ass in the gym. You should come spar with her. She might teach you a thing or two."

"Maybe she'd want to sign up for a fight night? I've been toying with the idea of opening it up to female boxers."

"Not on your life." There's no way my woman is going back to that ring.

"Fine, fine," my brother replies on a chuckle. "Have

you thought about taking her on a honeymoon? Mom thinks you've turned into some kind of brute or some shit because you two barely leave the house."

"We haven't had time. Until a week ago, she didn't tolerate my presence, let alone did I think she'd have been inclined to take a trip with me."

I didn't have to tell my brother things with Alessia took a wild turn. He was at the casino a few days ago and saw the difference in us immediately. He didn't comment, just smirked and patted me on the back before telling me our mother would be happy I'd decided to settle down with my wife. Apparently, marrying her wasn't enough or some shit.

"You should take her to an island or something. Don't most women dream of a tropical honeymoon?"

I laugh quietly into the phone. "My wife is hardly most women."

"I don't know, brother. She might surprise you."

Not that I'd be opposed to seeing Alessia in a little bikini for a week straight, but I'm not sure tropical vacation is her speed. Hell, now that I think about it, I'm not entirely sure what is.

"I'll give it some thought. Did you just call me to talk about my vacation plans, or is there another reason you interrupted my workout?"

"I thought with you being laid regularly, you wouldn't be so grumpy all the time."

"Watch it, little brother," I grumble.

Eoghan laughs at my tone, never taking me too

seriously. If he wasn't my brother, I swear I would have put him six feet under a hundred times by now for his insolence alone. He updates me on the fights he has lined up and a few changes he wants to make with a distributor.

"It all sounds good, brother." He may be a cocky little shit most of the time, but he's a smart businessman who treats saving a few dollars to make more money like a challenge. My little brother never met a good deal he could pass up.

"Are we going to be graced with your presence for Sunday mass?"

I missed last week, and my mother was none too happy about it. I was too busy being buried inside my bride to care about attending a church service, but she made it clear it was only a forgivable offense if there wasn't a repeat.

"Yes. Alessia will be with me as well."

Since being married, she hasn't attended mass or brunch with my family, instead driving out to her parents' on Sundays. It's time we started acting like a real couple and finally intertwining our lives like other married people do.

"Mom will be ecstatic. She hasn't wanted to push—"

"No, she leaves that to you."

"What can I say? It's tough being her favorite."

"Except you're not."

"I will be if you miss any more Sunday brunches. See you then, asshole."

"Bye." I hang up the phone and shake my head. My brother's an idiot.

Alessia walks out of the gym, sweaty and beautiful, and I swear my heart skips a beat when she greets me with a wide smile.

"Who was on the phone?"

"Eoghan. I told him we'd make it to church and Sunday brunch this week."

"That kind of makes it official, then."

"I think our wedding made it official, but it would be a good idea to show our faces in public, aside from the casino. Plus, Eoghan inferred that my mother thinks I'm holding you here against your will or something." I roll my eyes and Alessia laughs, walking up to me and running a hand through my hair before tilting her head up for a kiss.

"Maybe I'm the one holding you here to be my sex slave," she purrs just before she bites my lower lip.

I growl and lift her, allowing her legs to wrap around my body. "I'll let you tell her that one."

Alessia lets out a bark of laughter. "I most certainly will not."

When I head to the staircase, she pulls back from where her lips had been trailing wet kisses up and down my neck.

"I thought we were going for a run after the gym?"

Stopping at the bottom of the stairs, I take her mouth in a bruising kiss. "I think I have a better idea to get some cardio in that doesn't involve running. Or clothes."

The casino is quieter tonight than it has been since word got out about Alessia being the new host. Don't get me wrong, we're still busy, always are and hopefully always will be, but it's a manageable pace tonight. People are curious to see my wife in the flesh, wanting to catch a glimpse of the Italian Mafia princess I married. Doesn't bother me in the least. If their curiosity puts money in my pocket, who am I to argue?

"Boss, I think there might be a problem," one of our security guys says. This is the first night Alessia's been on the floor without Enzo being here. His niece was celebrating her seventh birthday, so my wife insisted he have the night off. I gave one of my other guards the sole task of watching Alessia, but she doesn't like anyone crowding her when she's working the floor. Says it makes her seem unapproachable when she's trying to attend to our guests. There haven't been any issues since she started. Everyone's been respectful, but I have a sinking feeling that's going to end tonight.

I pull up the camera feed on my computer and quickly find my wife. She's talking to a man who I recognize as the son of a guy my father did business with years ago. If memory serves, he runs a couple brothels. Not as high end as the ones my organization has, but he makes a pretty penny. He'd have to in order to afford the membership here.

Alessia is wearing that *don't fuck with me* look and the guy has a sneer stamped across his face. Her guard tries to intervene, but she shakes her head in his direction, so he takes a step back.

I grab my jacket from the back of my chair and put it on, heading to the casino floor.

"I told you I wanted Tatiana tonight. If she's not here, then call her in," I hear him say loudly as I cross the room. Others are beginning to notice his drunken behavior and they spot me quickly walking to where the scene is playing out before averting their eyes. Everyone knows I don't tolerate disruptions like this in my establishment, but every once in a while, someone likes to test me. With Alessia involved, I'm less likely than ever to handle this gently.

"And I told you, she's unavailable this evening, and that's not going to change, no matter how much money you try to throw at me or how loud your voice gets."

Alessia looks as though she would love nothing more than to knock this prick on his ass. If he keeps it up, I might let her.

She's obviously had enough and turns to one of the security guards waiting in the wings, signaling for him to remove the asshole in front of her from the premises.

He grabs her arm, and I see fucking red. "Listen here, you Italian whore—"

I get there before he has a chance to finish his statement, fury coursing through me when I grab the back of his head and slam it into the bar he's sitting at. I yank his head back up as blood drips from his broken nose and wrench his face toward mine.

"Hello, Rick. I believe you've met my wife."

Fear blazes through his eyes when he realizes the trouble he's just found himself in. I bash his head into the bar again, cutting his forehead when it slams into his glass. When I yank it up, I turn him to Alessia.

"Apologize," I bark at him.

"I'm sorry," he mumbles.

"Not loud enough. I want some feeling behind it, Rick. And you'll call her by her name."

"I'm sorry, Mrs. Monaghan."

Alessia quirks a brow and stares Rick in the face. "Thank you, but I have a feeling you haven't even begun to be sorry."

She flicks her gaze to me and tilts her lip in a private smile.

I haul the piece of shit from his chair and throw him on the carpeted floor. Two security guards flank Rick from both sides and haul him away, taking him to the back room without me having to instruct them. They know what the punishment is for anyone who disrespects my wife.

"Make sure everyone has a fresh drink on the house, yeah?" I say to Alessia, who rolls her eyes.

"I already planned on it."

"That attitude, wife," I growl as I touch my palm to her cheek and hold her stare. "Are you okay?"

Alessia's gaze softens for a moment at the concern in my question. "Perfectly fine."

I dip my lips to hers and take her mouth in a brief kiss, with the promise of more lingering between us.

"This won't take long," I tell her.

"Good," she growls. "Meet me in your office when you've finished."

I quirk a brow and a seductive smile toys with the corners of her mouth. So, violence in her defense is a turn-on. Noted.

Straightening my jacket, I turn around and march back across the casino floor to the end of the hallway with a hidden door on the left next to my office. I move a painting aside and press my thumb to the scanner, which unlocks the door to a soundproof room.

The lights are much brighter here than anywhere else in the building. It heightens the anxiety of the men I've had cuffed to the chair the way Rick is now.

"You know, Rick, our fathers used to do business together. Some would even say they're friends. How disappointed yours is going to be when he finds out what a miserable asshole you were to his friend's dear daughter-in-law."

"I'm sorry, Finn. It's been a long night of drinking, then one of my buddies got his hands on some grade A coke. I was out of my head for a minute there. I swear to you, it won't happen again."

His terrified gaze tracks me as I walk over to the table that holds several instruments we keep on hand for situations such as this.

"Oh, I have no doubt. You can consider your membership revoked, Rick."

He nods his head frantically. "That's fair, Finn. I deserve that."

"But that would have been the case if you had spoken to any of my employees like that. The difference here is you spoke to my wife like that. You put your hands on what's mine. What was it you called her again?"

I turn toward the trembling man with my arms crossed across my chest and stare into his eyes.

"A-an Italian whore."

My jaw clenches so hard I'm liable to break a tooth. In two long strides, I'm standing in front of Rick, hammering my fist into his mouth one, two, three times. Blood drips down and runs over his chin before he spits a couple teeth from his mouth.

I grab him by the throat, not caring in the slightest that his blood is getting all over my hand and squeeze hard. Leaning down, I put my face mere inches from his.

"That's for the filth you spewed at my wife."

I revel in the panicked look in his eyes. He has no idea if I'm going to release his throat so he can breathe or if I plan on watching the life drain from him here and now.

Letting go of his neck, I spin around and walk back over to my table.

"Which disgusting hand did you use to grab my wife with?"

I turn slightly to watch him choke and gasp trying to

get air back into his lungs so he can answer me.

"My right," he coughs out.

My head tilts to the guard on his right. "Release his hand."

The guard unlocks the cuff securing him to the chair, but firmly holds his wrist.

I grab a wooden barstool from the corner of the room and haul it to Rick's side. My guard lifts his hand to the stool as Rick uselessly struggles against him.

"Knock it off, asshole. Take your punishment like a man, or I promise this is going to get so much worse for you."

Rick stops trying to get his hand free, but his low cries grate on my fucking nerves.

Pussy.

I walk back to my table and grab a heavy rubber mallet. "Let this be a lesson to you and any of your buddies who may share the same views about the woman I married. No one speaks to my wife with anything less than the respect I demand from everyone in this city. If anyone thinks putting their hands on her will ever be justified or forgiven, they are wrong. No one touches my wife without severe consequences. The only reason I'm inclined to let you live is so you can serve as an example. If I catch you saying one rude thing about her, and believe me, Rick, I will find out, I will not hesitate to put a bullet between your eyes."

I swing the mallet down on Rick's prone hand over and over until the white bones on his knuckles are visible through his torn and bloody skin.

"Have I made my point clear?"

"Y-yes, Finn. Fuck. I get it."

"Good." I pull my fist back and punch the asshole in the temple, knocking him out cold. He slumps in the chair, an unconscious and bloody mess.

"Tie him up and dump him in front of his old man's place. I'll get you the address. He can explain to his dad what he did to cause this to happen."

My men nod and take Rick out the door on the other side of the room into the back alley, where a car is waiting.

After washing my hands thoroughly in the industrial sink, I call one of my men to clean this room then call Cillian.

"Heard you were handling a problem," he says when he picks up.

"All in a day's work."

I hear Cillian chuckle on the other end. "What's up?"

"I need a favor. Can you charter me a plane and cover the casino tomorrow?"

"Sure. Where are you going?"

My mouth splits into a wide grin as my idea solidifies in my brain. "Atlantic City."

Chapter Fourteen

Alessia

Finn and I were at the casino for another hour after he met me in his office, and I nearly tore his pants from his body to get to his cock. Seeing him handle that asshole flipped some sort of switch in me, and I showed him my appreciation on my knees. It was as though some baser instinct completely took over my actions and the need to own him somehow consumed every thought in my head.

Being with him is so different than I'd imagined. All the men I've known who are a part of this life would've seen what was going on with that Rick guy and gotten angry that someone was disrespecting their property. They wouldn't have given two shits about making them apologize to me. Sure, they would have demanded an apology, but it would've been to them, not me. Finn was obviously angry that someone caused a scene in his casino and disrespected his wife, but he was also angry *for* me. He doesn't tolerate anyone having a cross word to say about me, not because I'm his, and it's a personal insult to him, but because he demands people respect me for my sake. Because that's what I deserve as my own person.

Typing on his phone on the way home from the casino, Finn looks at me with an I *know something you don't know* smile.

"I'm taking you somewhere tomorrow," he informs me.

"Oh, you are? What if I already have plans?" I don't, but I also don't appreciate him demanding instead of asking. "Just because we're married doesn't mean you have control over my time, Finn." My lips are set in a thin line as I shoot him a glare.

"Let me rephrase then, wife." His smile turns up a couple notches, and I can tell he's proud of whatever plans he has in store. "I'd like to take you on a date tomorrow. We'll be leaving around noon and won't be back until the next day. If that's alright with you, of course."

"Are you sure this is the best time for us to be leaving town? Carlo is still missing. I have the casino to think about—"

Finn cuts me off with a kiss. I let out a little growl of frustration, which, of course, makes him laugh. "Alessia, there's always going to be something. You and I both know that. If we don't steal time for ourselves where we can, we'll never do anything except work and plot and scheme. That's the way this life is. Let me do something for you."

I look into my husband's pleading eyes and can't find it within myself to deny what he's saying is true.

"Are we the type of couple who goes on *dates* now?"

"We're whatever we want to be. Since we didn't have a chance to do that before we were married, I figured, why not try it out?" He shrugs like it's no big deal, but one thing I know about Finn is he wouldn't put something together unless it was important to him. Unless I was important to him.

Exhaling a long sigh, I shrug and face forward in my seat. "I suppose I can spare the time, then."

"Gee, thank you so much. Your enthusiasm astounds me."

I glance in his direction and catch the hard eye roll. It's too easy to rile him up sometimes.

Leaning over, I place a small kiss on his cheek. "Thank you, Finn. I'm excited to see what you have up your sleeve. I'm sorry if I came across as ungrateful."

He grunts and turns to face me. "You can make it up to me by wearing that little red dress you had on the night we met."

A surprised chuckle escapes me before I place a lingering kiss on his lips. "Deal."

"He's taking me away for the night and I have no idea what to pack," I huff into the phone, talking with Gemma.

"My guess would be not much of anything. He didn't

give you any clues?"

"None. Just told me to bring the red dress he likes."

"So somewhere fancy, then."

"Maybe. At least he's not trying to take me somewhere like the Caribbean or something. Though that would be a lot more than an overnight trip." Not that I don't think beaches are beautiful, but I'm not one for lying around all day staring at the ocean. I like to actually *do* things. Plus, sand irritates the living hell out of me. The grainy feeling that takes forever to get rid of is just gross.

"Things are going well between you two, I take it."

"Define 'well.' I mean, the sex is unreal. I swear that man is fucking insatiable." My body heats remembering last night when we got back from the casino.

"Do you get along? I mean, other than between the sheets?"

I think about that for a moment. "I don't know. We've been spending a lot of time together but not a lot of time talking. Honestly, we don't know each other very well." I know how to piss him off, and he knows how to give me countless orgasms, but beyond that, we haven't taken the time to find out what makes the other person tick.

"That makes sense. You guys skipped several important steps in the beginning."

"Is it weird I'm nervous about going on a date with my husband?"

Gemma laughs. "If it was anyone else, I would say yes,

that's weird. But you and Finn didn't exactly start off your relationship in a typical fashion."

That's the fucking truth.

Finn walks into the bedroom as I'm zipping up my suitcase. He moved my things in here the night after we slept together for the first time. I may have thrown a small fit over it, but I never bothered moving my things back to my room.

"We need to get to the airport," he says, tapping his watch.

"We're flying? What if I'm afraid of planes?" I ask and hear Gemma laughing on the line.

Finn gives me a flat look and swirls his finger in the air, signaling for me to wrap it up. "Tell Gemma goodbye and get your sexy ass in the car, Alessia."

Damn bossy asshole.

"You're not afraid of flying," Gemma reminds me as Finn grabs my suitcase from the bed and exits the room.

"I know that, but he didn't," I grumble.

"Think of all the things you two get to learn about each other on your little trip."

I let out a calming breath and remind myself it's a good thing my husband wants to take me away. And Gemma was spot on, we did skip the get-to-know-you phase.

"You're right. God, I feel so dumb for being this nervous."

"It's been a while since you've done anything like this. Nerves are normal."

"Alessia!" Finn calls from downstairs.

"Alright, I have to go. I'll call you when we get back."

We hang up, and I toss my phone in my purse before making my way out of our bedroom.

"Jesus, hold your horses," I gripe, walking down the staircase.

Finn looks like a kid in a damn candy store waiting for me at the bottom.

"You look pleased with yourself," I say when I reach him.

Finn wraps me in his strong arms and places a kiss on the tip of my nose.

I guess we're the type to do cutesy shit like that now, too.

"Excited for tonight," is all he says before turning and ushering me out of the house.

"I still don't get a hint?"

"Patience is a virtue, wife." He opens the car door, and I slide inside.

"And what about me screams virtuous, husband?"

"You'll love it, I promise." Finn shuts the door and walks to the driver's side, wearing a grin the entire way to the airport.

I guess we'll see.

I'll admit the private jet is a nice touch. This isn't the first time I've flown private, but it's the first time I've had a man bring me to orgasm on a plane. As soon as we're in the air, Finn throws a blanket over us and leans in close, his hot breath tickling my neck when he whispers, "It's been nearly eight hours since I gave you an orgasm, wife. I think that should be rectified, don't you?"

I look around for the flight attendant who was pouring our drinks just before takeoff but don't see her.

"Right now?" I ask in a hushed tone.

Finn lets that damn smirk answer for him as he glides his fingers under my knee-length skirt and trails them up to my panties.

"Can you keep quiet while I slide my fingers inside of you? You don't want the attendant to know I'm fucking your hot cunt with my fingers," he whispers.

Nodding, I spread my thighs, allowing him access to my center. His index finger slides my panties to the side before he plunges his long middle finger into my already wet core. He pulls it out and circles my clit a few times before entering me again, pumping in and out. The wet noises coming from his ministrations are decadent and I have to turn my head into his neck, biting down on the collar of his suit jacket to keep myself from crying out.

"Your pussy is so wet for me. I can't wait to get to the hotel so I can fuck this tight little cunt and make you scream my name over and over. Fuck, you come so pretty for me, Alessia."

A contained whimper escapes when Finn curls his finger and finds that bundle of nerves that sets me off every single time.

"Give me your eyes," he commands.

I lift my head and his heated gaze locks with mine, imploring me to let go.

The second he feels my walls tighten, he slams his mouth to mine, swallowing my muted moans as my entire body quakes with intense pleasure as wave after wave of bliss rushes through me.

When I come down, he slides his fingers from me and swirls them in his glass of whiskey, sucking them into his mouth before draining the glass. I stare at him in disbelief, not quite able to form words just yet. This man plays my body like his own personal fiddle, and I'm too addicted to him to care. He rights my skirt and adjusts the blanket, then lifts his arm so I can lean into him. Something I've learned about Finn is that he's extremely tactile. Even in the small moments, like driving to the casino, he always has to be touching me in some way.

A limo picks us up from the private airstrip and we're whisked away to our resort. Naturally, Finn booked the penthouse suite, which overlooks all of Atlantic City. It reminds me of the hotel in Boston the night of our wedding—the giant window overlooking the skyline, the white leather couches with white carpet throughout the living room. There're two bedrooms as well, but unlike our wedding night, we won't be sleeping in separate rooms.

"When we get back tonight, I'm going to hold you against this window and fuck you like I wanted to do the night of our wedding."

"You say the most romantic things," I let out a dreamy sigh before laughing.

Finn smirks. "You love it," he says, then kisses me breathless.

He's right, I do love it. And I would be lying if the idea of love and my husband in the same sentence didn't scare me a little.

"I have a massage therapist coming up in a couple minutes."

"There you go, planning stuff without my input. What if I don't want a stranger touching me?"

"I'll be here too. I thought a couples massage would be a nice way to start our date."

I quirk my brow. "So, you wanted a massage?"

"Well, yes. But you've been working hard, and we've been at the casino late every night this week. I want to pamper you a little, Alessia. Lord knows you won't think to do it for yourself."

He has a point. I've never been the pampering type. Or the type comfortable with people doing things for me out of care for my stress level.

"It would be nice if you were marginally excited with some pampering and a surprise date," he says with a small pout.

And doesn't that just make me feel like a huge asshole.

I wrap my arms around his middle, and he reluctantly allows me to pull him into my body.

"Hug me," I growl at him.

He does, and I smile at him, holding his dark-blue stare. "I'm sorry. I'm not used to having someone look out for me like this or wanting to do nice things for me just because."

"I'm not used to wanting to do this stuff, so I guess we're even."

"You're just a big marshmallow, aren't you?" I ask, my mouth turning up in a wide smile.

"Not with anyone other than you."

Finn leans down and places a sweet kiss on my shoulder before the shrill sound of the hotel phone ringing breaks us apart.

"Yes?" he answers, silent for a beat. "Yes, allow them up." He turns to me. "Time to get in one of those robes. Your pampering is about to begin."

An hour and a half later, I'm lying in a bath, wondering why the hell I've never scheduled massages into my weekly planner. Finn is sitting opposite me in the large marble Jacuzzi tub that's big enough for at least five more people.

"Well?" he starts, and I open my eyes. "Did you like it?" A smile plays on the corner of his lips. There's no way he thinks I wasn't in absolute heaven when I was having every knot and tense muscle worked out of my body.

"I'll give you this one. It was absolute magic."

The self-satisfied smirk he's wearing makes me want to kiss his lips or smack him. It can always go either way with us.

"We have about an hour before our dinner

reservation," he tells me, gliding his fingers up and down my calf. The touch isn't meant to lead to more, which is usually the case with us. It's a simple caress, a way to connect us with no reason other than because he likes to.

I reluctantly raise myself from the bath, and Finn stares at my naked form with a heated look in his devastating gaze.

"Oh no, Mr. Monaghan. I only have an hour to get ready. Keep those thoughts in your filthy mind."

In reality, every time he looks at me like that, it takes a ridiculous amount of willpower not to lose myself in him.

"Don't worry, Mrs. Monaghan. I can control myself." He bites his lip as his eyes trail up and down my body. "But when we get back tonight., it's going to be an entirely different story."

The restaurant Finn takes me to is exquisite. The space is bathed in dim light with dark-blue walls and rich oak furniture. Giant beams run across the ceiling, and white gauzy fabric is draped from them, giving the room a Mediterranean feel. The rich Spanish cuisine melts in my mouth as I sip the expensive wine. Everything is perfect, from the menu to the private booth, right down to the company.

"You sure know how to wine and dine a lady. Have a lot of practice?"

"Ah, is this the part where we talk about our pasts?" Finn smirks and takes a bite of his paella. "I've had exactly one serious girlfriend. She wasn't fond of the late nights or the focus I had building our business from where we were when I took over. Eventually, she wanted me to choose, so I did. Since you're the only woman wearing my ring, you can guess what my decision was. She was a nice enough girl but not right for me."

"Yes, a marriage of convenience is much more advantageous for you."

"It served your family as well. And our marriage has been anything but convenient." He sends me a challenging stare as he sips his red wine.

"If you wanted a little house mouse, then sorry to tell you, you picked the wrong girl."

Finn smiles, ignoring the ire in my tone. "I'd say I picked exactly the right woman."

My attempt to hide the smile fails miserably.

"How about you? Any hearts you left broken on our wedding day?" he asks, taking another bite of the delicious cuisine.

"I dated a few men here and there. There was only one serious relationship, but that ended badly."

Finn's gaze darkens. "Define 'badly.'"

This isn't exactly what I'd consider polite dinner conversation, but Gemma said we need to get to know each other. Maybe if Finn knows a bit about my past with Orlando, he'll understand my reaction to certain situations at the beginning of our marriage.

"He was part of this life. It was the typical story of a rich mobster's son thinking he could do anything he wanted, so he did. Late nights with his friends, though I have a strong suspicion he was with other women long before he admitted it. A lot of drinking and erratic behavior."

"Did he hit you?"

I swallow hard and nod. "He did."

Finn clenches his fork and takes a breath. "Give me his name, Alessia."

I quickly shake my head. "Absolutely not. It was years ago, and my brother took care of it."

"If he's still breathing, then he didn't finish the job. I want his name."

This could go one of two ways. Either I tell him he's being absolutely ridiculous and he can't possibly avenge something that happened before he knew I existed, or I can try to calm him down.

"Finn," I say, covering his tight fist with my hand. "Please. Let's drop this. Gio handled it the only way he could at the time. It's best for everyone if you let it go."

Finn stares into my pleading gaze for a few moments and takes several breaths while I hold mine in my lungs.

"It goes against every part of who I am to not get revenge for a man putting his hands on you. So when I say this, I hope you understand what it means—I will drop it for you. I trust you have your reasons for not wanting me to react and leaving this in the past. But that means you have to leave it *all* in the past. No more not trusting me, no more closing yourself off to me, and no more comparing me and our relationship to whatever you had with that piece of shit. You are *my* wife, and that means more to me than a signed piece of paper and a couple of rings."

Tears threaten to erupt with his sweet and slightly violent declaration. I hold them back, but just barely. "Thank you."

It's not that what happened with Orlando still makes me want to sob my eyes out, though that was the case for a long time. It's that every time Finn says things like this to me, the fact that he's so different from what I was prepared for smacks me over the head. I don't know how to process all of it. Unfortunately for me, the emotions come out as tears. It's so damn annoying.

Finn smiles and lifts our hands to his mouth, kissing the back of mine. "Anything for you."

We move onto lighter topics, him telling me about the antics he and his brother got up to as kids and me telling him all the ways I used to love annoying my older brother.

"Gio would get so frustrated with me. There was one time when he was in high school and had a girl over. They were in the theater room watching some scary movie. Now that I think about it, it was probably so she would hide her face in his arm when something would jump out." I laugh at that realization. "Anyways, I had just been to a sleepover, and we snuck out of my friend's room and watched that movie with the girl crawling out of the well or something with her hair in front of her face. You know the one?"

"I do," he replies with a shudder.

"I thought it would be hilarious to sneak into the room and reenact that scene. I didn't have a well, obviously, but I wore a long nightgown and did this ridiculous crab walk from around the back of the couch." I'm in near hysterics as I remember the girl's terrified scream and my brother hollering at me at the top of his lungs. "I ended up falling over in a fit of giggles, and his date laughed a little, too. I never did see her again, though."

Finn's laughter is booming, and his face is as relaxed as I've ever seen it as he leans back, those dimples of his on full display.

"It must have been a younger sibling thing. I swear my brother came out of the womb with the singular purpose of tormenting me."

Finn finishes his wine, the bill taken care of and sets his napkin on the table.

"We should get going," he says, checking his watch. "The main event is about to begin."

That piques my interest, and an excited smile spreads across my face.

He points at my smile. "That's the look I've wanted to see from you since I told you about our date last night."

"You've been doing such a good job so far, I have every confidence I'm going to love what comes next."

He lifts both of his hands and looks toward the ceiling. "Finally, she gets it," he says as though he's thanking the heavens.

The restaurant is busier now than when we walked in. The way he guides me through the tables with his hand on my hip feels so natural it catches me off guard for a moment. There's something so innate in the small action I've never felt before, and that scares me less than it would have twenty-four hours ago.

Finn and I chat in the limo ride to our next destination, so I hardly notice where we've pulled up. The doorman opens Finn's door first, and he holds his hand out, helping me from the car. We're at a brightly lit casino and my eyes turn to my husband with a questioning stare. "Are we checking out how the other half runs a casino?"

Finn smiles but doesn't answer. He leads me through the busy floor, then down a long hallway connected to what looks like some sort of arena at the resort. We take a turn into a smaller hallway and Finn shows the man in front of two nondescript doors the tickets he pulls from his pockets. He opens the door, and we're let into a giant private lounge with servers walking around carrying trays filled with flutes of champagne and hors d'oeuvres. Several well-dressed people are milling about with drinks in their hands and excitement on their faces. When I look at one of the televisions hanging from the wall, I spot a familiar logo.

"You brought me to a sold-out heavyweight championship MMA match?"

Finn smiles widely down at me. "You like?"

"Are you kidding? I've never been to a live event before. This is perfect."

"Did I mention we're front row?" His cocky grin is back in full force as he holds the tickets in front of me.

It could be the wine, the thrill of being here, or the lightness in my chest, but I throw my arms around my husband's neck and place a kiss soundly on his mouth. Finn's hand tangles in the back of my hair, not caring that we're in public and thrusts his tongue in my mouth.

When we pull apart, he leans his forehead against mine. "I'm glad you're happy with it."

"I'm more than happy with my surprise. And just so there's no confusion, seeing as this is our first date and all, you're totally getting laid."

He throws his head back, and a loud laugh explodes from him.

"You are something else, Alessia Monaghan." His smile is shining so bright it's nearly blinding.

That's the first time I've heard anyone say my full married name, and I think that might just be my favorite part of this night.

CHAPTER FIFTEEN

FINN

THE EXCITEMENT OF THE crowd is palpable in the packed arena as the match comes closer and closer to being called. The smile on my wife's face as she watches the two fighters in the octagon attack each other is fucking breathtaking. I knew this would be right up Alessia's alley. She loves sparring as much as I do, and with her training and skill, along with her taste for violence, there was no doubt in my mind this was the perfect date. As exciting as the fight is, I can't seem to pull my attention away from her face for more than a few brief moments. The gasps and murmurs falling from her lips as she watches the men try to dominate one another send delight and amusement through me. There's no doubt she's scrutinizing every move they make to find their mistakes, not that there are many. But Alessia wouldn't be who she is if she didn't point each one out, even if it's only to herself.

When the bruised and bloody fighter is called to be the new world champion, Alessia and I are on our feet, cheering loudly with the rest of the crowd. Her beaming smile is directed at me when I lean down to kiss her.

"That was amazing," she says with a breathless quality to her voice like she was the one in the ring. "I've never been to any sort of fight like this. The only boxing I've ever seen in person was at your fight."

"That's hardly on par with this, though. Our fights are barely a step up from any back-alley brawl." Maybe a touch higher, but Eoghan insists on keeping the fights as gritty as possible. He says the crowd comes for the bloodbath then stays for the alcohol. It's his deal, so I let him run things how he sees fit. Plus, we make a pretty penny from those nights, which tells me he must be doing something right.

"I don't know. I liked watching you fight that night." Her arms wrap around my neck while mine circles her waist in the bustling arena. "There's something about seeing you in the ring, all sweaty and focused."

"Did watching those guys turn you on, wife?"

She shakes her head. "No, that was fun. Watching you is something else."

Her face tilts toward mine, and I kiss her red lips.

"I've never met a woman with a vicious streak quite like yours, Alessia," I murmur in her ear. "You have no idea how bad it makes me want to fuck you against that octagon."

Her head tilts back on a laugh, which gives me the opportunity to playfully nip at the smooth skin of her neck.

She pulls away all too soon for my liking. "I'd rather not get arrested in Atlantic City tonight for public indecency. Each of us has gone this long without a criminal record. Let's not break that stride."

"You're right. Cillian would never forgive me if he had to drive out here to bail us out of jail. And there's no way I'd let Eoghan do it. Knowing him, it would be the first thing he'd bring up at Sunday brunch."

"That settles it. You'll just have to take me back to our suite and fuck me there like a good, law-abiding citizen."

"I think it's time to go then because I don't know how much longer you can expect me to stare at your ass in this red dress and not flip it up so I can sink inside your pussy."

Alessia's eyes flare with unmistakable heat before she spins around in my arms and grabs my hand in hers, yanking me toward the exit. My wife's sensual appetite knows no bounds, and I'm one lucky son of a bitch for it.

The ride back to the hotel is filled with wantful touches and needy glances. I may have gotten away with fingering her on the plane, but I don't want to press my luck with it in the limo. We aren't far from our hotel, and there's something to be said for building anticipation. Hell, it's been building in me all day. Especially when she slipped into the red dress I fucking love so much.

When we step into the elevator, I back her against the wall as the door slides shut. I don't touch her, instead pressing my hands against the wall on either side of her head. Her lips are parted, and her sweet breath tickles my mouth when I lean in close and connect our gazes.

"When we get upstairs, you're going to stand in front of the window and press your hands to the glass." I've had that image in my head since we walked into the suite earlier today. "You're not going to say a word. I want you to wait for me and imagine all the things I'm going to do to you against that glass. How hard I'm going to make you come while you look down on all the poor saps who will never be lucky enough to have a woman like you to play with and worship. All those poor souls who'll never know what it's like to have a man who would maim and kill anyone who threatened harm to her."

Alessia's pupils dilate to the point they nearly block out her moss-green irises.

The elevator door opens into the suite. I push myself off the wall and turn my head, looking back at my wife, who hasn't moved an inch. Her hand goes to her lower belly as she closes her eyes and blows out a breath through puckered lips.

"I think I gave you an order, wife. Don't keep me waiting."

Her eyes open and snap into focus. There's a touch of defiance that only lasts a moment before she walks to the window and does as instructed. She places her hands on the glass, and I make my way to the bar and fill my glass with ice, then splash a healthy pour of whiskey over it. I usually drink it straight, but I have plans for the freezing cubes that clink in the glass as I bring it to my lips for a sip.

Alessia cranes her neck to watch me and I click my tongue. "I thought I told you to watch all the people outside, wife. You're not very good at following directions, are you?"

"You're just now figuring that out?"

I lean against the bar and take another sip from my glass as I study the curves of her body and the subtle way her ass is tipped up. I've pumped my cock so many times to the memory of her in that dress after we first met that it's almost embarrassing. She looks even better tonight because I know I'll be deep inside her before the evening's over rather than driving home with an ache in my dick like last time.

Her eyes track my movements as I walk over to stand behind her. She still isn't looking below us. Instead, she's watching my reflection in the mirror.

"Do you remember our wedding night? How it felt to look over the city we were about to claim as our own?"

"I needed help with my zipper," she replies on a whisper.

"And I didn't think I'd ever feel as desperate to touch you as I did that night, but I was wrong. I'm just as desperate, just as consumed with the feel of your skin as I was that night, maybe even more so now that I've tasted it."

My hand brushes the hair from her back over her shoulders before I slowly begin dragging the pull of her zipper down, letting my finger run along her exposed skin. A shiver runs through Alessia, and I smile, loving the sight of what my simple touch does to her.

Grabbing a cube from my glass, I brush it against her neck, then slowly run it down her spine, allowing the heat of her skin to melt the ice as I watch the rivulets of water drip down to her ass. She lets out a hiss at the sensation, her back arching, but she doesn't move otherwise or tell me to stop. When the ice has nearly melted, I bring it to my mouth and crunch it between my teeth, then bend, dragging my cold tongue up her spine to the back of her neck.

"I love the taste of your skin."

Alessia turns her head, looking at me over her shoulder, molten desire swimming in her green gaze.

"Slide your dress off," I tell her.

"You're quite demanding tonight." Her teasing voice elicits a growl from my throat.

"And impatient." I step back a few inches. "Dress. Now."

Alessia narrows her eyes but doesn't argue further, instead removing her hands from the glass and slipping the red fabric off her shoulders and over her hips, letting it pool on the ground around her feet. The tiny black lace panties she's wearing barely cover her round ass.

"You know what else I love, Alessia?"

"Hmm?" She kicks her dress to the side, and I pull her against my chest, her back to my front, before she circles her arms around my neck.

"I love the taste of whiskey and your cunt," I say, removing another cube of ice from my glass. "In fact"—I slide it across her chest to the valley between her breasts encased in black lace to the top of her matching panties—"when I tasted the two combined on the plane earlier, I decided it was my new favorite flavor."

Her breaths come in short pants as I run the ice along the skin of her lower belly, watching her eyes fall closed in the reflection of the window. Her thighs are rubbing together, seeking some sort of friction to help alleviate the ache in her center. The movement causes her ass to rub against my hard cock. I'm not sure she's even aware she's doing it until I catch the smirk playing on her lips.

"You want to get fucked hard, don't you, wife?"

"God, yes." Her voice is a hoarse moan as I continue to tease her with the ice, dipping it into her panties ever so slightly.

"But I'm not done playing with you yet."

I slip the cube all the way inside the lace fabric and through her hot center. She lets out a surprised gasp and tunnels her fingers through my hair, clutching the strands in her tight grip as I circle her clit with the ice.

"Holy fuck, Finn," she hisses.

Removing the cube from her pussy, I drop the half-melted ice back into my glass and swirl it around before taking a long sip, finishing the whiskey.

"Fucking divine."

I toss the glass to the floor because, at this point, I don't give a shit about making a mess. I spin her in my arms and yank her by the back of her neck, crashing my mouth to hers. The kiss is wild and desperate, both of us beyond any sort of reason or sanity. We're feeding off each other's passion and it's almost as though it's turning us into animals. Alessia's hands go to either side of my shirt and she rips the damn thing open, scoring her nails over my chest and down my abs until she reaches my belt. With deft fingers, she quickly undoes the leather and rips my zipper down before freeing my raging hard-on. When her fist squeezes my dick, we both let out a hiss.

"Stop teasing me and fuck me," she demands.

Hoisting her up, she wraps her legs around my waist. Taking two steps forward, I slam her against the tall window. I can't wait another second to be inside my wife. Moving her panties to the side, I slam into her in one hard thrust.

"Yes," Alessia screams as I begin to pump with an intense brutality meant to bring us to the peak as fast and as hard as possible.

Her nails claw over my shoulders, and her heels are digging into my ass as I crush her against the glass, rutting into her like a fucking rabid beast. Our foreheads press together, and her wide eyes tell me she's close to the edge. Thank God because I'm not sure I can hold off much longer.

"I need you to get there, baby. Fuck, the way you strangle my cock feels so fucking good."

Her walls begin to flutter around me, and a second

later, her teeth press into my shoulder, biting hard. I barely register the pain as I erupt inside of her, taking us both over the edge on a shout of indescribable pleasure. I honestly don't think I've ever come so fucking hard in my entire life.

When my mind settles back into clear consciousness, Alessia's lips brush over the angry red mark she left on my skin.

"Sorry about that," she begins. "I may have gotten a little carried away."

"I don't know why you think I need an apology, wife. I'm not sorry in the least."

I slip from her core but keep her wrapped tightly around my waist.

"You can let me down."

"I could do a lot of things, doesn't mean I'm going to."

Walking over to the couch, I sit down with her straddling my lap. "Now, take your bra off. I haven't spent nearly enough time in our short marriage playing with your tits."

I've come to realize when we wake the next morning, there simply isn't enough time to play with my little wife all the ways I want to in one night. My imagination is far too extensive, and we have to get back to reality today. We eventually succumbed to exhaustion sometime in the early hours of the morning. When my phone rings as the sun is peeking in from the window, the last thing I'm prepared for is having a coherent conversation.

I grab my phone from the nightstand next to the bed we crashed into last night, seeing Cillian's name flash on the screen.

"This better be good," I tell him, scrubbing a hand over my face.

"Cataldi was spotted at a bar on the border of Farina and Amatto territory by one of our guys. Said he was there meeting with Orlando Farina himself. I don't like this, Finn. If the Farinas and what's left of the Cataldis team up, they'll be pushing into Amatto territory in no time."

Shit. I sit up in bed and look over to my wife, who is beginning to stir. A month ago, I wouldn't have given two shits about anything that happens in Worcester, but now? Now, I have a very good reason sleeping next to me to make sure not only my organization is strong but her father's as well.

"I'll call the pilot and have him get the plane ready for an early takeoff."

I wasn't planning on being back in Boston until later, hoping to spend more time with Alessia, making use of every available surface of this suite. "I'll call you when we land."

I immediately dial the pilot, who assures me the plane can be ready within the hour, then I call a car service to take us to the private airport.

Alessia groans next to me and peels one eye open. "Why does it sound like you're going to make me get out of this nice, warm bed?"

"Sorry, baby. We have to get home. Cillian called and it sounds like Carlo's poked his head out from whatever hole he's hiding in again."

"Fuck. I can't wait until that bastard is six feet under," she mumbles, turning toward the edge of the bed to get up.

"Have I told you how much I love your taste for violence?" I ask, admiring her perfect ass as she stands from the bed.

"What can I say? I don't appreciate him disrupting my mornings." She sends me a small smile before walking into the bathroom.

When my cock stirs, I look down then back to Alessia, who has just turned on the shower.

She catches my gaze in the mirror and must see something in my expression. "Don't even think about it. If we have to meet the plane in an hour, that's just enough time for me to shower and get ready, so get that look off your face."

She closes the door on me. Even though my hope for a quickie has deflated, my damn dick hasn't gotten the message.

"Sorry, buddy," I mutter and get off the bed to get the coffee started and pack our bags.

Stepping into the cabin of the plane, there's a large breakfast spread waiting for us. Thank God, because I am fucking starving. Neither of us has eaten since last night, and we spent the rest of the evening after the fight burning several thousand calories, I'm sure. We have just enough time to eat and enjoy a little peace and quiet before the plane lands, and Enzo and Cillian meet us at the airport.

"Take Alessia home and stay there with her. I'm going with Cillian."

Enzo nods and puts our bags in the trunk.

"Are you coming home tonight?" Alessia asks when I walk her to her car.

"I'll try. Cillian and I need to do some digging on Cataldi's associates. Maybe question a few people." I wrap her in my arms before she gets in the car. "But if I'm not going to be home before the sun comes up, I'll make sure to call you."

She smiles and leans up, standing on her tiptoes to place a soft kiss on my lips. "Be safe."

I shoot her a smile then deepen the kiss before leaning back. "Always am, wife."

CHAPTER SIXTEEN

ALESSIA

FINN DID, IN FACT, come home last night, this time with some new cuts on his knuckles. Most of the time, when a man in this life says he's going to "question someone," it means he'll be coming home with bloodied hands.

I cleaned the wounds and bandaged him up before drawing us a bath. Something I learned about my husband on our little getaway is his desire to live life and enjoy it to the fullest rather than do nothing but work. He allows himself to take time to relax, which surprises me, considering when we were first married, he was hardly home. I know he was getting things settled at the docks in those first few weeks, and it's not like I was waiting up for him like I do now. But what he said before going to Atlantic City struck a chord with me. We need to steal moments of time to just be us and enjoy life when we can because there will always be something or someone trying to tear that time away from us.

When I was little, my father was gone more than he was home. It never bothered me, I was too young to know any different, but I saw the look in my mother's eyes after my father was away for a couple days and the phone would ring. She never knew if it was the call that he was on his way or that he was never coming back again.

Then, when Gio died, he was gone even more. I was nineteen when it happened, and it was right after being beaten by Orlando and losing the pregnancy. I'll never forget the wail that fell from my mother's lips when my father told her Gio was dead. It was as though her soul was shattering right before our eyes. She lay in bed for weeks, completely inconsolable. My father was gone all of the time, leaving us to grieve on our own.

Finally, when he came home one night, she was up and waiting for him in the library. I was in the kitchen getting a glass of water when I heard her laying into him, telling him he needed to realize he had a daughter and a wife who needed him here. She'd let it slide when we were younger, but that was over. If he didn't start coming home every night and being with his family so we could heal from our loss together, then she was leaving. I doubt she actually would have, though. She loved him too much—not to mention the church and just about everyone in our life frowns upon divorce.

When I silently crept to peek into the library, I saw my parents embracing, tears falling from both of their eyes.

"I'm sorry, Lilliana. I don't know how to handle this. He's our son and he's not coming home. I-I—"

"Shh. I know. But you have a daughter who needs you

and a wife who is falling apart without you. We need you here, Mario."

I went back up to my room, feeling like I was prying on a private moment between my parents. I cried myself to sleep that night like I had done every night since Gio was killed. But when I woke the next morning, my father was still home, and he never spent another night out of the house.

Of course, that meant his men came to our home much more frequently, but by that point, I was on my way back to college. Every night when I'd call my mother to check in in the months following Gio's death, I would hear my father's voice in the background, and as the weeks wore on, we all eventually found a new routine.

From that night in the library forward, my father was a changed man. His priority became my mother and me, even offering me a job in one of his real estate development companies when I graduated with my MBA. Of course, it was mostly a front for moving his money around from other less-than-legal gains, but he wanted to keep me close and give me purpose. And I wanted to make him proud. I knew I was never going to be allowed to rise to the top like Gio would have, but I was a part of this family. My father made sure I knew how much he appreciated my dedication and having someone in my position whom he shared unwavering trust with. Not exactly easy to come by.

I shake myself from my thoughts and look at my

husband with a glass of whiskey in one hand and his head tilted back.

"Can I help?" I ask, relaxing on the opposite side of the large bathtub as I run a comforting hand along Finn's leg under the water.

Finn's gaze travels to mine, and he smiles. "This shit with not knowing what Cataldi is doing or where he's hiding is fucking with me. Being here with you and having you take care of me is helping, though."

"I haven't done anything."

"You bandaged me up." He raises his hand to show me the proof.

"I just didn't want you getting blood on the furniture," I reply, shrugging my damp shoulder.

"You drew a bath for me."

"That's because you stink. You needed the wash."

Finn barks out a laugh, the tension in his face melting a smidge.

"You can deny it all you want, Alessia. I know you like taking care of me just as much as I enjoy taking care of you."

I don't answer him, but he's right. I love being here and doing these little things for Finn. Not that I'll ever tell him that.

"We're going to your parents tomorrow for dinner. I need to update your father on what's been going on."

"Are you going to let me in on your little meeting? It is my family, too, you know."

"Actually, yes, that is my plan. I'd appreciate you and

your father's perspectives on some leads we've had."

"Why don't we talk about it now?"

Finn sets his glass on the side of the bathtub and prowls toward me.

"Because you're naked in here with me, so I've formulated a few plans of my own that don't involve talking unless the words falling from your lips are yes, please, more, and just like that."

I could argue and insist that figuring out the Cataldi situation is more important, or I can give my husband the stress relief he needs and earn myself a couple orgasms in the process. I think about it for a moment then brush my lips against his, whispering, "Tomorrow it is, then."

"*Piccola demone*," my father greets me with open arms. Finn and I make our way up the stairs, his hand resting on my lower back as he walks beside me. I fall into my father's embrace with a wide smile. "Hi, Papa."

My mother stands in the doorway, and I walk over to her, kissing her cheeks. "So good to see you, Mama."

Her smile is bright as she glances between me and my husband.

"Something has changed, sweetheart. I can see it in the way your husband looks at you."

"We've been getting along," I say with a light smile, but

my mother continues to stare at me, studying my face.

"Oh, I think it's more than that." She leans in for another hug and whispers in my ear, "It looks like love."

My brows are furrowed when we separate, and she turns to greet Finn.

Love? There's respect and admiration between us, absolutely. There's an unquenchable desire and a fierce passion, no doubt. But I've never considered love until this moment. Sure, there was attraction from the first time we met, that much we've admitted, but we weren't exactly compatible personality-wise. Nearly every word that came out of his mouth irritated the hell out of me, and I doubt he would disagree that I worked hard on getting on his last nerve. What would it take for two people who started the way Finn and I did to fall in love?

My parents walk into the house while I'm left standing on the front porch, still thinking about the words my mother whispered.

Finn catches my gaze with a concerned one of his own. "You okay?"

I stare at him for a brief moment, trying to find in his eyes what my mother saw. I see concern for my momentary lack of ability to form words, but other than that, I have no idea what she's talking about. He's looking at me like he always does.

Shaking my head, I let out a quiet chuckle. "Fine." I tilt my head up for a kiss and he doesn't leave me waiting, softly brushing his lips against mine.

We turn toward the front door, my arm looped in his when he asks, "What does *piccola demone* mean?"

"Little demon," I reply with a fond smile. "My father's been calling me that since I was little."

Finn chuckles then bends to kiss the top of my head. "Fitting."

I laugh but don't say anything. It's not as though I can deny it, and he wouldn't believe me if I tried. After these past several weeks, Finn has become well acquainted with who I am and vice versa. Even if he could change it, I have a sneaking suspicion he wouldn't.

After finishing the exquisite meal my parents' cook prepared, Finn leans back in his chair and rests his hand on his stomach.

"That was absolutely delicious. Maybe your cook would be inclined to teach Alessia how to prepare some of her recipes," he says, smiling at my mother.

"What do you mean? Alessia's been cooking with her since she was, I don't know, eight, maybe? Remember when she wanted to open her own restaurant, Mario?" My mother looks at my father with a warm smile. "Honestly, we were both surprised when she went to college for finance instead of culinary school."

Finn's eyes shoot to me. "You said you couldn't cook."

"No," I correct. "I said you had two hands and could fend for yourself. I never said I couldn't. Besides, it's been years since I made a full-course meal like this one."

"You could give it a shot," Finn murmurs, taking a sip of his wine.

"I could do a lot of things. I'm also quite adept at carving meat. Would you care to see my knife skills, husband?"

Finn shakes his head with a smirk playing on the corner of his lips. "Little demon is right."

I shrug and sip my wine as Finn turns to my father. "We should talk about a few things before Alessia and I head home, Mario. There's been some new developments."

My father nods, and my mother rises from the table, grabbing the plates to take to the kitchen. We have staff for this kind of thing, but whenever business conversations come up, she takes her leave. It's not that my father hides things from her; it's that she's not the type of wife to involve herself in the business. She's perfectly happy hosting parties and being a mother and wife to the head of a family, but that's where her involvement ends. Unlike me, who's been involved in a lot of what goes on in my father's illegal pursuits since working for one of his companies. He was always honest about what my job truly entailed. It never bothered either of us that I knew most of the details of his business, which is far from common in other families. My mother has her way of contributing to this life, and I have mine.

The three of us make our way into the study where I first met Finn. We've come a long way since that night and still have a long way to go. But instead of fear of the unknown, I'm walking in here happier than I ever remember being in my life.

Finn and my father have a seat on the couches facing each other while I pour us three glasses of whiskey and hand one to my father then my husband before sitting next to him. It's so different from where we were positioned barely a month ago.

"Cataldi has been seen in both of our territories," Finn tells my father. "We still don't know where exactly he's been hiding, but we have a feeling he's planning something. It looks to us like he's trying to drum up support. Many of his father's capos knew about his side of the business," Finn says, referring to the sex trafficking Carlo's been facilitating through the ports. "And my source tells me they aren't happy about it. Not all, but most of the men in the Cataldi organization don't agree with what Carlo's been doing or the fact his father was turning a blind eye to it. There's been infighting about who is going to take over Francesco's territory since he went to prison. Some think they should stay loyal to Carlo, while others want to move in a different direction. It's the perfect time for our families to move in on all the Cataldi businesses, not just the ports. I think it's time the Cataldi organization answers to a new boss, and it isn't Carlo."

My father absorbs his words and blows out a long breath. "You're talking about a war. That can get expensive and bloody."

Finn nods. "If we're going to act, the time is now. Their organization is in tatters, and we think he may be trying to find support with the Farinas."

My head whips toward Finn, and my father's eyes widen for a moment before he schools his expression.

"Why do you think that?" I ask.

"He was spotted near your border at a bar meeting with Orlando. It would make sense that he's trying to find allies somewhere, and since the only other family in Massachusetts is your father's, Farina is the only viable option. I also know that Orlando was visiting Carlo at his home often before his father was convicted."

"How do you know that?" my father asks.

Finn looks between the two of us and leans forward, resting his forearms on his knees. "I have an inside man in the Cataldi organization. He's made it possible to get information we wouldn't otherwise have. It sounds like Orlando and Carlo were planning on uniting two families to be the driving force of the Massachusetts criminal world."

My father and I look at each other when he mentions Orlando again.

Finn catches the look between us, studying the expressions on our faces. "What aren't you telling me?"

My father holds my gaze and nods his head, prompting me to be completely transparent with my husband.

"Do you remember when I told you I was in a relationship and he beat me?"

Finn nods, his jaw ticcing as he waits for me to continue.

"It was Orlando."

Finn's eyes stay glued to mine as he studies me intently. "There's more you're not telling me, Alessia. I knew, when we were in Atlantic City, you were keeping his name a secret for a reason. There's more to the story."

My eyes close and I tilt my head down toward my wringing hands resting on my lap. I need to get it out. Finn needs the truth about the entire situation and Gio's death.

"I was pregnant. He didn't believe me and beat me so badly I miscarried," I whisper before clearing my throat and meeting my husband's gaze. "I called my brother, and he took me home to his house. My mother was on a holiday visiting her parents in Italy, so Gio called my father. He had a doctor come to his apartment to treat me since I refused to go to the hospital. I told them everything. After sitting with me night and day until I was on a steady road to recovery, Gio left to handle Orlando. My brother beat him to bloody hell and could have killed him, but Gio knew that would have started a war between our families. He came home and told me he took care of Orlando. When I asked if he was still alive, Gio assured me he hadn't taken it that far, but he was a bloody mess, so I'm sure Orlando didn't fare too well. Then, two days later, he was dead, stabbed in a 'mugging' outside of a bar he frequented often. It was too coincidental, him being murdered right after beating Orlando. Orlando is a vindictive son of a bitch, and I knew, in my gut, he was responsible for Gio's death. Not to mention, everyone knew my brother and knew who our father was. No one would've had the balls to kill him, knowing the hell that would rain down on them. The only people who knew what Orlando had done were my father and I. And until that point, the only people who knew Orlando and I were involved were Gemma and Enzo. My father called Massimo Farina and accused Orlando of killing Gio. Of course, Orlando denied it."

I take a deep breath, and thankfully, my father fills Finn in on the rest of the story since he was the one who spoke to Orlando's father.

"Massimo said Gio nearly killed Orlando and implied maybe Gio had made some dangerous enemies. But I knew that was bullshit. Everyone loved Gio. He had a way about him that made people gravitate toward him. The only enemy he had was Orlando Farina." My father squeezes his eyes shut, the pain of losing his son evident on his face. He clears his throat and opens his eyes before continuing. "I explained to him who his son was and what he did to my daughter, but he felt that it was between a man and his woman. Said his son told him she was cheating on him and there was no way he could have gotten her pregnant. He said if any harm came to his son, then Alessia would be next." His gaze travels to me for a moment then back to my husband's. "It was the first time in my life I had to choose between being the boss and my only remaining child. I couldn't let my wife lose her daughter because I wanted revenge for our son's death. I couldn't lose her, and I knew Massimo would make good on his threat. I love my daughter more than the air I breathe, and I wasn't going to risk her life. I couldn't. In the end, I made Massimo give me his word that he would keep Orlando away from Alessia and stay out of Amatto territory."

"That motherfucker was at our wedding!" Finn booms, losing the last thread of his composure. "He spoke to my wife. Touched her right in front of everyone there." Finn shoots from his seat with his fists clenched at his side. "How could you invite that piece of shit to be anywhere near your daughter?"

To my recollection, no one has ever spoken to my father the way Finn is, especially in his own house. I'm equally shocked and impressed at the level of composure my father has right now as Finn looks ready to tear this room apart in a rage.

"It's the way we've done business for generations. We keep polite and friendly appearances in the faces of our worst enemies while plotting to stab them in the back. And make no mistake, the Farinas are my enemy. I had no proof that Gio was murdered by Orlando, and too many men in this world think the same way as that piece of shit's father. That what happens between a man and his woman is private and no one should involve themselves, even when he beats her. But there was no doubt that when the time was right, I'd make Orlando pay."

Finn walks back over to the couch and stands behind me, placing his strong hand on my shoulder. "You had your chance, Mario. I understand you were backed into a corner and wanted to protect Alessia's life. I respect the choice you made, but he's still breathing. We'll handle this my way now, and I have no intention of my knife going into his back. He'll look me in the eyes and know I'm the one ending his miserable existence."

CHAPTER SEVENTEEN
ALESSIA

THE RIDE HOME FROM my parents' house is quiet as Finn works through whatever's tumbling around in his head.

"Are you okay?" What I want to ask is if we're okay, but for some reason, I'm afraid of the answer.

There are people in this world who believe a woman puts herself in a position to be hurt and abused. That she should have left the first time and not "let" it escalate. What they fail to realize is the abuser does a fucking remarkable job of turning you around on yourself. I questioned everything about what I thought I knew about myself when Orlando love-bombed the hell out of me after the first time he hit me. I thought I would never fall for a man who could possess the type of demon in his soul that would make him hurt the woman he was supposed to love. It wasn't until I left and started healing from his abuse and my brother's death that I realized what kind of monster he truly was. Gio was what a real man was made of. He saw what Orlando did and refused to stand by and let him get away with it. And he paid with his life for his convictions.

"It's a lot to process. I didn't know about you and Orlando. It changes things," Finn says, still not looking at me.

His reply hurts something deep within me. I thought my husband was different from the other men in this life. The ones who turn a blind eye to men who abuse women because it isn't any of their business.

"If you've changed your mind about going after him—"

He whips the car to the side of the road and slams on the brakes.

"Jesus Christ, Finn!"

He turns his blue gaze to me and pins me with the most intense stare I've ever seen from him. "Let's get something straight real quick, Alessia. He hurt you and put you through unspeakable pain. There is no scenario where I let him live. I was referring to extra security and coordinating with your father and his men for when we go to war with Farina and whatever's left of the Cataldi organization. It's not just Carlo whose days are numbered now."

Relief sweeps through me from Finn's reassurance and I reach my hand to cover his, still clutching the steering wheel. He is the man I thought he was. The man I'm coming to realize I'm falling in love with.

"Not everyone in this life shares your view. Thank you for being different."

He brings my hand to his lips and kisses the back of it. "Fuck, baby. It's a sad day when a woman has to thank a man for not being a piece of shit." Finn shakes his head as cars zoom past us on the highway leading home. "There isn't a single man in my organization who would get away with the kind of things Orlando did. I'd take care of them personally if I ever found out they treated their girlfriends or wives the way he did. I will never abide by that kind of thinking or behavior. Ever. Understood?"

I nod my head, giving him a small smile and he merges back onto the road.

More relaxed than I've been the last half hour driving, I lean back in my seat and face my husband. He isn't mad at me for not telling him my ex's identity or how this is turning into a much bigger issue than he originally thought. He's mad *for* me and for the women who've been where I was. He's angry that men like Carlo and Orlando have gotten away with hurting women for generations, and no one has stepped in to stop them. A soft smile moves across my lips, and Finn catches me staring from the corner of his eye.

"What?" he asks, removing one hand from the steering wheel and laying it on my thigh.

I cover it with my palm and link our fingers together. "I'm surprised by you. I have no idea why I would be, but every time I think you're going to respond to something one way, you turn around and amaze me by doing the opposite. I don't know, I kind of like it."

Finn huffs out a laugh and his smile is wide and happy. It's not one the world sees, but when it's just the two of us, he lets it out more and more often.

"Well, wife. I can't wait to get home so I can amaze and surprise you all night."

"My husband, the romantic," I reply in a dry tone, but there's no stopping a grin from lighting up my face.

After speaking with my father last night at dinner, Finn decided we needed more security. His guards are working longer shifts, so there are more on duty at one time. Enzo also now has a room in the house, so he's never far if we need him. Finn insists I have a shadow when he isn't home, and I'm glad it's Enzo, considering I've known him for most of my life. If my husband feels the need to be overprotective, I'd much rather have someone I know in the house with me at all times rather than a guard I've only met a few times.

"I hope he's paying you overtime," I tell Enzo as we head up the stairs from the underground gun range. Finn told me he wasn't comfortable with me making any unnecessary trips off the property. And apparently, being able to shoot at my favorite range is deemed unnecessary. Of course, he didn't tell me that outright, but Enzo let me know when I suggested we go over there this evening. When I argued, he told me I should take it up with my husband. That's probably exactly what Finn wanted. The man loves to rile me up then kiss me breathless, and he knew damn well telling Enzo instead of me that we were on a sort of lockdown would piss me off.

How convenient that Finn left an hour ago with Cillian to follow a lead on Carlo's whereabouts.

"Mr. Monaghan has been very generous," Enzo replies.

"You're just happy to not have to traipse all over with me when Finn's around. Has it been nice having some time to yourself?"

"It's always nice getting to spend more time with my sister and her kids. But I doubt I'll see very much of them for the next little while."

That's true. With Finn most likely being gone more and the shit that's about to hit the fan with not only the Cataldis but the Farinas as well, Enzo will be spending day and night at the house with me.

"Sorry about that. But you know it won't be forever." I shut off the light to the stairwell and close the door to the basement.

"My job is to make sure you're safe. I've never minded, Alessia."

They don't make guards like Enzo anymore. He's turned into more than an employee over the years. I consider him a trusted friend.

When we get to the kitchen, I'm making coffee for the both of us. It's going to be a long night waiting up for Finn, and I know Enzo won't rest until Finn is home, either.

"Here you go." I'm handing him the cup when the

house suddenly goes dark. "What the hell?"

"Let me call the guardhouse." Enzo takes his phone from his pocket and the light illuminates his face, highlighting the furrow of his brow.

I watch him wait for one of the guards to answer. The longer he's silent, the more nervous I get. There's always someone in there. Why aren't they answering?

"Let me try one of the other guards patrolling," he says, dialing another number.

It's not time to freak out yet. The guards at the gate are probably just trying to figure out what happened with the power.

Enzo disconnects the call when it goes to voice mail.

Our eyes meet, and his worried expression mirrors mine.

"Something's not right," I whisper just as we hear a loud crash from a window shattering boom throughout the silent house.

"Get back to the basement. Now!" Enzo commands and I take off out of the kitchen and into the hallway leading to the basement stairs with Enzo at my heels. Before I get to the door leading to the basement, heavy footfalls sound inside the house.

Wrenching the door open, I find the steps and begin my descent, careful not to miss one in the dark and take a tumble. We just need to make it back to the armory connected to the shooting range. Once inside, we can lock it and use the emergency phone to call Finn. Cell reception is shitty because of the steel-enforced walls. I've never been happier that Finn built a safe room down here as I am now. When he first showed me, I thought he was being overly cautious, though I should have known better. I was naive to think we wouldn't be attacked at home, stupidly thinking no one would come in here and try to get through the already heavy safeguards Finn has in place. Just because something has never happened doesn't mean it never will.

When I get to the bottom of the stairs, my shaking hands feel along the wall to find the steel door leading into the safety of the armory. The footfalls are directly over us, running toward the basement door then charging down the stairs. I find the handle of the heavy door and pull it open just as two shots ring out. My palm slams into the power switch next to the inside of the door, and I flip it on so the room is lit up with fluorescent lights running off a separate power grid. I turn, expecting to see Enzo right behind me, but instead, I'm faced with two men at the bottom of the stairs wearing night-vision goggles, pointing their weapons at me and my bodyguard lying on the floor. One lunges for me, jumping over Enzo's prone body. Before he can reach me, I slam the door and hear a thunk on the other side as I'm sliding the locks in place. My head whips to the camera monitors set up in the room that activates when the interior lights are turned on. The camera right outside the safe room shows the two men standing in front of the door and Enzo bleeding on the floor, not moving at all.

"You let her get away," one man shouts at the other.

"How the hell am I supposed to get through a steel fucking door, man?"

The men look around the dark basement, barely acknowledging the man they shot lying on the cold cement floor. My heart is in my throat, hoping against hope for Enzo to still be alive and praying they don't decide to put a bullet in his head to make sure he's dead.

"There's a camera in the corner." The man who lunged for me points up, and it eerily looks like he's pointing directly at me through the screen as I watch his partner walk up and peer at the lens.

That's right, assholes. Pay attention to the camera and not the bleeding man.

"I thought you made sure the power was cut."

His voice sounds familiar, but it's muffled through the mask he's wearing over his face.

"There must be a separate power source for the room. I heard he likes his toys."

Another man enters the basement behind them, but this one isn't wearing a mask, only a pair of night-vision goggles.

"She locked herself in the room, boss. No way in through what I'm guessing is at least eight inches of solid steel. Monaghan has surely been notified by now."

Adrenaline is coursing through my blood as my heart races while the men on the other side of the door speak to their boss, the one person in this world who can still evoke this type of fear from me. The one who has been the cause of so many nightmares in my life.

The man in the suit walks up to the camera and takes off the goggles. Not that he needed to. I would recognize his voice anywhere.

"Tell your husband I said hello," Orlando says into the camera, making every hair on my body stand on end. "I'll be seeing you, sweetheart."

He blows a kiss into the camera then places the goggles over his eyes once more. I want to gag, or scream, or open this door and shoot him between the eyes.

The three of them turn and walk up the stairs and out of the camera's line of sight.

The shrill sound of the phone ringing breaks the silence in the safe room, startling me out of my momentary stupor. Grabbing the phone hanging on the wall, I pick up the receiver.

"Alessia!" Finn yells into the phone. "I see you, baby. You're going to be okay."

I look around frantically, trying to find another camera in the room.

"Look above the door to the gun range," he tells me.

Looking up, I spot the small camera, feeling a sense of relief that he can see me, that I can hear his voice.

"I'll be there in fifteen minutes, Alessia. Cillian is with me and Eoghan is on his way with the family doctor. All you have to do is stay in the room and wait for me, okay?"

My head bobs up and down, and a sob that I've

been holding on to since the power went out upstairs escapes from my throat. "They shot Enzo. He's not in here with me. God, Finn. I think he's dead."

"I know, baby. And I know this is going to be hard for you, but I need you to stay in the room. It looks like they're gone, but I don't want you taking any chances, okay? You need to wait for me."

I nod again, tears pouring down my face. "It was Orlando."

"I know. I'm almost there. It'll be okay. I'm almost home."

"Please hurry."

I keep the phone in my hand but turn back toward the monitor, where I see Enzo. He still hasn't moved and the amount of blood under him is scaring the ever-loving shit out of me.

God, Finn. Hurry.

CHAPTER EIGHTEEN
FINN

I'M IN A NEARLY blind rage. The only thing keeping me fucking grounded in this moment is the fact I'm on the phone with my wife. Cillian got a call from the dancer who tipped him off the first time that Carlo was at the strip club again. Eoghan met Cillian and me there with a couple of our guys, intent on ending this tonight. I'm sick and fucking tired of Carlo and Orlando Farina walking around this planet thinking they're untouchable, they sure as shit aren't, and it's time I proved it.

When we pulled up, we saw a sea of flashing lights outside. Declan, one of the guys who works on Eoghan's crew, jumped out to ask what was going on. He talked to the security guy for the club, and he said one of the girls was found in the alley with a bullet between the eyes. Turns out it was Cillian's friend who tipped us off earlier tonight.

I don't know if Carlo knew she called us or made her call us, then killed her. But either way, the girl was dead, and shit was not sitting right with me.

We all jumped back in the car to head to my house. I

needed to be close to my wife, to know she was safe. We weren't more than fifteen minutes from the house when I got an emergency notification on my phone. The lock to the safe room had been activated. Cillian immediately pulled up the camera feed to the house, and what I saw shook me to my core. Two men were standing outside the safe room door in one frame and my wife was behind the steel-reinforced door in the other. I could hear them trying to figure out what the hell to do when a third man walked into the basement.

Orlando Farina. My wife's soon-to-be-dead ex-boyfriend.

He fed her a line of bullshit about seeing her soon and turned, walking past Enzo's body, lying motionless on the ground. I immediately called Eoghan and told him to go pick up the doctor we keep on payroll and meet us at the house. Before he could ask any questions, I hung up and called Alessia on the direct line going to the safe room.

I've been on the phone with her for the last ten minutes, trying to calm her down, but she can't take her eyes off the monitor for the camera pointing at Enzo.

"How much longer?" she asks again. "He's still not moving." Swiping the tears pouring down her face, she stares at the screen. Knowing my wife, she's probably trying to will him to move, to wake up and show some kind of life.

"I know, baby. I can see both of you."

I refrain from telling her I'm not sure Enzo will ever

move again. Goddammit. We've gotten to know each other a bit since the three of us began working out together. The man doesn't say much, but he's reliable and has a dry sense of humor that reminds me of Alessia's. I can see why she's so fucking distraught over the idea of losing him. I've always felt at ease when I couldn't be with her, knowing he was there to protect her. Even now, if he dies, I know he did everything he could to make sure she was safe.

"How close are you?"

"I'm pulling up to the gate now."

Thank fuck.

Passing through the wide-open front gate, I spy the two guards on the floor of the guardhouse with their throats slit open.

We drive slowly up the drive, keeping our eyes peeled for any movement, but only find three more of my guards dead on the ground.

"Finn, be fucking careful," Cillian calls as I shove the car door open and fly to the front door, my gun in hand and ready to shoot any motherfucker I see moving. Cillian is right behind me, his gun raised and ready to fire.

"I'm at the front door," I tell Alessia, not willing to hang up until I have her in my arms.

"Please be careful. I don't know if they're still in the house."

I don't like there being too many cameras in the house, but I have a few. I watched Orlando and the other two men he was with walking out the front door and toward the gate. They must have parked on the street and come onto the property somewhere along the fence line. I'll be figuring out how they got to my guards without being detected.

Rushing into the house, I fly down the stairs, trusting Cillian to have my back just in case I missed someone lying in wait.

"Open the door, Alessia." The basement is dark, but light spills from the steel door when she cracks it open, and Alessia stands there with the phone still to her ear. As soon as she sees me, she runs into my arms and nearly knocks me over. Her body is shaking, and I hold her for a moment, reaffirming to myself she's safe and unharmed.

She pulls back and steps a few feet to the right, where Enzo's body is lying face down with two bullets in his back. Alessia drops to her knees next to her bodyguard.

"Enzo," she cries as she feels for a pulse. "Oh my God, Finn. He's still alive."

I drop down next to her and place two fingers on his neck.

"There's a pulse. It's faint, but it's there."

"Thank you, God." Alessia grabs Enzo's hand. "You're going to be okay, Enzo. We've got you."

I don't have the heart to tell her that I'm not so sure he's going to pull through, judging by the amount of blood we're kneeling in. Instead, I keep my mouth shut, tear off my jacket and place it on the two wounds on the man's back.

"Finn, you good?" I hear Cillian call from the top of the stairs.

"We're okay. Enzo is still alive."

"Holy shit." He saw the same thing I did when we pulled up the camera feed in the basement. "I'm going to turn the generator on."

The sound of his footfalls echo through the basement as he moves toward the back door, where I have a backup generator. Moments later, the lights in the basement flick on, and I look into my wife's teary eyes.

"Did you see them leave?" she asks, probably scared they're going to come back any second and try to finish the job.

I nod. "There were three. I watched them walk out the front door and head toward the gate."

"Were you already on your way back? What happened?"

I could tell her not to worry about it, and I'll handle it. It doesn't matter to me that she grew up in this life and knows what to expect. She's still my wife, and I want to protect her from all of this. I don't want any part of this to touch her, and I don't want her to hear all the gory details about what's bound to happen. But Alessia wouldn't be the woman she is if she let me get away with keeping anything from her. And I wouldn't be the man I am if I didn't respect the hell out of her for that—and so many other things.

"We went to the same strip club as last time. When

we got there, the dancer was dead. Found shot in the head in the back alley. Police were all over the place, so we came home."

"This was a setup to get you out of the house." Her eyes narrow as she mulls something over in that sharp-as-hell brain of hers. "Why not shoot me when they shot Enzo? I may be a fast runner, but I'm not faster than a bullet." She looks at her friend then her gaze snaps to mine. "Holy shit. Do you think Carlo and Orlando are working together?"

"My guess?" I ask, and Alessia nods. "They wanted to take you. Hold you hostage, or, I don't know, sell you off. If Carlo is involved, that would be the most logical reason." Not that logical and that piece of shit's name belong in the same sentence. "That's what he tried to do to the prosecutor who put his old man away. She's also involved with the president of an MC we work with. The Black Roses and the Cataldis have a history that goes way back. It's not the first time someone from their organization tried to take one of the women and sell her in the skin trade."

"Jesus fucking Christ. Well, at least he's consistent. Sounds like Carlo and Orlando are a match made in hell."

"Maybe, but they fucked up more than they can possibly imagine when they went after you. I don't care what I have to do; they'll both die before this is over."

Alessia looks me straight on with fire and vengeance swirling in her green eyes. We're kneeling over her dying friend's body, both of us with blood on our hands, and I don't think I've ever seen a person with such resolute determination and anger on their face.

"I want to be there, Finn. When you have Orlando. I want to see him take his last breath."

Fuck. My wife is stunning. "Consider it done."

The air seems to crackle between us with the power behind my words. Alessia will have her revenge. I'll make damn sure of it.

"Finn, I have the doctor and we're coming down," Eoghan calls out, probably so I don't raise my pistol and scare the poor doc.

Eoghan appears at the bottom of the stairs with a portable stretcher in his hands and Dr. Simmons and Cillian behind him.

"What do we have?' the doctor asks, kneeling beside me.

"Two gunshots to the back. I didn't turn him to check if the bullets went straight through," I answer.

He removes the jacket I'd placed over Enzo's wounds then checks his pulse.

Nodding to no one in particular, he looks back at Eoghan. "We need to move him. Lay the stretcher here," he says, pointing next to Enzo.

Dr. Simmons and his team have been responsible for stitching up all manners of knife and bullet wounds for my family since my father's time at the helm.

I help the doc carefully roll Enzo over and onto the narrow cot before Eoghan and Cillian pick it up and head up the stairs.

"He's lost a lot of blood, and I won't know the extent of the damage until I get in there. Finn, you come with me. You're O neg, and we may need some blood from you."

"So am I," Alessia says, standing from the pool of blood at our feet.

"Then you come, too."

Dr. Simmons turns and follows his patient up the stairs. "They should have the operating room ready when we get there, but we need to hurry."

"Are we going to a hospital?" Alessia asks.

With all the money he's made from my family the last several years, plus his time in his own legal private practice, the good doctor built a house not too far from here. Pretty convenient for me. Of course, I made sure to contribute to the cost of the surgical room he had built onto the house as well.

"He has a setup in his house. Do you want to get changed before we go?"

Alessia shakes her head. "No. I don't want the doctor waiting in case he needs us."

"Come on then. We'll take Eoghan's car. I don't care if we get blood all over his."

Alessia lets out a small, barely there chuckle, but it's the first hint of lightness I've seen since I got home.

"Glad the thought of ruining my brother's car amuses you. Let's see how he feels about it."

I reach my hand out and she slides her bloody palm into mine. Some people may get a little squeamish with the blood, but not us. I wouldn't care if she was covered head to toe in the most disgusting substance known to man. As long as I can touch her and have her safe next to me, then all is right in my world.

One of Simmons's nurses scrounges up some scrubs for us to change into after we've washed up as best we can in the bathroom. Alessia insisted they take some blood from both of us to have on hand and ready if necessary. If they don't need it this time around, that's fine. It's not like it won't be used at some point down the road. We're about to go into a war with two Mafia families. Who knows how long it's going to last or how much bloodshed is in our future? If the past serves as any indicator, my guess is a lot.

It's been an hour since they wheeled Enzo into surgery, and so far, the only thing we know is he's still alive. Now that I've had time to process the events of the evening, I can't help but wonder how Orlando and Carlo found themselves in cahoots and why I didn't know about it. And where the hell was Carlo when all of this was going down?

"Alessia, is there anything you recognized about the other two men?"

Her head lifts from my shoulder that she's been resting on since we sat on the large couch outside of the operating room at the doctor's house.

"Not really. They were wearing masks and night-vision goggles, except Orlando. It was like he wanted me to see he was after me. He probably thought it would scare me even more or something. Orlando always did enjoy psychological warfare."

His name falling from her lips sends rage coursing through my blood. And the fact she knows that about him. It gives me a terrifying insight into their relationship.

"One of their voices did sound familiar, but I couldn't place it at the time."

"Could it have been Carlo?"

Alessia is silent as she considers my question. "It could have been. Honestly, Finn, I'm not entirely sure. I wasn't exactly in my right frame of mind. Plus, I've only met Carlo a few times. Even my father couldn't stand him, so he was rarely invited to any functions my family had."

That makes sense. The Cataldis weren't well liked by the other families if the word on the street was accurate. That's why I'm confused as to why Farina is helping him now.

"I need to make a couple calls."

I pull out my phone. Normally, I would walk out of the room. But the thought of leaving Alessia alone is too much. I know she won't be attached to my side for every move I plan to make against Cataldi and Farina, but I need more time next to her before I'm willing to let her out of my sight.

Dialing Luca, he answers right away. I usually wouldn't make contact with him on the phone he uses when he's at the Cataldi estate, but this can't wait. "Hey. Hold on a second." I hear him tell someone he'll be right back and to not even think of leaving the house. "Okay, I'm back."

"Fun times babysitting?" He's been on guard duty for Carlo's little sister, Giada.

"You have no idea. She's being a pain in the ass for the simple sake of getting a rise out of me."

I chuckle, thinking of Alessia and me the first few weeks of our marriage. Shit, she still likes to get a rise out of me for the hell of it.

"Have you seen Carlo, or has his sister heard from him?"

"Haven't heard anything, and as far as I know, he hasn't been in touch with Giada. Why?"

"There was an attack on my house tonight. Alessia's bodyguard was shot, and it looks like they were there to try to take her."

"Fuck, man, is he okay?"

"It's still up in the air."

"It might be time to get out of here. Sounds like you need the help over there. He hasn't been home in weeks and his men haven't been around either. There's no one here who would know anything."

I think about that for a few moments. I haven't wanted Luca to join us for several reasons. He wanted revenge on Francesco, Carlo's father, and I wanted an inside man. What better way to kill two birds with one stone? He gets his pound of flesh, and I get the information I need to take down their organization. Unfortunately, since Francesco went to prison, Carlo has been MIA.

"Stay there a little longer. At least until we can figure out where Carlo has been hiding. He might decide to come home, and if he does, I want a shot at him."

"As long as Giada doesn't get caught in the cross fire, you can have whatever you want. She may be a pain in the ass, but she isn't part of this."

"Trying to protect the princess?" A smirk plays on my lips at Luca's protectiveness over his sworn enemy's daughter.

"Someone needs to. It certainly isn't going to be anyone here."

"Alright. Keep me updated."

We disconnect the call, and I look at my wife.

"Your inside man is Giada Cataldi's personal bodyguard?"

"He is now. Having him in the house gave us some useful information about their operation, but with Carlo on the run, it's been hard for him to stay there. He fucking hates those bastards."

"Why? Other than the fact that Carlo is a piece of shit, of course."

"Long story that goes back years. But they were responsible for the death of his parents."

She blows out a harsh breath. "They've been

responsible for ruining countless lives. Especially Carlo." She's referring to the sex trafficking ring Carlo set up under a lot of our noses. It was up and running for some time before I caught wind of it. Just one more reason to want the man put down.

"We're going to stop him, Alessia. Make no mistake. He isn't long for this world."

My wife nods and rests her head back on my shoulder.

My thoughts keep trailing back to what she said about possibly recognizing one of the men's voices. Carlo takes a sick satisfaction in inflicting pain. Makes me wonder if he was one of the masked men and wanted a front-row seat to them hurting my wife. But it doesn't make sense why he would still be hiding his identity. Unless he doesn't think we're on to him and Orlando working together yet. When Cillian heard from the stripper, she only mentioned Carlo. She didn't say anything about Orlando. Carlo has proven he likes flying under the radar until he tries to make some big move. Maybe he would have revealed himself if their plan had worked. What he fails to understand and what will eventually be his downfall, is we're smarter than he is. I kiss the top of my wife's head.

We have a lot more to lose, which makes men like me even more dangerous and ruthless, especially to those who try to take what's mine.

CHAPTER NINETEEN
ALESSIA

"HE MADE IT THROUGH surgery. The next few days will determine whether he survives or not," Dr. Simmons tells Finn and me about four hours after they took Enzo into the operating room.

The doctor doesn't have what I would call a great bedside manner, but he's used to dealing with patients who aren't fond of being coddled, at least when he gets a call from Finn. It doesn't bother me, though. I'd rather have the facts straight and to the point, especially because, so far, it's the outcome I've spent the last several hours praying for.

"I'll keep him here while he recovers. Does he have family you'd like to call?"

"He has a sister," I tell him, even though he's talking to Finn. The doctor is perfectly capable, but I'm the one with the information, not the man standing next to me. He's obviously old school and defers to the men in the room. "I'll call her. She's going to want to come visit him."

The doctor nods. "That's fine. I'll let the guard gate know."

Dr. Simmons lives in a vast gated community, not one of those cookie-cutter ones, either. Each house sits on about five acres, so you aren't in your neighbor's business like so many other subdivisions. Handy when you're performing illegal medical care from your home.

"I'm assuming she knows the protocol?" He raises the question to Finn. Again.

"Her brother has been working with my family for over ten years. She's well versed in the importance of keeping her mouth shut about what she may see or hear and the consequences if she doesn't," I inform him.

Finn looks at me with a small smirk ghosting his lips, and the doctor looks completely nonplussed by my answer.

"Very well. He should be ready for visitors within the hour."

"Thank you, doctor. I'd like to keep a couple guys rotating in and out. Just as an extra precaution," Finn informs him.

"That's fine. I'll give the gate their names as well when I call down."

Dr. Simmons turns and walks back into his surgical area, presumably to check on Enzo. I fall into Finn's side, emotionally and physically more exhausted than I can remember being in years. It's been nearly a decade since I allowed myself any sort of breakdown, but damn, does that sound good right about now. Being attacked in my own house, then to see Enzo shot and lying on the cold ground. The life was bleeding from his body while those men carelessly stepped over him like he was nothing more than a fallen obstacle in their way. It was too much. All the while, I watched from inside a secured room, hoping with everything in me that my bodyguard and friend wasn't dead.

"You need to rest," Finn says, interrupting my thoughts.

"I'll rest when I know Enzo's going to be okay. I need to call his sister. Shit, I don't have my phone."

Finn studies me like he wants to argue. Instead, he pulls his cell from his pocket and opens his contacts. "Enzo gave me his sister's contact information just in case...well, in case something like this happened and he couldn't call her himself."

"Thank you," I mutter and hit Emilia's contact.

"Hello?" she answers, sounding a little confused and nervous at receiving a call from an unknown number. When you're in the life we are, unknown numbers could mean so many different things, most of them bad.

"Hey, Emilia. It's Alessia."

"Hi. Is everything okay?" Her voice carries a weight of worry. Considering I'm calling at the break of dawn, it makes sense that she's scared I'm calling with bad news.

"There was an incident at my house, and Enzo was shot. He's just gotten out of surgery, but the doctor said the next few hours are critical. I thought you should know."

"Oh my God," she whispers. "Okay...okay." She takes what sounds like several deep breaths, trying to calm herself down. "I can call my sitter and have her come stay with the kids. What hospital are you at?"

"We're not at a hospital. My husband has a doctor outside of the city. That's where we are."

"No hospital? Alessia, are you sure—"

I cut her off before she can finish her thought. "Trust me, Emilia. He's in just as good of hands here as he would be at any hospital. I wouldn't have let them bring him here otherwise."

She takes a deep breath. "I know you wouldn't have," she says before a sob escapes her. There's a freedom in her vulnerability, a certain knowledge she has that someone will pick up her pieces. It's probably not even a thought or consideration. Enzo has always been that for her, and I suppose she thinks I can be the same. She's a strong woman, don't get me wrong. From everything Enzo has told me about her and the few times I've met her, she's hardly a demure wallflower who lets everyone make decisions for her. No, she's the opposite. But she does have the luxury of falling apart and it being okay for her. I don't have that, especially not with a virtual stranger.

"I'll have a car sent for you." It doesn't sound like she should be driving, and it's the least I can do since her brother was shot protecting me.

"Thank you, Alessia."

"Of course." It doesn't feel right to reply with *you're welcome* when I've delivered devastating news to her.

We hang up and Finn makes the call for Emilia's car.

Apparently, Enzo gave him all of her information.

"Do you want to go home and change?"

"No, I want to sit with him for a bit before his sister gets here. I don't want..." I trail off, feeling silly about where my thoughts are going.

"You don't want him to be alone," Finn finishes for me.

I stare at my husband for a few beats, amazed at the overwhelming feeling that washes through me. Before I have time to sift through the heady rush of emotion, his phone rings.

"Yeah," he answers. Gone is the caring husband; the mob boss has taken his place. "Thanks, Cillian. I'll call the families myself."

My husband disconnects the call and turns to me. "Cillian had everything at the house cleaned up. I'll be honest, Alessia, I don't want to leave you there now that they think they can get to you."

"Where do you want to go?"

"I'd feel better if you went to your parents—"

"Absolutely not," I cut in before he can finish that thought. "My place is with you, Finn. You aren't going to hide me away until this is settled. I won't show them that kind of weakness." How he could even consider it baffles me. If he wants it to look like I run scared every time there's a threat, then all his enemies for the rest of our short lives will come after me to get to him. I won't be used against him. "We're Monaghans. We don't run."

The smile that covers his face with my statement is blinding before he wraps an arm around my waist and kisses me soundly on the mouth.

"That's right, baby. We are." He lays another kiss on my mouth before dialing a number.

"Cillian, we're staying at the penthouse."

When Finn hangs up, he's still wearing his smile, pride shining in his eyes. "I need to make a few calls, but I'll be right outside Enzo's room. Why don't you wait with him, then, when his sister gets here, I'll take you into the city."

Taking my hand in his, he leads me to where Dr. Simmons keeps the patients. It looks like any room in a hospital, filled with medical equipment and monitors with the same disinfectant smell permeating the air.

Enzo is still pale, which is to be expected, and so still. If the monitor next to him wasn't beeping with every beat of his heart, I'd be worried. Finn kisses me before stepping out of the room to make his phone calls. I have a seat next to his ventilator and focus on the rhythmic whooshing noise to reassure me that he's alive and recovering.

"I'm going to make them pay for this, Enzo. I promise you. They aren't going to get away with hurting you."

He doesn't answer of course, but I need to say the words for him as much as I need to hear them myself. Orlando has taken too much from me as it is, and I refuse to let him live so he has the opportunity to hurt me or anyone I care about again.

With nothing else to do or say until Emilia gets here, I sit and allow the monotonous noises to lull me to sleep.

When I wake, my gaze meets Emilia in a chair on the other side of the bed.

"Hi." My voice is raspy and thick with sleep.

Emilia looks at me and gives me a soft smile. "Hi," she whispers. I'm at a loss of what to say to the woman whose brother almost lost his life protecting me.

"I'm so sorry for what happened, Emilia. I know how close you two are and the kids..." I let my words trail off because what's there to say, really? This isn't an uncommon position for someone in our life to be in.

"Enzo was well aware this could happen, Alessia. You have nothing to apologize for."

She's right; I don't. But that doesn't mean I still don't feel responsible.

She smiles at her brother and brushes his dark hair back from his forehead. "You know, he cares about you. He thinks of you as another sister. I used to be so jealous of you." She looks at me with wide eyes. "I'm sorry. I shouldn't have said that."

"Why not if it's your truth?" I shrug. I've never had issues with people being honest with me. It's when they smile to my face and lie behind my back that I have a problem with them. Enzo and Emilia are cut from the same cloth, so I have no doubt she's a straight shooter like her brother.

She waves her hand in front of her face. "I was just being a bratty younger sister. Here was this gorgeous girl taking my brother away all the time." She laughs and shakes her head. "For a while there, I thought you two would end up together. Like one of those romance books where the girl falls for her bodyguard who's always been by her side."

She sees the horrified look on my face and laughs even harder. "Yeah, that's the same look Enzo gave me when I told him my theory. He said he saw you as the less annoying sister." Her laughter cuts off and her eyes well with tears.

"I'm so sorry."

God, why do I keep saying that?

"I'm not, and neither would Enzo be if he was awake. He loves you, Alessia. And we all know my brother would gladly lay down his life for the people he cares about."

My own eyes fill with tears, but I feel foolish letting them fall in front of Emilia. Until tonight, I haven't cried in front of anyone since my brother died. What's the point? Tears wouldn't have brought him back, and they won't help Enzo now.

"I met your husband. Nice guy."

A scoff escapes me. "That's usually not the first impression he gives off."

"Enzo always had good things to say about him."

"Those two like to give me shit, so it makes sense."

"He said you were different with Finn." She shrugs. "I don't know, but he made it seem like you were happy. Said he thought there was finally someone in your life who understood what made you tick. Also, he said Finn was the only person he knew who could give you a run for your money on the mat. That's high praise from my brother."

I roll my eyes, but it's in good humor. Typical Italian man.

Finn peeks his head in the door and tilts it toward the hallway, silently asking if I'm ready to go. I nod and turn to Emilia, who is busying herself, fussing over the sheet covering her brother.

"I'll give you some time alone with him. If you need anything, call me or Finn. Again, Emilia, I'm so—"

"Please don't apologize again. All I need to know is whoever did this doesn't get away with it."

Standing from my chair, I walk to her and lay a hand on her shoulder. "This is one of many things I promise they'll pay for."

Finn and I pull up to a nondescript brick building. It's a large square structure in the more industrial part of the city. The other buildings surrounding it look like small, closed-down factories.

"I have to say, Finn. So far, I'm not impressed."

He turns to me with a smile. "Just wait."

Finn presses a button in his car, and a steel garage door opens. Driving into the underground parking, we're met with two guards holding semiautomatic rifles.

When he parks the car, he greets the guards and

heads to the elevator. After putting his hand on the scanner, the doors open, and we're carried to another floor. Finn steps out first and presses his hand to another scanner, which unlocks yet another door. The telltale sound of a lock disengaging fills the small hallway. If I was in a better headspace, I'd probably appreciate all the safety measures he has in place here. But as it is, I can barely keep my eyes open.

"You know, wife, there is a small matter of a marriage custom we overlooked."

My brow quirks as I stare at his knowing grin. "What's that?"

Instead of answering, he picks me up and holds me bridal style, carrying me through the doorway before his booted foot kicks the door shut.

"I never carried you over the threshold." Finn bends his neck and kisses me softly on the mouth.

"You decided the best place to do this was at your penthouse?"

"I plan on doing it at every home we own."

"Jesus. Marriage has made you sentimental. Or just plain mental, I'm not quite sure which."

He smirks and sets me on my feet. I spin around and take in the penthouse. It's an open floor plan with tall brick walls throughout. Stairs lead up to what looks like an open loft. Giant windows cover one wall, letting in a beautiful glow of natural light that reflects off the stainless steel appliances in the kitchen. This space screams Finn. There's only a small dining table with four chairs, and black leather couches along with a few club chairs make up the living area. There's no overpriced artwork on the walls, empty glass vases or anything equally useless. The function of the space is more important to him than having it overly decorated. The only thing that surprises me is the large television on one of the walls with a gaming console on the shelf next to it.

"I never took you for a gamer."

"Eoghan spends time here when I'm in the city. He owns another building not too far from here."

Finn walks to the giant window and tilts his head, indicating for me to follow. Standing shoulder to shoulder, he points to four of the surrounding buildings. "I own all of these. Those two"—he points to the left— "are apartments for some of my men. And those two"—he points to the right—"are where we store some of our inventory. They also double as apartments on the top two floors."

"So you basically own the entire block?"

He nods and walks over to a door laid into the brick wall. "Let me show you something else that I think you're going to like."

The door opens to what looks like another set of elevator doors and another fingerprint scanner.

"God, Finn, this place is like Fort Knox, with all the security features."

He presses his palm to the scanner and the narrow elevator doors open.

"This can only be accessed with a palm print." He grabs his phone from his pocket and dials a number. When whoever is on the other end answers, he tells them, "My wife needs access to all the scanners." He listens for a moment, then nods in my direction. "Press your hand here," he instructs.

When I do, nothing happens for a few moments, then a small light above the scanner turns green.

"Thanks," he says into the phone and slides it back into his pocket. "Me, you, Cillian and Eoghan are the only ones who can access this particular elevator, but your print has been uploaded into the system, so you have access to all my buildings."

We step inside, and the doors close, taking us a level lower than the garage. My head is spinning with the idea that my husband has some high-tech secret hideout that I now have access to. When the doors open again, we step out into a bright room filled with nearly a hundred different guns, all ranging in size. Make that a *heavily armed* secret hideout.

"Do you have a small armory in every house you own?"

"Pretty much. And I also have one of these." He opens another steel door into an underground shooting range. It's a bit more narrow than the one at his house, this one having only one lane for target practice.

"An armory and a gun range in every house. Are you building an army I don't know about? Did I marry someone with designs to take over the world?"

Finn laughs, and the sound echoes off what I'm guessing are soundproof walls. "No, you married the head of a criminal organization who makes a shit ton of their money in the gun trade. I like to test the shipments, and having a range here is more convenient. The one at the house is for practice. Well, there's also one in most of our safe houses, but that's more for fun for whoever is out there. It can get boring as hell."

I can't fault his logic there. There have been days when practicing at a range is what saves my sanity and helps me work through whatever problems are tumbling through my brain.

"This is quite the setup you have." I wander over to one of the walls with several pistols hanging up and loaded magazines lying on the shelf below.

I grab a 9mm and test the weight in my hand. "This one is my favorite." Memories of all the times Enzo would take me to the range for target practice filter through my mind. A chuckle escapes when I think of one of my first times at the range. "After Gio's death, I felt so damn helpless. I didn't know any sort of self-defense and I'd never held a gun. When I was healed from my injuries, I'd jump at every little thing. Even Enzo could see the constant state of fear I was living in. He and my father refused to let me escape into the shell of a person I was becoming." I put the 9mm back and pick up the 44 Magnum next to it. "My father decided if I was afraid of my own shadow, it was time I learned different ways of defending myself, so I'd never feel powerless again. Our first stop was a gun range. This was Enzo's favorite gun. I don't know, something about *Dirty Harry* and being the ultimate badass. He let me shoot a gun just like this and it nearly knocked me on my ass, but after a few more tries, I kind of got the hang of it. Then my father handed me a 9mm, and it was much easier for me to handle." I smile at the gun in my hand. "But this one was always Enzo's favorite."

I look down and find a bullet, taking it from the box.

"Do you have a knife?" I ask Finn.

He walks to a display case I hadn't noticed and takes out a short utility knife, handing it to me. I flip the blade open and lay the bullet on the shelf, carving an O on the side.

"I want the kill shot, Finn."

He looks from me to the gun, then back to me. "Taking a life isn't an easy thing, Alessia. It can change you, haunt you."

"Does it haunt you? Do you see the faces of the men whose deaths you've been responsible for?"

He looks me straight in the eye. "Each one deserved it, so no. I don't give them a second thought."

"Then why do you think I would? Orlando deserves this." I hold the bullet between us. "And I deserve to be the one to deliver it."

He's silent as he studies the hard resolution in my eyes. "Then you'll have it," he answers. "Anything you need, I'll stand next to you and make sure it's yours."

That feeling I'd had at the doctor's house returns

in full force. Finn doesn't attempt to shield me from anything that being a part of this life means. He knows I would never be okay with that. When I need to show the world the hardened woman who I have to be to survive in this life, he stands right next to me. When I need somewhere soft to land, he's right there next to me then, too. He doesn't want a wife he has to coddle; he wants a partner. This man loves my stubbornness, my determination, and my fire. If I need bloody vengeance, he'll make sure I have it because that's who Finn is. Anything I need or could possibly want, he would move heaven and hell to make sure I get it. He's broken through my walls brick by brick without me even realizing it. Now, standing in front of him, telling him I want to be the one to take the life of someone who's caused me and the people I love so much pain, someone who has taken so much from me, he doesn't blink an eye. If I want it, he'll make sure it happens. That's who I need by my side. He's who I've always needed.

"I love you," I blurt out. He doesn't say anything, instead staring at me with his mouth hanging open. "I know this was never about love, and maybe I'm emotional from the horrible fucking day I've had and seeing someone who's like a brother to me almost dying, or—"

"Alessia." Finn slides his warm palm around the side of my neck and cups my cheek. "Shut the hell up."

Chapter Twenty

Finn

"T HAT'S A FUCKING RUDE thing to say after someone tells you they love you, Finn," Alessia growls. "You know what? Never—"

Before she can finish her sentence, I slam my mouth to hers. My wife's lips part immediately for me. Not that she's ever one to deny me, even if she is in the middle of telling me off.

I pull away from her tempting lips and tilt my head toward the ceiling. "She finally admits it," I exclaim. Looking back into her deep-green eyes, I hold her stare as I rest my forehead against hers. "I love you, too." I pepper her face and mouth with little pecks, and she laughs.

"God, you're ridiculous."

But I don't stop. I'll never stop wanting my lips all over my wife, making her giggle, making her sigh, making her scream my name when I bring her body to heights of unimaginable pleasure. Every ruthless and bloody part of me is laid at her feet. Every piece that's wild and fierce matches the pieces of her she's never allowed anyone else to have.

"My heart, my loyalty, and my life are yours, Alessia. I'll burn down this entire fucking world if it means you're safe, and I'll kiss you in the ashes. You're mine, and I'll honor that until my dying breath."

"You're quite the poet, husband."

A smirk tilts my lips, matching the one she wears. "Well, I am Irish, after all."

The scrubs she's wearing hang loosely on her frame. We haven't showered, have barely eaten and probably need a good night's sleep. We're about to go to war, but the only thing I need in this moment is to slide into my wife's tight heat, to claim her and be claimed by her.

My hand trails under her baggy shirt and my finger finds the tie holding her pants around her waist. I grab one end and pull the knot loose.

"Here?" she asks with a breathless exhale.

"I can't wait another second."

Ripping the shirt over her head, I yank the lace covering her puckered nipples down and attach my mouth to the tight bud. Alessia's nails score through my short hair as she lets out a gasp of surprise. The scrub pants have fallen to the floor, but they're still around her ankles. I grab Alessia around the waist and set her on the counter, my cock hard and straining against the same type of shapeless pants she was wearing. When our lips collide, it's a frenzied kiss of lashing tongues and needy moans.

"I need you inside me, Finn," she says, bringing her hand to the tie on my pants and yanking the knot loose.

My pants fall to my ankles, and I grab my cock in one hand, moving her soaked panties to the side with the other.

"I swear I'll take my time with you later, wife."

Pushing in hard and fast, both of us let out loud groans of pleasure as I start fucking her on the shelf that holds ammunition for the guns behind her. A small box of bullets meant for a .22 falls from the shelf and spills across the floor, but we don't stop. We can't stop. The need for each other is too strong to care about the mess we're making all around us. I need to remind her she's alive and safe and here. Hell, I need the reminder just as much right now. It's been a horrible fucking day, and we're about to face more of the same, but here, in this moment, the only thing that matters is the all-consuming love I have for my wife. She's burrowed herself into every part of my being, and I'll be damned if she ever gets free from me.

My forehead presses to hers, and her eyes squeeze shut as the walls of her slick pussy flutter around my shaft, letting me know she's as close to release as I am.

"Open your eyes," I demand.

Her green gaze snaps to mine and the intensity I find there undoes me before I slam into her again, letting go. Her orgasm rips through her and she lets out a yell as she comes hard around me, digging her nails into the skin at my hips.

"Fuck," I bellow as all my senses are narrowed down to the singular feeling of coming inside Alessia. Nothing else exists here except me and her. There is no outside world, there is no war, or people we love being hurt. There's just us in the place we've carved for ourselves and the soul-deep love and respect we've found in each other.

My gaze never breaks from hers as my movements slow before stilling inside of her.

"That was…" She exhales, trying to catch her breath.

"That was us." I kiss her swollen lips again. When I pull away, she looks ready to fall asleep where she's sitting on the counter. I may be a selfish asshole for needing to bury myself in her body, but if the events of the last twenty-four hours have proven anything, it's that our lives could turn into tragedy on a dime. I, for one, am a firm believer in grabbing on to the good every chance I get. And my wife is everything good and right in our fucked-up world.

"Let's go upstairs." My lips brush against her sweaty forehead.

Alessia grunts as I set her down on shaky legs before I pull her pants back up, tying the knot again.

I find her shirt and slide it back on her, unfortunately covering all the delicious skin I need to spend the next several hours running my hands over. When she lets out a loud yawn, I have the distinct feeling my plans are going to have to wait.

"Sorry," she says as I pull my own pants back into place.

"Why? You've had a hell of a day. Let's take a shower

and get some sleep."

"There's so much to do, Finn. We need to—"

"Alessia," I say, my hands cupping her cheeks and staring into her exhausted eyes. "You need rest."

She narrows her eyes, and I know what she's going to say before the words leave her mouth. "Don't tell me what I need, husband."

It's nice to hear how well I know the fierce woman standing in front of me.

"Okay, then how about I tell you what I need? I need a shower, then I need to fall asleep with you in my arms, reminding me that you're safe and sound after almost being taken from me. I need to rest because in a few hours, my phone is going to ring and I'm going to have to leave to fulfill the promise I made to you. Until then, the only thing I want is to lie next to you and feel your heartbeat against me while I thank God for the millionth time that it's still beating."

Her eyes soften, and she lets out a long sigh, nodding in understanding. "Okay," she relents in a soft voice.

I take her hand and lead her to the elevator to take us back upstairs. The penthouse is cast in a warm glow from the setting sun outside. Her hand stays firmly locked in mine as we walk up the stairs to my loft bedroom and straight to the bathroom. After turning on the water for the shower, I strip her out of the scrubs.

"I'm burning these damn things," I gripe, ridding my body of the scratchy cotton material.

Alessia hums in agreement.

We step into the large shower covered in black-and-white subway tiles, and I position her under the spray, letting the water soak her from head to toe. Grabbing my shampoo, I work it into a lather and begin massaging her scalp and running it through her long, dark strands. She tilts her head back to rinse, and I quickly wash my own hair, switching positions with her so I can rinse away the shampoo. Her hands run over my entire body with soap, cleaning the day from me, then I do the same for her. Usually, my hands all over my wife or hers on me would lead to me being buried in her again. This isn't about sex, though. It's about finding comfort in her touch and me trying to give her the same. It's showing her I love her with light kisses and soft touches. After rinsing my body under the hot spray, I face Alessia again and see tears in her red eyes.

"Oh, sweetheart," I whisper, my heart breaking for the pain she's in.

My arms wrap around her while sobs rack her body. The day is catching up to her, and she's finally breaking. Alessia never shows the world this side of her. Her body shakes as she lets it all go and falls apart, trusting I'll catch every piece of her. And I will, without question or hesitation, I'll be the one standing next to her, helping her put herself back together, because I know how strong she is, and I know she can. I'll give her everything she needs. If what she needs right now is someone to hold her and try to carry some of the burden, then that's what I'll be for her.

When her shaking stops, she backs up and looks me in the eye. "Sorry," she whispers while I wipe the salty tears from her wet face.

Cupping her cheeks in my hands, I meet her gaze with a stern look. "Don't ever apologize to me for needing to let it out, wife. I'm your husband and the one person in this world you should always trust to hold you and take care of you."

"Thank you," she replies, her red eyes tired as her lips tip up in a ghost of a smile.

"And don't thank me either. I love you. I don't need thanks for doing exactly what someone who loves you should."

She moves both of her hands to cover mine. "I've never had that before. I...I never expected to find this with anyone, especially you."

"Ouch." I chuckle, and Alessia groans.

"Shit, that's not what I meant." Her hands drop and she wraps her arms around my middle, laying her forehead against my chest. "Fair warning, I'm really bad at showing emotion. Unless it's anger. That one comes naturally."

"I've noticed."

A sharp laugh bursts from her, making me smile.

She lifts her head from my chest and meets my eyes. "What I'm trying to say is I never expected to trust someone with my heart. Especially not the brash head of a rival criminal organization."

"We didn't exactly start on the right foot, I'll give you

that. But trust me when I tell you, there isn't another man on this earth who is going to protect your heart as ferociously as I will."

Alessia studies me for a moment then smiles. "I believe that."

Her green eyes shine bright with trust and the belief that no matter what, she has me to lean on for the rest of our lives. Fuck, I really love that look.

Turning off the water, we step out of the shower, and I wrap Alessia in a giant towel before heading to my room to find her something to put on. Pulling an old gray T-shirt from my drawer, I hand it to her, and she drops the towel, sliding the material over her skin. It's everything I can do to not suggest she lose the shirt, and we finish what we started in the basement. In all our time together, the one thing Alessia and I never did was make love. I want that so badly right now, but this night isn't about what I want. It's about what she needs, and the dark circles under her eyes are telling me that it's sleep.

She climbs into the king-size bed under the midnight-blue comforter as I find some sleep pants and pull them on.

"This is the first time we've slept in clothes," she comments, exhaustion in her voice.

"I know. I mean, you can sleep naked if you want, but I can't promise I won't be buried inside of you when you wake up."

Rolling her eyes, she turns onto her side, facing me as

I lie down next to her. I open my arms, and she wiggles to the middle of the bed, settling on my chest so I can hold her.

"Thank you for giving me what I need tonight."

"I already told you, you never have to thank me. I'll give you everything."

I feel her smile against my chest. "I love you," she whispers.

"I love you too, wife."

Fuck, I like the sound of that.

The phone vibrating on my nightstand wakes me from a restless sleep.

"Hello?" I keep my voice soft so I don't wake Alessia, who is still tucked into my side.

"We found Orlando," Cillian says into the phone. "He's got a girl in Springfield. One of our guys has been watching her place since yesterday after the shooting, and he just saw him run inside her building."

"Is Cataldi with him?"

Fuck, it would be nice to kill two birds with one stone.

"He didn't see Carlo. Do you want to hold off until they're together? I could keep Sean on him and see if he leads us to him."

Now that we know those two are working together, they're bound to meet up at some point. I could wait it out and get them at the same time, but who knows when that will happen? I look at my sleeping wife and imagine the fear she must have felt when she saw his face on that camera, knowing he was only a few inches from her as her bodyguard lay in a pool of his own blood. I'm not willing to ever give him the chance to get that close to her again. It may drive Cataldi further underground, but knowing him, he won't stay there for long. Orlando is my priority, and his life ends tonight.

"I want him tonight," I tell my lieutenant.

"I'll get everything together. Who do you want?"

"You and Eoghan."

"I'll make the call. We'll meet you at the penthouse."

We hang up and I know my brother will be fucking thrilled to take care of this with me. Even though he's happy running the bars and the fights, when it comes to shit like this, he's always ready to go. And there's no one else I trust to have my back more than Eoghan and Cillian.

Rising from the bed, my gaze sweeps over Alessia's sleeping face. I fucking hate to leave her, but this can't wait. She's safer here than anywhere else in the city, but that doesn't make me any less nervous. Last time I went after one of our enemies, they almost got to her. I can't allow myself to think about the what-ifs, or I'll barricade us both in this penthouse and never leave. There's no room for that kind of fear in this life. It's stand up and fight or roll over and die, and I've never been the type to back down. But I'd be lying if it didn't feel different leaving my wife this time. Unfortunately for that piece-of-shit Orlando, I don't let my fear dictate my actions, and I'll be damned if he gets away with the terror he's caused her.

Walking to my dresser, I pull out some clothes and put on a pair of jeans and a long-sleeved T-shirt before grabbing my boots and heading down the stairs.

There's just one call I want to make before waking Alessia to tell her what's going on.

"Yeah?" Ozzy answers sleepily. I hear a feminine voice in the background asking who's on the phone. "It's Finn. Go back to sleep, pretty girl," he answers before the sounds of him getting out of bed come through the line.

"What's up?" he asks.

"Some shit went down with my wife tonight."

"She okay?"

"Yeah, but her bodyguard took a couple shots. We're going after the motherfucker now."

"You need backup?"

"No, but I appreciate the offer. It's Orlando Farina. He's been working with Carlo."

A hiss sounds through the phone. "We knew someone must have been helping him."

"We think Farina has been helping him hide out. Carlo has been spotted a few times around Boston, but we never get there in time. They attacked my house and tried to take Alessia. I'm pretty sure Carlo was one of the men there."

"Makes sense. Carlo enjoys having a front-row seat.

Your wife didn't get a good look?"

"No, they were wearing masks, but she thinks she recognized his voice."

"What do you need from me?"

"I want these assholes in the ground, Ozzy. If anything goes south tonight, I want to make sure you put them there."

"That's no way to walk into that kind of situation, Finn."

"I don't foresee this going any way other than what I have planned, but if it does, I need to know that you'll take care of Cataldi and keep Alessia safe. I'm sending you a file with everything we have on Farina and Cataldi. I just want your assurance that if I can't finish the job, you will."

"You don't need to ask."

It's not that I don't trust Amatto to take care of his daughter, but Mafia politics have already tied his hands once. Ozzy and the Black Roses have no such ties, and I trust him to do what needs to be done to end this if I can't.

"Thank you. I'll keep you updated."

"It changes when you have someone who carries your heart in their body, doesn't it?"

"It sure as fuck does."

"Some men, like Cataldi, think it can make you weak. Like it's a power they can hold over you. But he's wrong. It makes you stronger and that much more vicious. That's what stupid fucks like him and Farina will never understand. The second they threaten what you love, it wakes a beast inside of you that will only rest with ending their life. Money and power are all well and good, but once you find the other half of your soul, you'll do anything to keep her safe. They'll never understand, and that's what will be their downfall."

"You sure you're not Irish? That's very poetic."

Ozzy lets out a small chuckle. "Nah. I'm just lucky enough to have found my other half, like you. Keep me posted, and if you need help, the offer stands."

I thank him again and hang up, letting his words tumble around my head. Loving Alessia and being loved by her is like finding the other half of my soul I hadn't even realized was missing.

And tonight, I'm going to prove that no one threatens that and walks away with their life.

CHAPTER TWENTY-ONE
FINN

E OGHAN AND CILLIAN GOT to the penthouse about thirty minutes ago. One of the perks of living here is the vast armory downstairs. We've loaded up everything in bags that we may need. I don't necessarily expect this to be more than an extraction, considering he's at his girlfriend's apartment, but you can never be underprepared.

The Kevlar vest fits snuggly under my black button-down and my holsters are loaded with my trusty 9mm, ready to go.

Sitting on the edge of the bed, I watch my wife sleep. It's not a peaceful slumber. Her brows are tight, and her body twitches every few minutes. I've been next to her longer than I should be, but I can't seem to tear myself away. Looking at my watch, I realize we should have left fifteen minutes ago. It's now or never. I don't want to wake her, knowing she's going to hate the fact I'm leaving to hunt down the man who tormented her, but if I don't tell her, there will most definitely be hell to pay when I come home.

And I refuse to believe I won't be walking through

those doors again soon.

"Alessia," I say softly, brushing the back of my hand over her cheek. "Baby, wake up."

Her eyelids flutter open, and for an all too brief moment, I'm completely hypnotized by her soft green eyes and the sweet smile playing on her lips. When she realizes I'm dressed, worry seeps into her gaze.

"Where are you going?" she asks, her voice thick from sleep and the tears she shed last night.

"We know where Orlando is. I'm going after him."

No use sugarcoating it.

My wife blows out a deep breath and sits up. "What do you want me to do?"

"Nothing," I reply, shaking my head. "The guards in the building are heavily armed, and I have men watching the cameras on the surrounding streets. No one will get within four blocks of the building without them knowing about it."

The idea of leaving her still doesn't sit right with me, but unless we were followed here, which I made damn sure we weren't, no one knows she's here. Hell, no one outside of our organization knows the setup we have here. But there's always that tiny chance, and when it comes to her safety, I hate not having eyes on her at all times.

"If the power is cut like it was at the house, the doors will automatically lock you inside. You'll still have power in the penthouse and the elevator to the armory. If anything seems even slightly off, go down there and lock yourself in. It's the same type of setup as what's at home. I'll be notified immediately."

"Are you worried someone will get in again?"

"No, but I didn't think anyone would be ballsy enough to try anything at the house, either. This place is set up as a fortress, with several safeguards in place. If I have to leave you alone, this is the one place I feel best about you staying at."

"Why does this feel different?" Alessia asks.

That's the question I was asking myself as I sat here watching her sleep. There was only one answer I could come up with.

"Because you finally admitted you love me and can't live without me." My mouth tips up in a smirk, and Alessia rolls her eyes.

She shakes her head and lets out a small huff of laughter. "I could certainly live without your cockiness."

"Nah, it's one of my many charms."

She looks me in the eye, all mirth wiped from her face. "Do me a favor and bring all those charms back to me in one piece, yeah?"

Cupping her face in my palm, I bend my forehead down and touch it to hers. "I love you, Alessia. Nothing is going to stop me from coming home to you." I grab the bullet with the O carved into it that I picked up from the shelf when Eoghan, Cillian, and I were preparing to leave and hold it in front of her. "I'll be back for you and this bullet in no time, wife. Then you can end that miserable piece of shit's existence, and I can bring you back here and do all the things to your body that I dreamed about last night."

"Ever the romantic." She chuckles and takes the bullet from me, staring at it for a few moments. When she meets my gaze again, her eyes are hard and resolute. "I love you, Finn. I'll see you when you get home."

My lips crash to hers, but before the kiss can get carried away, I pull my mouth from hers and stand from the bed.

"See you in a few hours." I nod and turn to walk down the stairs, meeting Cillian and Eoghan at the front door.

"Let's go."

The drive to Springfield takes us a little over an hour. Thankfully, the roads are clear as we pull up in front of the apartment building just as the dawn breaks. The entire block is quiet; everyone surely still sleeping at this early hour.

Cillian spots Sean, who's been keeping an eye on the place to make sure Orlando doesn't sneak away. He nods at Cillian, then at the apartment, indicating he's still inside. Cillian sends him a quick text telling him to stay put just in case we need someone on the street. Eoghan and Cillian refuse to let me go in there alone without knowing who else could be inside. I personally don't give a fuck. Anyone who tries to stop me from getting to that asshole is going to be met with a bullet between the eyes, no questions asked.

When Eoghan parks the nondescript sedan on the side of the tree-lined street, we all check our weapons. The three of us are going in armed to the teeth with various pistols and knives strapped to our bodies. There's even a syringe in my pocket filled with a little night-night concoction so we can get him out of there as quietly as possible. I'm going to do everything in my power to take him alive so I can fulfill my promise to my wife, but if shit goes sideways, I won't be too broken up about killing the man myself.

There's no doorman or lobby for the building, and Eoghan makes quick work of the lock so we can enter the building without having to ring an apartment. For some reason, it doesn't surprise me that Orlando wouldn't have put the girl up in a nicer place. He's a cheap son of a bitch with an ego the size of Texas. He probably thinks he's untouchable in his own territory, and until tonight, that was most likely true. Though, I am surprised he isn't hiding somewhere with a few more safety protocols in place. From what Alessia has told me about him, he likes to hit the bottle and has a nasty little drug habit to go along with his alcoholism. It's doubtful he's in his right mind, especially if he was celebrating getting what he thought was the upper hand by attacking my home.

We silently make our way to the second floor of the building.

Eoghan tries the handle before opening the door, but it's locked. "Worth a shot." He whispers. "You'd be surprised how often you can avoid picking a lock because the door's unlocked." He leans down and quickly disables it using his considerable skill. As far as I know, he doesn't go around breaking into people's houses, so Lord only knows why he decided to learn this. That's Eoghan, though. He decides to pick up a new skill and has to master it.

When he steps back from the door, we all draw our weapons. Eoghan opens the door and waits a beat before entering.

The apartment is dark. Nothing is in the living room except several empty beer bottles and a tall vodka bottle knocked on its side. And wouldn't you know, I spy a pill bottle with several crushed tablets on the table. Looks like someone was on a mission to get fucked up last night.

A short hallway leads to two doors. The first is a bathroom, and the second door sits ajar. I peer in and see two figures sleeping soundly on the bed. We enter the room, and neither person stirs. When I get to Orlando's side of the bed, I raise my gun with the silencer attached to the barrel and point it at his head. Cillian has his gun trained on his girlfriend. Neither of us relishes the idea of hurting a woman, but if she tries to draw on us...I'm just hoping it doesn't come to that.

I press the muzzle to Orlando's forehead, and his eyes open with a start. His body jerks, which wakes the sleeping woman next to him. When she opens her mouth to scream, Cillian clamps his palm over it and lays the muzzle of the gun on her temple. "Don't make me use this."

Of course, we both know he wouldn't, but she doesn't.

"What the fuck?" Orlando hisses. "She has nothing to do with anything. Don't hurt her."

Interesting. He's worried about her safety.

"Get up slowly and keep your hands in the air. We're walking out quietly. I don't want to have to carry you." I inch back but keep my gun trained on Orlando's head. He stands to his full height in nothing but a pair of boxers.

"Can I get my pants?" he asks, pointing to the denim that's strewn over a chair in the corner.

I grab them and check the pockets for weapons before tossing them in his direction. "Get dressed."

He slides the pants on and just as he finishes buttoning them, he darts for the bedroom door. Eoghan steps in his path before he can cross the threshold and smashes his gun over Orlando's skull, knocking him out cold.

"Goddammit, now we have to carry him," I mumble, taking the syringe from my pocket and jabbing it in his neck.

Eoghan shoots me a questioning look.

"I don't need the fucker waking up halfway to the car and screaming his head off," I say, plunging the contents into his bloodstream. "This should keep him quiet for the ride."

I look over to the woman shaking on the bed and notice the bruising around her neck and wrists as she clings to the sheet, tears streaming down her face.

"He do that to you?" I ask, pointing at the discoloration.

She nods. "I hope you kill him," she chokes out, staring at the unconscious man on the floor.

My gaze travels to Cillian, then Eoghan, both of them looking a little uncomfortable while Cillian still holds the gun to the woman's head.

I look back at the woman. "I have a proposition for you."

We make it back to my building after lugging the big Italian down a flight of stairs, followed closely by Cillian and Sandra, Orlando's girlfriend. Or would she be considered his ex-girlfriend? I feel like her telling us that she hopes we kill the man sharing her bed is a surefire sign the relationship is over.

Cillian pulls the car into the underground parking garage of my building. Eoghan helps Sandra from the car, and she stands back while I open the trunk. Orlando is alive but still unconscious in the trunk. Two of my guards help lift him out and carry him to the elevator to take him to a room on the same level as the armory. There's a small room I had built specifically for instances when we need to get information out of someone and to make cleanup from our "questioning" easier.

"I'm going upstairs for a minute," I tell the group. "I'll meet you down there."

I take the elevator to my penthouse and open the door. Alessia is sitting on the couch waiting for me, the 44 Magnum sitting next to her. I know there's one bullet in that gun, and I know exactly who it's going to be used to kill.

She jumps from the couch and rushes me, throwing her arms around my neck.

"Thank fuck," she breathes, and I lift her from the floor, slanting my mouth over hers.

When I set her on her feet, she smacks me in the arm.

"What the hell was that for?" I ask, rubbing the stinging spot.

"You need to work on your communication skills, Finn. I've been worried sick over here, not knowing if everything went okay or if you were on your way back. You should have called."

"I'm sorry, wife. Next time, I'll call you when I'm on my way home from a B and E with a side of kidnapping." My mouth kicks up in a small grin while Alessia continues to scowl in my direction.

"Thank you." She looks around me but doesn't see anyone else.

"Where is he?"

"I have him in the basement."

"And the girl he was with?" Alessia knew I was headed to her place to track Orlando down.

"Seems he doesn't treat his present girlfriends better than his past ones. I made a deal with her to help her get out of Springfield and set her up somewhere far away if she helps us."

"Let's go, then." Alessia makes a move to the other elevator that goes straight to the basement, but I stop her with a gentle tug at her arm.

"I'm not sure I want you down there yet. I don't know what it's going to take to get the information I need."

Alessia shoots me a questioning look, like she doesn't understand why that should stop her.

I pull her into my arms and kiss the crown of her head. "The entire ride here, it was all I could do not to pull over and end his sorry existence. You've never seen the man I am when someone hurts you."

The other two times when I had to educate the stupid fucks who thought they could touch her, I was unhinged but in control. This man not only beat her several times over but caused her to lose a pregnancy. He killed her brother, nearly killed her friend, and tried to take her from me. I don't think there's going to be much control maintained once I get in the room with him.

Alessia runs her hands up my chest, over my neck and cups my cheeks in both of her small palms. "If you're afraid I'm going to see the man you'll become down there, get that thought out of your head this instant. I love you, Finn. It doesn't matter if you're an unhinged psychopath or the loving husband who dotes on me. You belong to me, and I belong to you. Nothing changes that. You may not like who you have to be when you walk into that room, but you're still going to be mine when you walk out."

I blow out a breath, my arms still wrapped around her body. "That's the problem. I'm going to enjoy every second of pain I inflict on him. I'm fucking happy he's not going to live to see another day."

"So am I." She places a small kiss on the corner of my mouth. "And that's what makes us perfect for each other."

CHAPTER TWENTY-TWO
ALESSIA

F INN AND I STEP inside the elevator that leads down to the armory and shooting range. Considering neither of those combined took up the entire space of the subterranean level, I'm assuming that's where he keeps a room for "questioning," otherwise known as a kill room. It's not uncommon for men in Finn's position to have one, but based on the way he was hesitant for me to see the person he becomes when he's making use of such a place, he didn't want me to know about this one.

I don't fault him for wanting to keep that part of himself hidden, but I think he's finally coming to understand his brutal and violent side doesn't scare me. He has one, sure, but it's not directed at me, and I have every faith in my husband that it never will be. That's what makes him different from so many other men in this life. He doesn't get drunk on power or surround himself with yes-men. He uses his power to protect his family and make his organization stronger, not out of fear of retribution but out of respect. And he returns that respect to the people that deserve it. So no, I'll never fear him because I know his heart and his mind. This is a cutthroat world, but Finn refuses to let that change who he is at the core. He's a good man who does violent things to protect his people. And I love him more for it.

When we enter the armory, there's a door flush with the wall I hadn't noticed when I was down here in my exhausted stupor. Finn places his hand on yet another scanner and I hear the locks disengage. He pushes the door open, and we enter a small, dark room. There's a woman sitting in a metal folding chair and Eoghan is standing next to her. The door closes and locks again. I look to my left and see the man responsible for so many of my nightmares through a two-way mirror. The room that Orlando is tied up in is brightly lit and exactly the type of room I imagined. Smooth tile lines the walls with a concrete floor and a drain in the center. Perfect setup for easy cleanup.

"Hi, I'm Sandra," the woman sitting in the room says, extending her shaky hand.

I clasp her hand in a firm shake and notice the bruising on her neck and wrist. "Alessia Monaghan."

"I figured. He was furious when he found out you'd married the head of the Monaghan family." She tilts her head to Orlando in the other room but doesn't look in that direction.

"I'm sure he was." I sit next to her in an empty chair. It's not in my nature to comfort a stranger, but my heart goes out to the woman who, by the looks of it, hasn't known a kind touch in a long time. I was in her position, too, and remember all too clearly being afraid of everything and everyone. "You don't have to be scared. He won't hurt you again." My voice is soft, trying to reassure her.

"I just want this to be over," she says, rubbing her hands up and down her thin arms.

"You and me both," I reply.

"I tried to leave him, you know? But he found me and brought me back. Said as soon as his old man died, he was going to make me his wife. Said he loved me and wanted to have a family with me. But then he would do this if he caught another man looking at me." She waves to the faint bruises on her neck. "Why would someone who says they love you hurt you like this?"

"He doesn't know what love is. He only understands power and trying to possess another human being. That's not love." Now that I know the difference, there's no mistaking it. Hopefully, Sandra finds someone who can show her what she obviously craves, what the man in the other room will never be capable of.

Finn walks over to me and bends at the waist, kissing me softly on the lips. "I love you," he whispers sweetly, as though he's reminding me of that fact.

"I love you, too."

He holds my gaze then nods, standing to his full height. Finn takes three purposeful steps to the door to the other room and swings it open. As soon as he enters, gone is the sweet and gentle husband he was a few moments ago and in his place is the head of a criminal empire.

"Orlando, you're finally awake," he says, walking up to the dazed man and slapping him in the face a couple times.

"Fuck you," Orlando spits, jerking his face away from Finn's hand. "Where am I?"

"Well, I'd tell you, but then I'd have to kill you." Finn snaps his fingers and smiles. "Oh wait, that's going to happen regardless of what I tell you." He chuckles at his own joke.

I roll my eyes. Is this some sort of comedy hour? Jesus.

"But what you tell me will determine how you die. I can make it fast, or I can make it slow and incredibly painful. You decide."

"I'm not telling you shit."

Finn chuckles darkly. "That's what they all say." He turns and grabs a pair of pliers from the tool chest sitting on the folding table in the room. "In the beginning, at least." He walks behind Orlando and grabs him by his sweat-drenched hair, wrenching his head back. "Where's Carlo?"

"Fuck you," Orlando spits.

"Wrong answer." The grin on Finn's face should chill me to the bone, but it has the opposite effect.

He releases Orlando's hair and grabs one of his hands tied behind his back. I can't see what exactly he's doing, but Orlando screams and seconds later, Finn holds a bloody nail in front of the panting man's face.

"Hurts like a bitch, doesn't it?"

Finn gets to work on another fingernail and Orlando screams again. He does this a few more times, and a small pool of blood begins to collect on the floor below the hand that Finn has ripped every nail from.

"Had a change of heart yet?" Finn asks as he walks back over to the table and sets the pliers down.

Orlando lets out a sardonic laugh and that sends chills up my spine. I remember that sound all too well.

"Is that all you got? Fucking pussy," Orlando says with a sneer. "Hey, I meant to ask. Is Alessia's pussy still tight as a drum? Does she still enjoy that thing when you—"

Finn's head snaps up and I catch the look of feral rage in his eyes before he spins to Orlando and begins punching him in the face with his powerful fist over and over. "You. Will. Keep. Her name. Out. Of. Your mouth." Every word is punctuated with a punch, along with a spray of blood from Orlando's face.

My husband stops and Orlando's head is limp, his chin falling against his chest.

Cillian walks over and waves a tube of smelling salts under that asshole's nose. He jerks awake and glares at Cillian.

"You're all dead when my father finds out what you did," Orlando sneers, spitting out a mouthful of blood.

This causes a bark of laughter to burst from Finn. "You think I'm afraid of your father? All this time, you've been hiding behind an old man, thinking he was going to save you. No one's coming to save you, asshole. And no one is going to avenge your death. The Cataldis and Farinas are as good as dead. Your old man can't do shit to me."

Finn grabs a large metal bowl that's welded to a stand with wheels and rolls it over next to Orlando. He then takes one of Orlando's hands from behind his back and secures it to the side of the bowl with a metal cuff.

"I know all about what you did to my wife. How you hurt her with these hands." He walks to the table and puts on a pair of industrial rubber gloves then picks up a bottle without a label. Orlando watches him with fear in his eyes, and the gratification I feel from seeing that look on his face should scare me, but it doesn't. Whatever Finn is about to do to him is going to hurt more than I can imagine, and I'm glad for it. I want to see him hurt and scared for all the times he had me in the same position.

When Finn reaches the bowl with Orlando's hand secured to the side, he pours the liquid over his flesh and Orlando lets out an almost inhuman scream. I watch as his flesh bubbles and starts to melt as Orlando tries to thrash, but between Cillian holding his arm and him being strapped tightly to a chair, his movements do little.

"You know," Finn starts as he stops pouring the acid over Orlando's hand. "It wasn't just you that we took from your girlfriend's apartment."

I'm not sure Orlando can hear him through the agony he must be feeling right now, but Finn continues. "You know how badly I can make someone hurt, Orlando."

He nods his head toward the mirror and Sandra stands.

"Remember what we talked about," Eoghan tells her.

Sandra nods, and Eoghan opens the door, grabs her by the arm, and shoves her into the room with a gun pointed at her head. My first instinct is to get up and yell at them to let her go, that she's a victim in this, same as I was. But then I look into my husband's eyes. He's staring into the mirror, and even though I know he can't see me, it's as though he's looking right at me, begging me to trust him. I take a deep breath and Finn turns toward Orlando.

"I want to know where Carlo is. For every minute you don't give me an answer, I'm going to remove a body part from your girlfriend. Could be a nail, could be a finger, could be her entire hand."

Orlando looks at Sandra, then Finn, but he refuses to say anything.

Finn looks at Cillian. "Get the pliers."

Sandra lets out a bloodcurdling scream and fights in Eoghan's hold.

"If you don't give me what I want, Orlando, we won't stop with your little girlfriend. I'll send my men to your house and take your little sister. Maybe let them have some fun with her before I do to her what I'm more than happy to do to Sandra. You know, just to show you the pain I can put someone through before their body gives up." Finn's voice is colder than I've ever heard, and I have to keep telling myself that this is a show to get Orlando to talk because fuck, my husband is convincing.

Orlando's pained breathing is heavy as he watches Cillian walk over to the table. When he turns with the pliers in his hand, Orlando breaks.

"Stop! Stop!" Orlando yells. "Fuck. I'll tell you what I know. She doesn't have any part in this."

"Tell me!" Finn hollers.

"Okay. Fuck. Okay. He's trying to partner with the Russians. He had it all set up before his dad went to prison, but he fucked up when he went after the Black Roses and the prosecutor. The Russians didn't want that shit hanging over them. He's been trying to sweeten the deal and even offered his sister to the pakhan's son. I don't know. He's been in New York at one of their safe houses. He said if I could help him take you out and drum up support from his father's capos and mine, he would make sure I have a seat at the table. They want Boston and the rest of Massachusetts, and they want you out of the way."

"Do you know exactly where he is?"

"No, I swear I don't. He wouldn't tell me. He knows the Russians' goodwill is only going to last for so long before they turn their back on him. He could be anywhere by now." Orlando looks at his girlfriend then back to Finn. "Please let her go. She can't do anything to you."

Finn nods at Sandra, who, up until now, has been whimpering and crying while Eoghan keeps a strong hold on her. Eoghan drops his hand and Sandra straightens, wiping the tears from her eyes. She gives Orlando a hard stare and walks closer to him.

"Fuck you," she says and spits in his face. "I only hope they make you suffer more before you burn in hell." She turns on her heels, and Eoghan opens the door to the room I'm waiting in before she stomps away from Orlando.

I stand from my seat, looking at the woman in awe. "Damn, you're one hell of an actress," I tell her.

"Oh my God," she says, breathing heavily. "That felt so good." Her hand rests on her chest as she sits in a chair. I watch her for a few moments, expecting...I don't know, a breakdown of some sort. She's been sitting in here watching a man being tortured, after all. Instead, her head tilts toward the ceiling as she takes a deep breath and closes her eyes with a serene smile playing on her lips. My God, what did he put her through?

"Come on, sis. Finn is ready for you." Eoghan is waiting on the threshold to the other room.

I turn to the door and take a breath, stepping through into the bright room. Orlando spots me but doesn't say anything, looking defeated where he sits. It's odd seeing him like that. All the bravado and self-confidence he possessed is now washed away. All that's left is a sniveling, powerless man tied to a chair who's about to die. I once loved him. Once thought I'd marry him, but he took that love and devotion and twisted it into something painful. Now, the only thing I want is to wipe his existence from this planet.

"Alessia," Finn calls.

I walk to meet him as he stands in front of the table, the gun he took from me sitting right there.

"You don't have to do this. I'd be more than happy to kill him for you," he says softly.

I look my husband dead in the eye. "His death is mine."

Finn nods and hands me the gun. He turns and faces Orlando, who is barely conscious at this point and stands with his legs spread and his arms crossed over his chest. Cillian and Eoghan mirror his stance, simply waiting in silent support for me to finish it.

Walking up to Orlando with the gun in my hand, I stand still for a few moments and study him. There are so many things I could say. I could tell him all the ways he hurt me, all the ways he nearly destroyed me before taking my brother's life and nearly ending Enzo's. But what would be the point? It's not as though he would care. Monsters don't care about the people they hurt. They only want to devour and destroy.

"I bet you never thought we'd be here, did you, Orlando?"

When his eyes meet mine, there's no regret in them. Only anger because he knows this is the end and there's not a damn thing he can do about it.

"Bet this really pisses you off. You couldn't destroy me, and now you're going to your death knowing no one will mourn you. You failed. You're a weak piece of shit, and now you'll die powerless in your own snot and tears. So, fuck you, Orlando." I raise the gun. "This is for Gio and Enzo." I pull the trigger, and brain matter splatters behind him, the bullet exploding the back of his skull.

Everyone in the room is silent. I stare at his lifeless body. I don't know what I expected to feel after taking a man's life, but it wasn't the relief coursing through me. Finn is the first to move, coming to stand next to me. He takes the gun from my grip and puts his arm around my waist. "Come on, wife. Let's go upstairs."

I nod and allow him to lead me through the room where Sandra is smiling at me and back to the elevator to take us to the penthouse.

When we get upstairs, Finn walks to the kitchen and pours a glass of whiskey before handing it to me. I've come to appreciate his taste in alcohol during our time together. I sip from the glass and let the rich, smoky vanilla notes roll over my tongue before swallowing.

My husband lays the gun on the counter and looks at me. "You okay?"

I consider his question. For all intents and purposes, I should be anything but. I just took a man's life and feel zero remorse. Just the opposite, actually. Then I remember what he did to me, the fact he killed my brother and nearly killed one of my oldest friends. He was going to take me and do God knows what to get to my husband and most likely kill him, too. So, no, there is no regret, only satisfaction that he's finally burning in hell where he belongs.

"I'm fine. Honestly." My hand covers Finn's, and I catch the wince. I look down and see his knuckles bloody and torn apart.

"Jesus Christ, Finn. Why didn't you use brass knuckles or something? Your hand is a mess."

I move around him and start looking through the cupboards. "Where the hell is your first aid kit?"

He opens the cabinet door where he pulled the bottle of whiskey from earlier and grabs the blue box. Opening it, I find various wipes, gauze, and bandages, along with a small bottle of rubbing alcohol.

"That's a stupid place for a first aid kit."

Finn smirks as I start taking out what I need. "Actually, it's the perfect place for it. If I'm bleeding and need the kit, I usually need a drink as well. Saves steps and all that."

I roll my eyes and pour some alcohol on the gauze before pressing it to his knuckles. He lets out a hiss, and I shoot him a bland look.

"Really? I just watched you melt someone's skin from their hand and a little alcohol on your cut hurts?"

"It fucking stings. I'm man enough to admit that."

A smile plays on my lips as I shake my head a bit but continue to clean his hand.

"You were magnificent." He says the words with a reverence I haven't heard from him before.

I raise my eyes to Finn's and meet his emotion-filled gaze. I'm not sure if he means when I killed Orlando, me not flinching at his rather creative torture techniques, or my impressive first aid skills. Knowing him, it could be any of them, so I simply say, "Thank you."

I finish bandaging him and put the first aid kit back in its stupid storage place. "Do you think it's over? That they won't come after us again now that Orlando's dead?"

"Honestly, I'm not sure what's going to happen next, but no, I don't think it's over, baby. Not by a long shot."

EPILOGUE

FINN

Iᶠ I DIED WITH my face buried between my wife's thighs, I'd go out the happiest man on the planet. And whoever is calling me as she comes down from her orgasm might just lose their life by my hands.

Placing a kiss on the inside of Alessia's silky thigh, I groan as I raise myself from the bed and grab my phone, seeing Luca's name on the screen.

"Yeah?" I say irritably into the phone.

"Hey. We need to talk about my leaving. And by talk, I mean I'm leaving with Giada. Today."

"Slow down, cousin. We talked about this."

I stand from the bed and walk into the bathroom, turning on the shower.

"Listen, Finn. We've been doing it your way, and I understand, but Carlo hasn't been here in months. Giada got word that she needed to pack her things and be ready for some Russian to pick her up later today. He was going to ship her off to marry a man who would do God knows what to her. I can't let it happen."

I was worried something like this would happen with Luca at the house guarding the younger Cataldi. I saw it in his eyes when he met me at the fights over a month ago. Looks like my cousin may have caught feelings for the little princess.

"I'm done fighting in the shadows, Finn. And I'm not going to stand back while he hurts an innocent. I'm getting out, and Giada is coming with me."

"Fuck, okay. Just don't do anything rash. I'll set up a place for you to hide out and—"

"Too late."

"What do you mean too late?"

"Well, she can't exactly marry the pakhan's son if she's already married."

"Luca..."

"I married her, Finn."

Well...shit.

"Where are you?"

"New Hampshire. Manchester City Hall, to be exact."

"Goddammit. You need to get off the street. Go to my penthouse and I'll meet you there. I'll call the guards so they know to let you in."

"Okay. Sorry, Finn. I just couldn't—"

"I know you couldn't."

I would have done everything in my power to keep the woman I love safe, even before I admitted to myself that I loved her. Shit, I did even more for Alessia than Luca is doing for Giada before I admitted my feelings for her.

"I'll see you in a few."

I hang up the phone and walk back into the bedroom,

my wife still lying naked on the silk sheets.

It's been two weeks since Orlando went to ground, and we came back to the house. Of course, I added a shit ton of extra security features and more guards to patrol the grounds, but as soon as it was all in place, Alessia wanted to come back. She likes the penthouse well enough, but this is our home, and she wasn't going to let those fuckers take that from her. Her words, not mine.

"What's going on?" she asks.

"Luca is done being a mole for me, I guess." After Orlando was put to ground, I explained the situation to Alessia about who Luca is and what we've been doing the last seven years. "Oh, and he went and got himself a little wife on his way out."

Alessia's eyes widen. "Don't tell me..."

"Giada Cataldi," I confirm.

She blows out a heavy breath. "Well, that's one way to make an exit."

"No shit. Let's get in the shower. We need to meet them at the penthouse. I figured since you know each other, maybe you could make her feel a little more comfortable with everything. Reassure her a bit."

"I don't know her that well, but sure, I can try."

She stands from the bed and walks toward me, every naked inch of her on full display.

Standing on her tiptoes, she presses her soft lips to mine and leans her body into me.

I let out a low growl. "Get in the shower, wife. I need

to call Eoghan and tell him what's going on." He needs to hear it from me before he overhears one of the guards talking about it.

She saunters into the bathroom, and I watch her step into the shower, her bitable ass tempting me from here.

I hit Eoghan's number on my phone, needing to make this call quick so I can go make my wife come once more before we leave.

"Fuck, why do you always call me so goddamn early?" he asks in lieu of a greeting.

"It's almost noon, you lazy asshole."

"What the fuck ever," he groans out. "Some of us aren't old married men who go to bed before eleven."

We may go to bed early, but that sure as shit doesn't mean we go to sleep until well into the early hours of the morning.

"I have to tell you something, and you might get mad, but I want you to know I kept it from you for your safety."

"Not exactly the most trust-inspiring thing you've ever said to me, but shoot."

"I had an inside man in the Cataldi organization. It was someone who contacted me several years ago. He grew up thinking he was one person when, really, he was born as someone else with an entirely different family.

"Okay..."

"Mom's nephew didn't die. Our cousin is alive and well and has been working with me to take down Cataldi. His name is Luca, and he's coming home."

The End

Thank you so much for reading Finn and Alessia's story! If you enjoyed their book, I would be so appreciative if you took a little more time and left a review on the retailer site. Reviews are a great way to help out indie authors like me spread the word about their stories.

Want to get to know the guys from The Black Roses MC? They have a series, too! AND I have a little novella that gives you a glimpse into what it was like growing up in Shine for a few of my guys. You can get a copy of that by signing up for my newsletter at www.katerandallauthor.com. Don't worry, I'm not an email spammer!

Stalk me on my socials!
TikTok
Facebook
Instagram
Goodreads

BookBub

Scan the QR code to follow me on all my socials and sign up for my newsletter!

xoxo

ALSO BY KATE

The Ones Series
The Good One
The Fragile One
The Other One

The Black Roses MC
Linc
Jude
Ozzy
And more coming...

The Boston Syndicate
Finn
Luca
Eoghan
Cillian

Acknowledgements

Holy heck! Where to start? First of all, thank YOU for spending this time with my story. You have no idea how much it means to me for you to take your time to get lost in my world for a few hours.

I also want to thank everyone who has reached out and told me how much they love my words! Y'all have no idea how much that has kept me going this last year. I love hearing from each and every one of you.

Thank you to the awesome team at The Next Step PR, Kiki, Megan and Anna. They hold my hand through all things marketing, and I would probably lose my head without them! They are the best at what they do, and I'm so grateful for them.

Major thanks to my amazing editor, Victoria. You take my words and make them shine! I absolutely love working with you, and I'm so glad I found you!

Thank you to my sister-from-another-mister, Molli. You keep me sane through life's ups and downs, especially when my brain is telling me to give it up. You believe in me and push me to keep going in your kind and loving way.

And of course, my amazing husband. If it wasn't for you, we wouldn't eat when I'm on deadline. LOL. Your support from the second I told you I'm going to be an author has meant everything. I couldn't ever imagine doing this life thing without you and you'd better make sure I never have to! Love you, babe.

ABOUT KATE

Kate is a lover of all things books. It doesn't matter what sub-genre, as long as there's a HEA, she's in. She started reading romance in high school and would hide novels in textbooks to read during class. Becoming an author was always a dream she had and finally decided to put pen to paper (or finger to keyboard) and write what she loves. She grew up in the beautiful upper peninsula of Michigan then became a West Coast girl where she lives with her amazing husband and hilarious son. She would love to hear from readers so check out all her socials and sign up for her newsletter so she can keep you up to date on her books and whatever other ramblings come to mind.